Dark Encounters

OF THE FATED KIND

THE CHILDREN OF THE GODS

I. T. LUCAS

Aru

Aru stood motionless and silent behind Dagor's chair, watching the laptop screen. The video quality of the bug perched on Doctor Julian's shoulder was remarkably clear, and what Aru saw twisted his gut with worry.

Gabi looked drained, so pale and gaunt that she seemed almost ethereal. Her once vibrant and animated face was drawn, and her small frame barely made a rise under the blanket.

The contrast between the woman he'd known intimately over the last few days and the vulnerable figure in the hospital bed was jarring. In his memories she'd seemed like a force, a spirit that filled his heart and any space she occupied with her quirky personality and vivacious energy.

He was a damn god, and yet he was completely helpless to do anything about it. What were all his godly powers good for if he couldn't help her? Make her better?

Worse, Aru couldn't even hold the hand of the woman he cared for in her time of need, and putting his faith in the doctor was not something he was even remotely comfortable with.

Julian was the immortal descendant of the rebel gods, and Aru didn't know where he had gotten his education. Did he even know how to take care of Gabi?

As the urge to go to her became overwhelming, his grip on the back of Dagor's chair tightened to the point of the wood groaning in protest.

"Cut it out." Dagor looked at him over his shoulder. "You're going to break the chair."

"She doesn't look good," Aru murmured.

"On the contrary." Dagor turned back to the laptop screen. "She's a looker. I can understand now why you are so obsessed with her."

Over on the couch, Negal chuckled. "A human female's beauty can't compare to that of a goddess. It shouldn't affect you."

That was true. Gabi lacked the perfection of the goddesses back home, but her imperfections, her uniqueness, only made her more beautiful to Aru.

"Beauty is in the eye of the beholder," Aru said without sparing Negal a glance. "And there is much more to it than physicality. It's the bright soul animating Gabi's body that makes her beautiful."

"If you say so," was the trooper's sarcastic response.

"Your sister is doing very well." On the screen, the doctor turned to look at Gabi's brother, who appeared to be standing, given the angle of the bug's camera. "Her vitals are strong, and her bouts of unconsciousness don't last more than a few hours at a time. You should get some rest, Gilbert."

As relief flooded Aru, he let out a breath. That was good news.

That was excellent news.

"I told you so," Negal murmured from the couch. "She's in good hands."

"I'm not leaving her side." Gabi's brother looked around the room. "Is there a cot I can put in here? I plan on sleeping next to Gabi tonight."

"There should be one somewhere in the clinic. I'll get it for you."

"Thank you," Gilbert said.

As the doctor turned toward the door, Aru leaned over Dagor's shoulder. "Move the bug from the doctor to the brother."

"Are you sure? It's a small room. They might notice it flying over."

The outdated medical equipment in the room was making enough noise to mask the barely perceptible buzz the tiny drone would make as it crossed the short distance between the doctor's shoulder and Gilbert's. The device was smaller than a mosquito, made less noise than one, and was undetectable by human technology because it was mostly biological rather than mechanical.

"Do it," Aru commanded in a tone that brooked no argument.

"Yes, sir." Dagor moved his finger on the laptop pad, and the spy's viewpoint moved accordingly.

The doctor paused at the door. "Did you eat?"

"I didn't." Gilbert put his hand on his stomach. "But that's okay. I could lose an inch or two around the middle."

The doctor cast him an amused look. "I'll tell the guys in security to order us something. Anything in particular you're in the mood for?"

"Whatever you get is fine." The vantage point changed as Gilbert sat back down. "I want to call Orion and ask him to remove the compulsion from Gabi. It wasn't a smart idea to have her remember and forget things depending on where she was. Now, her mind is all scrambled, and she's confused. I hope that no damage was done, and she will go back to normal as soon as Orion removes his compulsion."

That explained so much—the memory lapses and the headaches. But why had they compelled her to forget things?

What were the secrets she held in her mind that she was allowed to remember in some circumstances and not others?

And who was Orion?

Was he a god?

Compulsion was a rare ability, and Aru doubted the immortal descendants of the rebel gods could have inherited that trait. Then again, the Eternal King's children could have gotten it from him and transferred it to their offspring, making these immortal descendants both dangerous and useful. There weren't many compellers left on Anumati, and those who had been sent to remote corners of the galaxy had usually met with one calamity or another.

The doctor frowned. "That worries me. The compulsion should be removed as soon as possible. Call Orion, explain the situation, and have him on standby for when Gabi wakes up again."

"That's precisely what I intend to do."

Aru

"I'm taking the laptop to my bedroom." Aru closed the device and lifted it over Dagor's head. "You two can take a rest."

Dagor cast him an amused look. "Are you planning on watching your human in the privacy of your bedroom?"

"You bet." Ignoring the innuendo, Aru tucked the laptop under his arm and headed to his room.

He didn't want his teammates watching Gabi in her vulnerable state, especially when the doctor was doing things that required exposing her.

Besides, he wanted to hear Gilbert's conversation with the mysterious Orion without them present. If Gabi knew important secrets pertaining to the gods and immortals, he wanted to hear them first and then decide whether to share them with Negal and Dagor.

"How is it going, Orion?" Gilbert asked when his call was answered.

Regrettably, Aru couldn't hear what Orion's reply was. The spy bug's receiver was not sensitive enough for that.

"Yeah, I know. The lockdown is maddening. But I'm not in the village. Kian let me out because Gabi is transitioning, and I begged him to let me be with her."

There was a short pause. "She wasn't feeling well and decided to walk over to the pharmacy around the corner from her hotel, but she never made it. She fainted on the way and was taken to a human hospital. Kian sent an extraction team to get her out of there, and we brought her to the keep."

After another short pause, Gilbert continued, "Yeah, we know who induced her, but I don't know if I can tell you. Since you're mated to Alena, and you are also Toven's son, you probably know what's going on, and I don't need to spell it out for you." Gilbert turned around to look at Gabi, giving Aru another glimpse of her before turning his back to her again. "Yeah, that's right. It was one of the gods. Anyway, the reason I'm calling you is your compulsion. It's messing with Gabi's head, and since she's no longer exposed to him and isn't going to be anytime soon or at all, you can release her, at least until she's out of the critical stage of her transition."

Critical stage sounded ominous, and Aru's gut clenched with worry. The doctor had said that she was doing fine, though, and he'd sounded sincere. So perhaps the critical stage didn't refer to how dangerous it was but to how important it was?

"Gilbert?" The sweet sound of Gabi's voice had Aru's heart flutter.

Her brother turned around, giving Aru the gift of seeing her with her eyes open. "Oh, good. You're awake. I thought I would have to call Orion again. Let me transfer the call to video."

Her beautiful eyes widening, Gabi feebly lifted a hand to shield her face. "Don't! I probably look like roadkill. I don't want anyone to see me like this."

Aru laughed. This was so like Gabi. Everyone was worried about her transition while she was fussing about looking presentable on the screen for Orion. Thankfully, Gilbert had said that the guy was mated, or Aru would have gotten jealous, thinking that Gabi wanted to look pretty for the guy.

But wait, did she know that Orion was taken? Perhaps she thought he was single?

"You look lovely even when you're disheveled." Gilbert echoed Aru's thoughts. "Besides, you are transitioning, and no one expects you to look your best."

Gabi frowned. "You keep saying that I'm transitioning. What does that mean?"

She didn't know?

So, Aru wasn't the only one who hadn't heard about Dormants and their ability to transition into immortality with the help of an immortal or a god's essence.

"Talk to Orion. Hopefully, things will make more sense after he does his thing." Gilbert turned his phone screen toward Gabi and activated the speaker.

Regrettably, Aru couldn't see Orion.

"Hello, Gabi," he heard the guy's voice. "I'm sorry about the mess my compulsion created in your head. In hindsight, it wasn't a good idea."

"I know you." She frowned at him. "You were at the dinner in the hotel."

Feeling like an idiot, Aru let out a relieved breath. Gabi could barely remember the guy, and she didn't sound interested in him.

"That's right. You were told things that needed to be kept a secret, but since you were seeing a guy who we suspected of possessing a certain ability, we couldn't let you remember what you'd been told when you had company. That was what created the confusion and eventually made you forget everything, even when there were no strangers around. I'm going to remove the compulsion now, and hopefully, that will clear up the confusion."

If they had suspected that the man Gabi was seeing was not human and could enter her mind, why hadn't they set a trap for him and caught him?

It would have been so easy.

He'd had no idea that she wasn't fully human or that she was related to the people he was searching for.

As it dawned on him that their encounter must have been destined, Aru lifted a hand to his chest. No wonder he felt so strongly about Gabi.

They were fated to be together.

"How are you going to fix that?" Gabi asked Orion.

"Simple. Look into my eyes and focus on the sound of my voice. You can remember everything you've learned about immortals, and you can speak freely about them with anyone. You are not restricted in any way."

Scrunching her nose, Gabi squinted as if she was in pain, but then her eyes grew large, and she lifted a hand to her temple. "Immortality. That's what I'm transitioning into. But how? I didn't have sex with an immortal, did I? Or did you make me forget that as well, and the memory just hasn't come back yet?"

Orion chuckled. "I'll let Gilbert explain. It's one hell of an incredible story, and he has more details than I do. I wish you the best of luck on your transition."

"Thank you." Gabi kept rubbing her temples.

"I'll see you in the village soon," Orion said. "Or so I hope. Goodbye, Gabi."

"Goodbye, and thank you again." She lifted a pair of questioning eyes to her brother.

He put the phone aside. "There is no easy way to do this. Your lover boy is not a human after all. He's a god, and he induced your transition. What I want to know is, what the hell were you thinking having unprotected sex with a guy you'd only just met?"

She arched an indignant brow. "Are you serious? That's what bothers you about this situation? And what do you mean by a god? Do you mean immortal, a descendant of the gods?"

"You were induced by a god. Not an immortal, not a demigod, but a pureblooded god. So was I, though, so you don't have exclusive bragging rights."

What in purgatory's name?

Who had induced Gabi's brother? Other than Aru and his teammates, there were no other gods on Earth.

"Wait a minute." Gabi lifted her hand. "You said that all the gods were dead, and only their immortal descendants remained."

That was precisely what Aru had believed up until a moment ago.

"I didn't say that all the gods were dead." Gilbert waved a hand.

Gabi cast him an accusing look. "I don't remember what you and the others said, but it was implied that there were no gods left on Earth and that only their immortal descendants remained."

Gilbert sighed. "The gods living in the village are our most guarded secret, even more so than the existence of immortals. It's like the Holiest of Holies of secrets. They were supposed to be the only ones, but then Aru and his friends showed up, getting our attention by activating trackers that we knew were of godly origins."

So, there were still gods left on Earth.

But how?

Had they removed their trackers?

Could the heir still be alive?

Hope surged in Aru's chest and then quickly winked out. Perhaps some gods had managed to survive, but it wasn't likely that the heir was one of them.

"How did you know that they were of godly origins?" Gabi asked.

"The history of those trackers is a long story for another day. When we identified the signals, we panicked, and the village went into lockdown. Do you remember that?"

She nodded. "It got so confusing. When I was alone, I remembered what you told me about a clan location that got compromised and that the lockdown was a security measure. Was all of that because of Uriel?" She asked in a whisper that carried a betrayed tone.

"His real name is Aru, and he's not from Portugal. It's just a fake identity he bought. Anyway, a team of our people met with him today, and it seems like his intentions are not hostile, but further talks are needed to ascertain that. He and his friends are very dangerous."

"Why?"

"Because gods are to immortals like immortals are to humans. We are powerless against them. They can get into our minds and thrall us or compel us. Also, they come from a planet of gods who don't hold humans in the highest regard."

"He wasn't condescending with me."

Gabi defending him to her brother brought Aru hope. Perhaps she wasn't angry about the deception and understood why it had been necessary.

"I don't know all the details of what the gods told the team that was sent to meet them, but from what I've heard so far, it seems like they are on our side."

"Good." Gabi rubbed her temple. "I think. Will I be able to see him again?"

She sounded hopeful, which reinforced Aru's belief that she didn't hate him for lying to her. There was still a chance he could salvage what they had.

To what end, though?

He couldn't stay. In a hundred and fifteen years, give or take a few, the patrol ship would return for him, and he would have to leave. But even before that, he couldn't be with her and endanger her and her community by his mere presence.

The tracker in his body made him into a beacon, a pointer, and Gabi's people had to hide not only from their terrestrial enemies but also from the Eternal King.

"It depends on how the talks go," Gilbert said. "If Kian is convinced that Aru's intentions are good, he will not stand in the way of fate."

Gabi arched a brow. "Fate?"

"The Fates, fate, it's all the same thing." Gilbert waved a dismissive hand again. "Do you really think that your flight getting canceled and you getting a first-class ticket and sitting next to a god was all a coincidence?"

She frowned. "No, I guess it wasn't. When do you think I will be allowed to see Uriel? I mean, Aru."

"I don't know." Gilbert took Gabi's hand. "As I said, it's up to Kian and how well the negotiations go."

Gabi

T he cycle of slipping away into unconsciousness, waking up, and then slipping away again wasn't so much scary as it was annoying.

Mostly, it was the unpredictability of it that got to her. She could be in the middle of a sentence and then find herself in the dream world or just drifting away into nothing.

Still, Gabi was grateful to be waking up at all.

According to the doctor, she was luckier than most, and other transitioning Dormants hadn't been as fortunate, spending the entire process unconscious.

Come to think of it, it shouldn't have been too difficult for them because they had been unaware of what was going on, but it must have been hard for those who cared for them and were helpless to do anything other than wait for the process to run its course.

Usually, though, the transitioning Dormants were accompanied by a mate, who worried about them and stayed by their side, sleeping on a cot in their hospital room.

Gabi had Gilbert.

Her eldest brother was the rock in her life, and he would probably remain the only male she could rely on, with her other brother being the runner-up. As far as a romantic partner, though, Gabi had never had one she could rely on.

Dylan was a self-absorbed cheater, others she'd dated hadn't clicked, and Uriel was a damned god who lied to her and whom she would most likely never see again.

"I miss you too," Gilbert whispered into his phone. "Where are you now?"

Gabi tuned him out, giving him privacy to talk to Karen the only way she could, which was by turning inward to the place where her heart ached from Uriel's betrayal.

He'd told her so very little about himself, claiming that he couldn't reveal more because he didn't want to lie to her, but even the little he'd told her had been a lie, including his name.

Why had he lied about that?

He could have told her that his name was Aru. What would it have mattered to her whether he was named Uriel or Aru?

It's not like everyone on the planet knew that there was a god named Aru roaming around, and she would have immediately recognized him by his name.

He wasn't a flea-market flipper either.

What did gods do for a living? Could they conjure gold from thin air?

The gods she'd read about had been worshiped and attended by the humans who revered them, so they didn't need to do anything other than look godly.

The same went for contemporary monarchs. They were figureheads, symbols, and, in a way, modern myths. The British didn't need their monarchs for anything, but the royal family was worshiped almost like deities.

Ugh, her mind was drifting again, and she couldn't even blame the transition for that. Or maybe she could?

Gabi lifted her eyes to the IV bag hanging over her bed. Perhaps they were feeding her relaxants in the IV, and that was why she was feeling so unfocused and scatter-brained.

Bringing her focus back to Uriel, she remembered fondly his offer to avenge her honor. He sounded so sincere when he'd offered to beat up Dylan. In retrospect, though, he'd probably had a different retribution in mind.

What did gods do to humans they didn't like?

Could Uriel summon lightning from the sky like Thor and smite those who incurred his wrath?

Nah, probably not.

Obviously, Uriel and his friends were just aliens who called themselves gods, the same as her ancestors, but she didn't know what powers they had other than mind manipulation.

Perhaps she could ask Gilbert to tell her what he knew about gods after he was done talking to Karen. He'd said that a god had induced his transition, so he must know a thing or two about these aliens.

Oh, crap. Why had he told her that?

That was so bad. If he felt free to tell her about the gods, he didn't expect her to ever see Uriel again.

Now that she was free of Orion's compulsion to forget what she'd been told about immortals, her mind was open to infiltration by immortals and gods, and she would never be allowed to see Aru again.

Hell, she would probably never be allowed to return to Cleveland.

The knowledge she'd gained was too valuable to risk infiltration by aliens or humans who could read minds.

Suddenly, the world seemed like an even scarier place than before. She had to worry not only about bodily harm but also about thought thieves.

Would they at least let her talk to Aru on the phone?

From what she understood about thralling, he couldn't peek into her mind unless he was physically next to her.

But would they trust her to keep her mouth shut about what she knew?

Probably not.

So that was it. Instead of a child, Uriel's parting gift to her had been immortality. Not bad as a consolation prize, except Gabi didn't feel like a winner.

Too weak to fight the tears, she let them stream down her cheeks.

Gabi wasn't a pretty crier, but down in the clan's underground clinic, there was no one to see her and pass judgment.

Gilbert was there, but it wouldn't be the first time he'd seen her falling apart. In fact, he'd seen her in a much worse condition after she'd gotten proof of Dylan's infidelity.

Somehow sensing that she was distressed, Gilbert turned around and looked at her. "I gotta go," he told Karen. "I'll call you later." He ended the call and got up. "What's wrong? Why are you crying?"

"It's nothing. I hate being weak and sick, and that's how I feel now."

He arched a brow. "You know that I can always tell when you're lying. Out with it, Gabi."

There was no point in resisting because he would just keep on pushing.

"Now that you've told me about the gods, I can never see Uriel again. I can't even say goodbye to him over the phone because I might inadvertently blurt something out."

"Oh, sweetheart." He sat on the bed beside her and took her hand. "Orion is available whenever you need him, at least as long as the lockdown is in effect, and if you ask him, he can compel you again to forget what you've learned."

She lifted her hand to her temple. "But his compulsion is messing with my head. I don't want my brain to turn to mush."

Gilbert smiled. "And yet I can see that your mood has improved, which means that you like having the option, and you're considering it."

"Well, yes, of course. It's a door that was closed before and is now open if I wish to step through it. But I hope it can be done better so it's less bothersome to my mind. Maybe Orion can just make me forget about the gods. Uriel already knows about immortals, right? So that's no longer a secret, and I don't mind not knowing about the gods at all."

"I guess so." Gilbert shifted his position to get more comfortable on the sliver of space he'd claimed on her bed. "I'm not privy to the details of their talks. You and I will have to wait until we are told, and I don't know when that will be."

"Can't you ask? Perhaps Julian knows more?"

Gilbert leaned closer and kissed Gabi's forehead. "You can ask him yourself the next time he checks on you."

She shifted sideways to make more room for her brother. "Can you do me a favor and call Orion now? I want to forget about the gods."

Gilbert patted her hand. "There is no rush. We will worry about it when meeting Orion in person becomes an option."

Annani

Annani surveyed the somber faces of her family and let out a sigh. "We are gathered around the dining table, surrounded by our loved ones, and being served a delicious dinner by our dear Odus. We should treasure these precious moments with family and friends and not let outside worries ruin them, or we will never get to enjoy ourselves." She smiled. "Life is full of challenges, and that is never going to change."

The news Kian had delivered about the Eternal King and the future of Earth was far from encouraging, but nothing was imminent, and they had plenty of time to prepare. The grace period of one hundred and fifteen years might be a blink of an eye for the gods, but it was an eternity for humans. The technological advancements of the last century were staggering, and with the help of artificial intelligence, progress would be exponential. By the time the team of newly arrived gods had to report their findings, a solution might present itself.

Her grandfather might send a new plague to cull the number of humans and halt their technological progress, but Annani believed that Kian was right about their ability to make humans immune to disease and maybe even make them immortal. Doing so might introduce new problems that would have to be solved, but that was a worry for another day.

Amanda's lips twisted in a grimace. "It's hard to be joyful after hearing that Earth's population is in danger from none other than my great-grandfather." She shivered. "I always believed myself to be good, but with his genes inside of me, I'm no longer sure that I am." She turned to Dalhu. "I felt the call of darkness once, the need to rage and destroy. Fortunately, I didn't have the means to do damage, but what if I had? Would I have destroyed the world in my grief and anger? What if that darkness is still hiding inside of me, waiting to emerge in response to a strong enough trigger?"

When Amanda had lost her young son to a tragic horse-back-riding accident, Annani had sensed that darkness threatening to consume her daughter—its toxic allure sadly all too familiar. But she knew that she had raised Amanda and her other children to resist the lure of darkness and cling to the light with all their might, and she had trusted that her teachings would hold even in the face of such incredible tragedy and pain.

As sweet as the call of the dark side was, it was a trap, and one step too many into its hot embrace could be the point of no return.

Dalhu put his hand on Amanda's shoulder. "Your great-grandfather is not necessarily evil. He's brilliant and pragmatic and does what he thinks is best for his people. I wouldn't have minded having his blood running in my veins instead of the blood of the hoodlum my mother was forced to breed with."

Amanda's eyes softened. "Oh, darling. Thank you for reminding me that we are more than our genetics and that we always have a choice."

Toven, however, did not look encouraged by Dalhu's words, and his somber expression had not abated. "Even if we manage to make all humans immune to disease or immortal, we won't be able to save humankind. Once the Eternal King realizes that a pathogen his scientists have introduced hasn't worked, and humans haven't been infected by his plague, he will order a different way of culling the population, which will be no less devastating. Probably more so."

As silence stretched across the table, Annani searched for a rebuttal to Toven's grim prediction, but nothing came to mind. Humans, along with the immortals living alongside them, were no match for the might of the gods.

"Our only hope is the rebellion," Syssi said. "The king needs to be replaced with someone who sympathizes with the created species." She turned her gaze to Annani. "I happen to know his legitimate heir, and she is a big-time sympathizer."

Annani laughed. "Are you suggesting that I take the throne and become the queen of the gods?"

"Why not? The original rebels wanted to make your father the king. If they knew of your existence, the new rebels would choose you. You'll make a wonderful queen."

Annani had been groomed to take the throne, and as a young goddess, she had been ready to ascend if and when her father chose to step down, but she was not the same goddess she had been then, and she had no wish to rule anyone—not even her clan. She would not mind being a figurehead and being worshiped and admired, but she would leave the day-to-day affairs of the throne to others who were better suited for the job.

"I do not wish to rule the planet of the gods, but even if I did, it is not feasible. Not now, not in the near future, and probably not ever." She turned to Kian. "Aru said that the rebellion is thousands of years in the making and has many more thousands to go before it is ready. We do not have that long. We need to come up with a solution and implement it within the next century."

Kian shrugged. "Maybe we don't. As long as humans do not possess interstellar travel capability, the Eternal King will not deem them a threat. Perhaps all we need to do is ensure that they never get to that point. Besides, the Eternal King is not in a rush to do anything. He moves in godly time, and until he turns his sights on Earth, the natural shrinkage in human population due to declining birthrates might be enough for him to leave humans alone."

Toven reached for Mia's hand. "If the Perfect Match adventure the AI designed for us was a hint from the Fates, then in five hundred years, the human population will have shrunk in size to what it was when the original rebels were exiled to Earth, and a new crop of gods will arrive to once again rule over humans."

Aru

"Have you learned anything new?" Dagor asked as Aru handed him the laptop.

He'd spent the evening of the day before, most of the prior night, and into the early morning watching Gabi through the little spy's eyes. She'd been unconscious for many hours, but when she'd woken up, she'd talked with her brother and the doctor, and Aru had gotten to eavesdrop on their conversations.

He'd learned quite a lot, but he wasn't about to share it with his teammates.

"I've learned a few things, but none of them are of much use to us. There were several mentions of a village, which is what they call the place they live in, and along with it, talk about a lockdown, which was done in response to our arrival. As soon as they identified the signals, they panicked."

As Negal unlocked their car, the three of them got in, with Negal behind the wheel, Aru on the passenger side, and Dagor in the back.

Magnus hadn't sent them the location pin yet, but thanks to the spy drone and what they had learned from listening to the feed, they knew where Gabi had been taken and that the meeting with the immortals' leader would take place in the same downtown location.

Scoping the area and the building itself was standard protocol.

They couldn't get inside, though, because thralling and shrouding were not going to work on the security cameras or the people watching the feed, but their little drone spies could be their eyes and ears and get into places they probably couldn't.

Most standard doors were not precisely fitted, and the bugs could pass under or above them. Anywhere a mosquito or an ant could go, their spy drones could go as well.

"I wonder if Jade and the other Kra-ell reside in the same village," Negal said.

"It would seem so." Aru turned around to look at Dagor. "Do you need the laptop, or can I use it until we get to the building?"

Rolling his eyes, Dagor closed the device. "You checked on her less than five minutes ago. Nothing has changed since then."

"You never know." Aru flipped the laptop open and brought up the feed from the clinic.

True to his promise, Gilbert hadn't left Gabi's side except to use the bathroom. During those brief breaks, Aru had muted the feed and busied himself with watching television to respect the brother's privacy until the guy was done with his business.

Thankfully, Gilbert hadn't showered or changed his clothing, so there had been no need to maneuver the bug. By now, the drone was running low on energy, and having it fly would drain what was left.

Aru would be lucky if the thing kept transmitting for a couple more hours.

They could attach new drones to their hosts, but Aru didn't want to push his luck. Security around the leader would be much tighter than it had been during the meeting in the canyon, and he wouldn't be surprised if they got strip-searched.

It hadn't been an easy decision to forgo bringing more bugs to the meeting with the leader, and as Aru had debated the pros and cons, he was well aware of what would happen if he lost contact with Gabi.

It was much worse than attaching spy drones to these immortals.

He was a god, and if pushed, he would use his mind powers over them.

No, diplomacy was always a better solution, and he would have to negotiate something with the clan's leader. The problem with that was having to admit that he knew they had Gabi. It would force him to also reveal the truth about the spy drone he'd attached to Magnus.

As hard as Aru tried to come up with a convincing lie about how he'd learned about Gabi's transition, he couldn't come up with one.

It had occurred to him that he could claim to have attached the drone to Gabi to make sure that she was unharmed when he wasn't with her, but in a way, it was worse than admitting he had attached the spy bug to Magnus.

The leader would be more understanding about the bug than she would, and rightfully so. Attaching the drone to Magnus wasn't personal. It was a strategically smart move. Attaching it to Gabi would have been an invasion of her privacy.

Come to think of it, Aru was crossing the line by monitoring her as it was.

"You still didn't tell us what you hope to get from them," Negal said. "We know now that the Kra-ell are not dead, and we know who took them. The question is what we tell the commander. We can't tell him about the immortals because our communications with the ship are recorded, and he will have no choice but to report our findings to headquarters."

"I'm glad that you arrived at the same conclusion I did." Just then, Gilbert turned to look at Gabi, and Aru got a glimpse of her sleeping face. "We will report that there was an uprising and that Gor and some of his males were taken out by the others."

Negal nodded. "You know what the problem with that is. We will need to report their new location, and that's where the immortals live. The Kra-ell will have to find a different place to settle."

"I know." Aru sighed. "Which is a shame. I love the idea of the Kra-ell and the immortal descendants of the gods living together in harmony and mutual respect. Also, Jade has an immortal mate, and she might not be the only one. Separating the two groups is going to be tough even though they haven't been integrated for long."

Aru hadn't told Dagor and Negal about the gods who also resided in the same location, and he didn't intend to, not because he didn't trust them, but because the less they knew, the safer the secret was.

Kian

"Thank the merciful Fates for air conditioning." Anandur patted his light suit jacket. "Covering up the arsenal I have on me would have been miserable without it." He opened the limo door for Kian.

Surprisingly, Brundar nodded in agreement. Like his brother, he was armed to the teeth and covered it with a suit jacket.

Okidu was behind the wheel, and Turner followed Kian into the back of the limo. "Wasn't Onidu supposed to join us as well?" he asked.

"I decided against it." Kian leaned back in the seat. "I don't want the gods to think I'm bringing the Odus as part of my security detail. I want them to see Okidu in his primary function as my butler. If I brought Onidu as well, it would be obvious that their presence is about providing protection." He smiled at the brothers. "With Brundar and Anandur assuming their tough guy personas, they will be my obvious and only bodyguards."

Turner was former special ops, and if needed, Kian had no doubt the guy would rise to the occasion and fight alongside him and the brothers, but he was short and didn't look physically intimidating, so the gods would accept that he wasn't part of Kian's security detail.

Turner shrugged. "We could have pretended that Onidu is my butler."

"We could have," Kian agreed. "But I really don't expect any trouble from these gods. What worries me is the might they represent."

Turner cast him a questioning look. "Aren't you concerned with how easily they agreed to meet you on your turf? They will be walking into a building that they know is under your control, and the fact that they are okay with that troubles me. They might have something up their proverbial sleeve."

That had occurred to Kian, and he had taken all the necessary precautions. Guardians had been in place since morning, fortified by a group of young Kra-ell males who had already received basic training and had been vetted by Bhathian as ready to assist.

"The gods owe us. The first meeting was on their turf, and we assumed the risk by walking in without knowing what to expect. On the other hand, they have already met our people and can be reasonably assured that we mean them no harm."

"These gods have trackers in them." Forgetting about all the weapons he had strapped on, Anandur crossed his arms over his chest. That must have made him uncomfortable because he winced and uncrossed his arms. "Which means that their shipmates and the Eternal King know where they are at all times, and after this meeting, they will all know where the keep is as well."

"Regrettably, the keep is already lost to us as a strategic location," Kian said. "It's compromised beyond salvation, so meeting the gods there will not make it any worse."

"I wonder if we can remove the trackers from these gods." Turner crossed his legs at the ankles.

Kian cast him a curious look. "Don't you think they would have done it themselves if they could?"

"They probably can't, and I wonder whether they'll be interested in getting rid of them. How are they supposed to start an uprising when their location is always known?"

Kian shook his head. "If the king knows everyone's movements and whereabouts, it's next to impossible. I can't imagine living with no privacy like that. They can't do anything without someone knowing about it. They can't meet people in secret because everyone is being tracked, and they can't make contraband purchases because they use credits for transactions. It's so easy to program artificial intelligence to analyze the data from the trackers and from the purchase history and flag anything that might indicate rebellious behavior."

Turner nodded. "I have no idea how they manage the resistance and recruit new people."

"You've heard Aru." Kian let out a sigh. "Snail's pace is fast compared to how they are progressing. The rebellion is thousands of years in the making, and it will take many thousands more until they are ready to act. The problem is that we might not have that long until the Eternal King learns about the progress of humans and decides to curtail it."

Yesterday, Kian had told his mother and the rest of the family that the king was likely to move slowly and that he might wait patiently for the size of the human population to shrink naturally. It hadn't been a lie, but it was one of many possible scenarios, and Kian had given it voice mainly to ease their minds.

"Aru could have made it up," Anandur said. "Humans don't pose a threat to the Eternal King's hegemony, and they won't even once they gain interstellar travel capability. I don't see any reason for him to bother with them."

It was no surprise that Anandur had echoed Kian's thoughts. After being his bodyguard for millennia, the guy had learned a thing or two about how Kian's mind worked. But Anandur was an optimist, while Kian was a pessimist.

The best scenario did not always play out, and they needed to be ready for the more pessimistic possibilities.

If eleven thousand years ago the king had thought that the few hundred thousand humans on Earth were a threat, he would surely deem the eight billion of them a threat now.

Kian had no proof that the Eternal King had been responsible for the flood, but if the myths surrounding the disaster were true, then the king was definitely the prime suspect.

The gods had seeded Earth and jumpstarted the human population. They had been involved in human affairs long before the group of rebels had been exiled to Earth. It wasn't a stretch to assume that the vengeful god of myths who had ordered the flood had been none other than the Eternal King or his heir, whom the king had sent to implement the culling.

Reaching into his pocket, Kian pulled out a pair of new earpieces and offered them to Turner. "I want you to put them on."

"Why? I'm immune, and these gods don't seem to have compulsion ability."

"We don't know that for sure." Kian put the devices in Turner's hand. "We don't know if these gods are compellers because they didn't try to compel our team-mates. And if they are compellers, or one of them is, we don't know whether or not you are immune to that particular compulsion style. We have plenty of examples that immunity is not universally applicable, nor is compulsion. Some people can be immune to one compeller but not the other, and I always prefer to err on the side of caution."

The truth was that the earpieces were most likely useless because the gods could thrall them, and thralling didn't require sound. The gods could reach straight into immortals' minds.

"I was thinking," Anandur said. "If we take the trackers out of Aru and his teammates, we will have to implant them in animals. Otherwise, their comrades on the patrol ship will think that they are dead and come to investigate. But those animals have to be long-lived, or we will have to keep transplanting them. Large turtles can live for up to five hundred years, so they would be perfect for that." He looked at Turner. "Any idea where we can get some? Other than the zoo, that is." He chuckled. "Imagine the headlines." Anandur lifted his hands, shaping quotation marks. "Three Large Turtles Escape From the Zoo. Authorities in a Slow-Motion Pursuit! Or how about this one? Three Massive Turtles Make a Slow Getaway."

Kian laughed. "I have one. Three Turtles Execute Slowest Zoo Heist in History. Security Two Steps Behind!"

Anandur lifted a finger. "I have a winner. Zoo Turtles Make a 'Speedy' Getaway. Authorities Hope to Catch Up by Next Friday!"

Clearing his throat, Turner offered with a straight face, "Breaking news: Three Turtles Escape a High-Security Zoo. Expected to Cross State Line in Six Months."

As the three of them laughed, Kian was thankful to Anandur for defusing the stressful atmosphere and lifting their spirits. Turning to Brundar, he asked, "Any headlines come to mind?"

The Guardian turned around and treated Kian to an icy look. "No."

The answer only made the three of them laugh harder, and even Okidu emitted a few chortles from behind the wheel.

Aru

"So far, everyone seems to be human." Dagor watched the six squares representing the six drones they had sent flying into the building. "We should collect them when we get in."

They had to be frugal with the little spies.

The case of drones they had arrived with was down to sixty-seven out of the original one hundred, and since they couldn't replenish their supplies, they had to be careful with how they used the remainder of the drones and reuse as many as they could.

Once the little bugs ran out of juice, there was no way to retrieve them. They just stopped broadcasting, and their location was lost.

Aru nodded. "There are too many floors with too many apartments in the building for us to check each one. We know that they have it well monitored, and the security guards in the lobby look like they know what they are doing. Other than that, we will have to trust that their intentions are as peaceful as ours and that they mean us no harm."

Negal snorted. "Even if they are wonderful people with the best intentions at heart, it's in their best interest to get rid of us. Naturally, that would prompt an investigation from our ship, but thanks to you, they now know that it will be a long time before that happens."

The accusation was not completely baseless, but it didn't have as much merit as Negal believed it had. It wasn't a big deal that Aru had told the immortals about the patrol ship's schedule. Their time horizon was not human, and it didn't make much difference to them if the expected retribution was in a year or a hundred years. They would still take it into consideration.

"We are safe." Aru's phone pinged with the pin Magnus had sent him. "These immortals are not stupid, and they are still going to be around when the patrol ship returns. They know that if we are gone, teams will land on Earth to investigate, and they would be much less friendly than we are, especially if they have reason to believe that we were murdered. Also, we have valuable information that they want about Anumati and the Eternal King's motives and machinations. In addition, I will come up with more reasons for why they need to not only keep us alive but also to stay in our good graces."

"How?" Dagor closed the laptop.

"I don't know yet," Aru admitted. "I'll think of something."

Dagor groaned. "We are doomed."

"Should I drive up to the valet?" Negal asked. "Or should I wait a few minutes to make it seem like we weren't parked a block away from the building?"

"We are expected to show up in twenty minutes, and I don't want us to arrive more than five minutes ahead of time. When we get there, stop a few meters from the building. We need to collect the six drones and leave them in the car before we pull up to the valet."

The only spy drone remaining would be the one monitoring Gabi.

"Got it." Negal checked the time. "That gives us ten minutes to brainstorm what we are going to tell these descendants to incentivize them to keep us alive."

"Your human might be useful," Dagor said. "Since she's apparently a descendant, once she transitions, she will become part of their community. She can claim you as her mate, and therefore guarantee your safety. The problem is that it doesn't help Negal and me."

"As long as one of us is alive, the descendants are in danger, so if Gabi claims me as hers and that offers me immunity, they will have no reason to eliminate you. But I really don't think that we need any additional guarantees. I also don't think that Gabi claiming me as her mate protects me."

Besides, she might not want to have anything to do with him, let alone claim him as hers.

"It's an old Kra-ell custom," Negal said. "And it might be our old custom as well, so the descendants might have adopted it from their godly ancestors."

"Even if they do, I will not use Gabi like that. She has enough reasons to resent me as it is. I don't want to add fuel to her ire and guarantee that she never chooses me as her mate."

"Don't worry." Negal waved a dismissive hand. "Females are more forgiving than males. You can sweet talk her into accepting you with open arms."

"I wish I shared your confidence."

In the backseat, Dagor sighed. "Nothing stands in the way of the Fates' plans, and if they decree that you belong with each other, you do."

Negal snorted. "Since when do you believe in that romantic nonsense? I thought you were smarter than that. The fated mates story is a classic example of the Eternal King's propaganda."

Even Aru had to raise a brow at that. "How could the king benefit from promoting a story like that?"

"Simple." Negal crossed his arms over his chest. "It's so self-explanatory that I wonder how the two of you haven't figured it out yet. Fated mates are supposed to be rare, and finding your one and only is supposed to be the greatest gift imaginable, and it's offered only to those who have suffered great hardship or sacrificed a lot for others. That's the perfect combination to incentivize young gods to journey to faraway crappy settlements in the hopes of being rewarded with a truelove mate."

Aru shook his head. "The king doesn't need to incentivize that because we don't have much choice in the matter. We are drafted, and we go where we are sent. Searching for truelove mates might be a nice perk, but it's not like the king needs to sell us on the service. It's mandatory."

"Oh, but he does." Negal smiled. "That's precisely how the king operates. There is always a carrot along with the whip, a perk to soften the hardship so he can maintain his benevolent façade of the almighty father, the shepherd of us all."

Aru had to admit that Negal was onto something, but the myths about fated mates were so old that they even predated the king.

"I have no love lost for the Eternal King, but in this case, I don't think he invented that story. I personally know couples who are truelove mates."

Negal arched a brow. "Give me one example?"

"My parents."

The trooper laughed. "Is that what they told you?"

"They did, but I would have known that even if they hadn't. Their love is evident in every word and look they exchange, and they are loyal to each other. Gods in arranged marriages play around, and they don't even try to hide it. Having multiple lovers is not only common practice, but it is a reason to brag."

"And you know for sure that your parents don't play around?" Negal chuckled. "The young are so naive. Your parents are stationed on a faraway outpost, and your only contact with them is via holo-calls. You haven't visited them in many cycles, and you have no idea what they are up to."

"That's true, but I know what I know, and you are not going to make me doubt it. Once you see true love, you can't mistake it for anything else."

Looking amused, Negal shrugged. "If you say so. So, tell me, is your transitioning human your truelove mate?"

"She might be."

Kian

On the laptop screen, Kian watched his three guests shaking hands with Magnus in the lobby.

Without the hardhats and the glasses, they looked like gods, and yet they didn't. They were not luminous, but they could be suppressing their natural glow. Still, their features, although perfect, were not as striking as Annani's or Toven's.

Could it be that the royal family had been gifted with rare genes to make them more beautiful than the common gods?

In a society of genetic experts, it made sense that the more prominent members ensured better genetics for their offspring. Then again, if the Eternal King didn't wish to create competition for himself, he shouldn't have ensured his offspring's superiority. Although, given the way he operated and his keen awareness of public opinion, he would make them as beautiful and as physically perfect as Anumati's scientists could craft them, but he wouldn't enhance their intelligence or their leadership skills.

Except, it didn't look like he had done that either.

Toven, who was the king's grandson, wasn't a leader, but he was smart, and Annani lacked neither smarts nor leadership skills.

What she lacked was the will to lead. She was satisfied with being loved and worshiped, and she was perfectly content to let Kian and Sari lead in all the ways that mattered.

Her father, though, had been smart, politically savvy, and hadn't shied away from leadership, so either the Eternal King hadn't thought to alter those genes in his heir, or maybe those weren't the types of things that genes could be coded for.

Not everything was biological. Free will had to play a role.

"I'm a little underwhelmed." Turner looked at the laptop screen. "I expected to be awed."

"Maybe they are more impressive in person." Kian got to his feet and walked over to the bar. "Anyone care for a drink?"

"I'll wait for our guests." Turner glanced at Okidu. "Is your butler going to open the door?"

Kian smirked. "That's the plan. I can't wait to see their expressions when they encounter him for the first time."

46

He poured himself a shot of whiskey and returned to the couch.

On the screen of his laptop, he watched as the elevator doors opened on the penthouse level, and the three gods followed Magnus out.

"You can open the door, Okidu. Our guests have arrived."

"Yes, master." The Odu bowed before rushing to the door.

Behind Kian, Anandur and Brundar got in position.

Turner leaned over to look at the screen. "Do you think they will be disappointed that Jade and Morgada are not here?"

Kian shook his head. "They want to see me, not the Kra-ell."

"Good afternoon, masters." Okidu bowed at the open door.

"Impossible," he heard one of the gods hiss. "You are not supposed to exist."

"My apologies for existing, master," Okidu said. "Please, come in. Master Kian is awaiting you."

"Thank you." Aru earned points with Kian for thanking Okidu and not treating him like a machine.

He rose to his feet and offered the god his hand. "Welcome to my home, Aru. My name is Kian."

"Nice place you've got here."

The god's handshake was firm but not overly so, and he was much more impressive in person than on the screen. His face was the sculpted perfection of male beauty, but he still wasn't in the same league as Annani or Toven.

"These are my teammates. Negal and Dagor," Aru introduced his friends, who were each model-perfect in their own way, but again, not in the same league as his mother and her cousin.

It kind of made sense that in a society of millions, or perhaps billions, not everyone was as perfectly made as the elite. Variation was needed, and Kian wondered whether they had artists who specialized in creating perfect genetic models.

"It's a pleasure to meet you." Kian motioned for Turner to come forward. "This is my good friend and advisor, Victor Turner."

Surrounded by four tall males, Turner had to look up, but that didn't affect his confidence. The power of his personality and his intelligence more than compensated for that.

After shaking Turner's hand, Aru shifted his gaze to the brothers. "Hello." He smiled at them.

Anandur returned his smile. "I'm Anandur, and this is my brother, Brundar."

Brundar nodded.

Aru's eyes darted around the room until they landed on Okidu. "How did you obtain an Odu? I thought that all of them were decommissioned. Did the rebels smuggle it onboard their ship?"

Aru had just lost points for calling Okidu 'it.'

"Okidu is a 'he' and sometimes a 'she,' but never an 'it,' and the rebels didn't bring any Odus with them. Someone sent the Odus to Earth. They crash landed and wandered the desert until they were found by one of the gods. They have served my family through many generations."

Aru's eyes widened. "So, there are more of them on Earth?"

"Yes." Kian didn't provide a number. "Regrettably, their memories were either wiped or lost because of the crash landing, and they couldn't tell us anything about their creators. We only learned about their fate when we rescued Jade, and she told us their story. They were used, abused, and then used again as scapegoats."

Aru

It was obvious to Aru that the leader of the immortals cared for the Odu, even though he treated him as a servant, and Aru had made a mistake by referring to the Odu as 'it.'

Could he blame it on faulty translation?

Pronouns in his native language were different, and there were many ways to refer to a person, some gender-specific and some gender-neutral. The gender-neutral ones were actually considered more formal and respectful, and gender-specific addresses were reserved for one's close friends and family.

Except, Aru had referred to the Odu as 'it' precisely for the reason Kian had thought he had, and lying about it would only make him uncomfortable.

Aru nodded. "I couldn't agree more, but just so you know, most people on Anumati were brainwashed to believe that the Odus were monstrosities. That was what

I was taught, and that was what the historical records claim. So even now, knowing that most of what we were told did not happen the way it was presented, I can't help the instinctive, negative, fearful response that was programmed into me."

Kian's harsh expression softened. "I understand. Jade told us about the pervasive propaganda that is meant to show the Eternal King in the best light possible and explain his actions as necessary no matter how monstrous they might be." He motioned toward the couch. "Please, take a seat."

The gesture implied that he wanted all three of them on the couch, which was fine with Aru. Taking the middle seat, he waited for Negal and Dagor to flank him.

"Can I offer you gentlemen a drink? I have many fine whiskeys to choose from."

Aru smiled. "I'd prefer beer if you don't mind."

"Of course." The twinkle in Kian's eyes didn't bode well, and Aru wondered what the leader was plotting.

Poisoning by beer?

"I'll join you." Kian sat on one of the armchairs and waved the Odu over. "Beers all around, please."

The advisor sat on the other armchair, and Magnus pulled up a chair that he'd removed from the dining table. The two bodyguards remained standing.

The Odu bowed. "Of course, master. Should I bring a plate of appetizers along with the beers?"

"That's a great idea. Beers first, though. I don't want our guests to be thirsty."

"Right away, master." The Odu bowed again, turned on his heel, and walked over to the bar.

As Aru contemplated how to start the conversation, a long moment of awkward silence ensued. He hadn't formed an opinion about Kian yet or his silent advisor. He had taken an immediate liking to the big redheaded bodyguard and was wary of his blond brother.

The blond with the icy eyes had a lethal aura that was like a big warning sign—'don't mess with my boss, or you'll regret it.'

Aru had a feeling that the guy would be a challenge even for an enhanced god's strength and agility.

When the Odu returned with a case of six beers, Aru arched a brow. "Only six?"

"Anandur and Brundar are on duty," Kian said. "And they don't drink while guarding me. Okidu doesn't drink either."

"Okidu? Do you mean the Odu?"

"That's his name." Kian waved at the beer Aru was holding. "Go ahead. Take a sip. This is a very special beer. It packs a punch."

"Snake Venom," Aru read the label. "67.5% ABV. No wonder it packs a punch."

The drink tasted awful, and Aru did his best not to grimace. Putting the bottle down, he glanced in the direction of the kitchen, hoping the Odu would hurry up with the appetizer plate so he could bite into something that would wash away the taste.

Kian arched a brow. "What's the matter? You don't like the beer?"

"I don't wish to offend, but I'm not a fan."

"It's not bad," Negal said. "After the first few gulps, you get used to the taste. It reminds me of some of the beers back home." He sighed. "It makes me nostalgic."

Kian was still watching Aru with interest in his penetrating blue eyes. "What do you usually drink?"

"I prefer light beers and cocktails that are favored by the ladies." What was the drink that Gabi had introduced him to? It was delicious. Aru smiled sheepishly. "I drink for the taste, not for the alcohol. I don't like being inebriated."

"You like being in control." Kian was still staring him in the eyes.

Was it a competition? Was he supposed to look away?

Some cultures deemed it disrespectful to look a high-ranking person in the eyes.

"I like my mind to operate on all cylinders, as the humans like to say. I'm out of my element here, and I need all my faculties. I'm not much of a diplomat, and I don't know your customs, so if I do or say something that you consider offensive, please let me know so I don't repeat it."

Kian frowned. "Other than referring to Okidu as an object, you were perfectly polite. I don't consider you not liking my beer offensive."

"That's good to know." Aru let out a breath. "How about this staring competition? Am I supposed to look away? What are the rules?"

Kian laughed. "No, you aren't. It might have appeared as if I was staring you down, and I apologize if it made you uncomfortable, but I was just fascinated by you. You look more like an immortal than a god."

That was a fantastic slip of the tongue that Aru could have used to confront Kian about the gods living in his village of immortals, but he didn't want to do that in front of Negal and Dagor.

"And you look more like a god than an immortal."

Kian chuckled. "I'm far from perfect."

"You look quite perfect to me. I can't point out even one imperfection."

"Oh, gosh," said the redhead standing guard behind Kian's chair, in a mocking tone. "Do you two want to continue your bromance in private?"

Kian turned around. "Really, Anandur? You couldn't help yourself for once?"

The redhead affected an apologetic expression and shrugged. "Sorry, boss. I'll keep my mouth shut from now on."

"Right." Kian let out a long-suffering sigh. "I apologize for my associate. He enjoys turning everything into a joke."

"No apologies needed." Aru looked up at the guard. "We were practically asking for it, and I welcome a joke or a humorous comment whenever the situation calls for it." He smiled at the redhead, who didn't seem apologetic at all. "You have a gift, Anandur. You make people smile."

Kian

Anandur beamed at the god. "That's a male with a good sense of humor. You are my kind of guy, Aru."

Brundar groaned. "There will be no stopping him now. We will have to suffer through his infantile jokes for the rest of the afternoon."

Kian rolled his eyes. "Way to impress our guests, guys. Now they think that we are running a clown operation."

Across from him, Aru grinned. "On the contrary. Seeing how free your men feel to goof around with you tells me a lot about your leadership style. It reinforces Jade's favorable impression. Her vouching for you means that she trusts you, and after what she's been through, I bet that it's not been easy to earn her trust."

Aru claimed not to be much of a diplomat, but he was better at it than Kian. Despite Kian's wariness and mistrust of his three guests, he couldn't help but like

Aru, and it had a lot to do with the compliments the guy was showering on him.

Also, he didn't act like a god.

The only two examples of godly behavior Kian had been exposed to were Annani and Toven. His mother was a diva with a personality a hundred times bigger than her petite frame, and Toven was aloof and condescending without meaning to be. It was just the way he was.

Aru, on the other hand, was a nice guy without the inflated ego Kian had expected a god to have. Appearances might be misleading, but Kian's gut was rarely wrong. It might be off a little, but he'd never completely misjudged a person.

Aru's companions weren't afraid of him, and they afforded him only the barest of deference, which meant that his style of leadership was similar to Kian's.

No wonder Aru appreciated it. It echoed his own.

"I have to admit that Jade has grown on me." Kian took a swig of his beer. "Listening to her former tribe members' descriptions of her, I had expected a tyrant with no regard for her people's feelings, but when I met her, I changed my mind. She's made mistakes in the past, of which she's aware, and she is doing her best to guide the future of her people. She's honorable, capable, and trustworthy."

"How about the rest of the Kra-ell?" Aru asked. "How are they getting along with your people?"

"We are still learning to live with each other, and we are all making an effort to accommodate our differences. The Kra-ell are doing their best to assimilate the social etiquette that is accepted in the West, and my people are learning to be patient and accept that it's going to take a while. So far, the integration is going better than I expected." He smiled. "People are people no matter where they come from and what their customs are. We all want the same things in life, and the same is true for the Kra-ell."

"You give me hope." Aru put a hand over his chest. "If the descendants of the gods can coexist with the Kra-ell in peace and harmony and collaboration, then there is hope for Anumati to one day achieve that utopian state as well."

Kian tilted his head. "It's not the same. My people and I did not have preconceived notions about the Kra-ell's inferiority or an ingrained mistrust and animosity towards them. Also, the vast majority of the Kra-ell we welcomed into our community were born on Earth, either to two pureblooded parents or a pureblood and a human." He observed the change in Aru's expression and was glad to see surprise but not horror. "Igor was a vile creature, and I hesitate to attribute anything good to him, but thanks to his resolve to create a new kind of Kra-ell community, they weren't exposed to negative talk about the gods and what happened on Anumati. In a way, it was a fresh start for both of our peoples with only a handful of preconceived notions. That's not the case on the gods' home planet, especially for the old gods who had held on to those beliefs forever."

Aru frowned. "Are you suggesting that we shouldn't try to change things on our home world and should start anew somewhere else in the galaxy?"

Kian shook his head. "I know next to nothing about the politics and socioeconomics of Anumati, so I'm not qualified to make suggestions. It was just a thought."

He wondered whether he should bring up Gabi and her transition. The god had no way of knowing that his lover was a Dormant and that he had inadvertently induced her transition. If he knew, he would have seemed much more worried. Then again, perhaps Aru didn't care about Gabi as much as she cared about him.

"I appreciate your candor." Aru took a cube of cheese off the tray Okidu had brought and popped it into his mouth. When he was done chewing, he looked at Kian. "It's food for thought, but the people of Anumati deserve better, and the grassroots movement that started there is growing by the day. Eventually, there will be so many of us that the king will have no choice but to bow to our demands and become nothing more than a figurehead, step down, or be removed."

"How populous is Anumati?" Kian asked.

For some reason, he hadn't asked Jade that question. Maybe because it had never occurred to him that his ancestral world could become a threat to him and his people.

"It's very populous compared to Earth. There are over three trillion gods residing on Anumati and about one trillion Kra-ell. And then there are the colonies, which probably quadruple that number, and that does not include all the created species."

Kian couldn't comprehend a planet with such a vast population. How could they produce enough food to feed everyone?

"How large is Anumati?" he asked.

"Large." Negal spoke his first word since they had exchanged greetings. "It's about a thousand times larger than Earth."

"That explains it." Kian took a long swig of his beer. "I wondered how they fed all those people."

Aru nodded. "Many gods choose to go into stasis for prolonged periods. We have a labyrinth of deep underground structures that are built under the cities. They are filled with pods that are preprogrammed to wake their occupants at predetermined times."

What Aru had described evoked thoughts of the clan's crypt and human cemeteries. The gods' stasis structures were the equivalent of those.

"Fascinating," Turner said. "What percentage of your population chooses to hibernate?"

"Currently, the rate is about fifteen percent at any given time, but demand for pods is growing. The Kra-ell don't take part in this trend, though, in part because the service is costly and most cannot afford it, and in part because their lifespans are short. They don't get bored with their lives like we do."

"I wish there was a documentary about Anumati we could watch," Anandur said. "It would be easier for me to absorb all the strangeness if I thought of it as a science fiction movie."

Aru smiled up at him. "That's why I love watching human television. This method, more than any other, allows me to learn much faster about human societies. I don't need the deep understanding that comes from reading philosophy and history, and I hate trying to understand all those stuffy words that the authors use to aggrandize themselves. Movies convey the essence of the human condition, and I don't mind that the storylines are oversimplified. They are good enough for me."

Aru

So far, the meeting was going exceedingly well. Kian seemed like a decent guy, and the big bodyguard provided some much-needed comic relief, given the somber theme of the meeting. Magnus, whom Aru had gotten to know the day before, was contented to remain silent today and just listen to the talk.

Aru still hadn't formed an opinion about the advisor, and the other guard was a killer, but since he was the redhead's brother and tolerated the guy's quirky humor, he couldn't be too bad.

"Tea is served, masters." The Odu placed a tray with a teapot and several teacups on the table and offered a fake smile to Aru. "Would master like me to pour for him?"

"Yes, please." Anything was better than the horrible beer, and Aru was thirsty.

Watching the Odu pour the tea, he was fascinated by how closely the cyborg mimicked a human butler.

The representations in the historical records always portrayed the Odus with ugly faces, mean expressions, and a stocky, muscular build.

Up close, Okidu wasn't ugly. He resembled an older human male, and his expression was kind. He was stocky, but he didn't look overly muscular.

Still, Aru and his teammates had easily recognized the Odu for what he was, and it wasn't just his scent that was not fully biological. He resembled the depictions in the historical records, but not completely. It was amazing how slight changes had been enough to portray the Odus in a completely different light.

It always surprised Aru anew how easy it was to manipulate public opinion, especially since the gods were not designed to be easily manipulated like the species they created.

When the Odu handed him the teacup, Aru thanked him, and as Okidu continued pouring tea for the rest of the group, he sipped slowly and watched the interplay between the Odu and the immortals.

They were all fond of him, even the cold blond and the calculating advisor.

Interesting. The Odu might not be the creature of horror Aru had learned about, but he was still an artificial intelligence dressed in a butler suit. He wasn't a person, and as long as he was programmed to be a servant and not a killing machine, he shouldn't evoke any feelings, positive or negative.

"So, Aru," Kian said. "You wanted to meet me, so I assume that you want something from me and my people. Let's hear your proposition."

"I don't have one. Not yet, anyway. I wanted to see who you were and maybe bounce a few ideas around." He smiled. "Don't forget that until yesterday, I didn't know of your existence. Since my teammates and I couldn't find any contemporary mentions of gods or people with extraordinary abilities, we assumed that the rebels and all of their offspring had perished."

Kian regarded him with a raised brow. "You told the team I sent to meet you that it was a known fact that the rebel gods were gone. Their trackers stopped transmitting, and the Eternal King told the public that he had been informed by the oracle that they were gone. That contradicts what you just said about searching for contemporary mentions of gods. You knew there shouldn't be any."

The leader of the immortals was a suspicious guy, and he seemed eager to poke holes in Aru's story. The truth was that Aru happened to know more details about what had actually happened to the rebels, but he couldn't reveal that without casting suspicion on himself. Negal and Dagor weren't privy to the information, and they would wonder how he had come by that knowledge.

"You are right and wrong at the same time. We knew that the original rebels were gone, but they had over two thousand Earth years to produce offspring, who wouldn't have been implanted with trackers and therefore were not accounted for. Some of those gods could have survived, and that was who we were searching for. We assumed that the rebels honored the prohibition on procreating with created species, so we didn't expect to find any hybrid offspring, just young, pureblooded gods. Naturally, we were aware of the human myths surrounding the gods' dalliances with humans, but we didn't take them too seriously. We did a precautionary search for enhanced humans, but when all the leads we investigated proved to be bogus, we stopped searching."

Kian's expression softened. "We are very good at hiding. The Doomers are less so, but they also know to stay under the humans' radar. Your king is right about one thing. Humans might be weak as individuals, but they are formidable when organized. Still, given that there are trillions of gods and only billions of humans, your king has nothing to worry about."

Aru lifted a hand. "First of all, he's not my king. I don't belong to him, although he would like to think that all the gods are his to do with as he pleases. And secondly, he doesn't share his goals with the population. Well, he does, but it's all pretty lies about the beauty of creation and other platitudes. I don't understand why we create intelligent species all over the galaxy but curtail their proliferation and their advancement."

The Supreme probably knew the answer to that, but Aru wasn't in a position where he could ask the Supreme questions, and neither was Aria.

Kian's advisor rubbed his fingers over his clean-shaven jaw. "The king needs to keep his people busy. Seeding new planets and creating new intelligent species seem like exciting endeavors that gods would be glad to partake in. Besides, I'm sure he uses these created species to do work for the gods. Whether it is mining for materials, producing food, or making things. Am I right?"

Aru nodded. "The spin is that we, the benevolent gods, give these people knowledge and the tools necessary to build a civilization, and in their gratitude, they pay us tribute."

"In other words, taxes." Kian put his teacup down. "The more intelligent and productive species the gods create, the more riches they produce for Anumati in the form of taxes, or tribute as they call it. That keeps Anumati's citizens happy and loyal to the king, who makes it all happen. That being said, the gods, or rather the Eternal King and his government, don't want those species to become too numerous, too strong, and too advanced and feel emboldened enough to refuse to pay tribute to the gods. Of course, since Earth was declared a forbidden planet and no taxes are collected here, that doesn't apply to humans, but it's probably a general policy that is implemented universally."

Aru regarded Kian with new appreciation. "You are very astute, Kian. I guess it takes an outsider to see things so clearly. It should have been obvious to me, and yet I once again allowed myself to believe the propaganda."

"I have had the advantage of witnessing human history unfold and empires rise and fall. Instead of creating new species to exploit, humans have conquered and subjugated other humans. The history of Anumati probably was similar in its early days, and different groups of gods fought for dominance. At some point, the Eternal King or his predecessor united all the gods on Anumati and subjugated the only other intelligent species on the planet. When that proved successful, the operation was expanded to other planets in the galaxy."

"We were not taught that," Dagor said. "But Anumati's civilization is very old, and since we suspect that we were not always immortal, it's possible that in our early days, we were not all that different from humans and fought among ourselves."

"There is a saying I once heard," Anandur said, "about a fly in a dung heap who thinks he's in paradise because he's warm and well fed."

Aru tried to decipher what the saying tried to convey, but Anandur must have forgotten the punchline.

Brundar turned an icy stare on his brother. "You have just insulted our guests."

"I'm not offended," Aru said. "Just puzzled. What does the dung fly have to do with what we are talking about?"

Kian

"**N**othing." Kian lifted a hand to stop Anandur from elaborating. "It has nothing to do with our discussion."

They could probably keep talking for hours, and although Kian wanted to learn as much as he could about Anumati, the Eternal King, the rebellion, and how it all affected Earth and humanity, it couldn't all be done in one afternoon. He needed to establish a working relationship with the gods, reach a general understanding regarding future collaboration, and create a platform for future talks.

He couldn't invite them into the village, but he could offer them the penthouse as accommodation during their stay so he could have access to them whenever he pleased.

Under normal circumstances, the gods would not accept his invitation. They wouldn't want to give him so much control. But he had an ace up his proverbial sleeve.

Gabi was in the keep, and if Aru wanted to see her and have access to her, he would have to agree to be the clan's guest with all the limitations on his freedom and privacy that it implied.

The question was how to broach the subject.

"Do the gods still believe in the Fates?" Kian asked. "And in truelove mates?"

"We do." Aru frowned. "Why do you ask?"

"Our ancestors passed the belief in the Fates to us, but I was a skeptic up until not too long ago. Now I'm a believer, especially when it applies to finding one's truelove mate. I've witnessed it happening time and again, first when my own fated love appeared in my life under the most unlikely circumstances, and then when many more were found in similarly strange situations by my clan members. Dormant carriers of godly genes are nearly impossible to identify, and they are very rare, and yet the Fates found a way to make those unions happen, for us and for you."

He expected Aru to look surprised or puzzled, but given the gleam in the god's eyes, he knew precisely what Kian was talking about.

The only way he could have known about Gabi's transition was if he had managed to attach a bug to one of the team members despite all the precautions they had taken.

Once again, Kian's paranoia had prevented a disaster. His insistence on the team staying in the keep had saved them from compromising the village's location.

"What are you talking about?" Aru said in a tone that attempted to sound puzzled but didn't.

The god should never play poker.

"You know what I'm talking about. Or rather, who."

"How should I know that?" Aru was still trying to keep up the pretense. "I didn't thrall you. That would have been a hostile act on my part."

It was possible that Aru or one of his teammates had entered Magnus's mind and plucked the information about Gabi's transition from there, but since they hadn't had enough time with the Guardian to do it stealthily, Magnus would have felt it.

A bug was the more likely method.

There was a slight chance that the god might be a powerful thraller who could enter their minds without them feeling a thing, but Kian was willing to bet it was a spy bug.

"You couldn't have thralled Magnus or me without us feeling the intrusion. You planted a bug on one of the team members you met with yesterday, and that's a hostile act as much as thralling would have been."

Aru swallowed. "Did you find it? If you didn't, you have no proof."

"I don't need proof." Kian leaned forward. "You don't have a poker face, Aru, so I suggest you never play the game, or you'll lose all your money."

For some reason, that seemed to upset Aru more than anything else that had been said so far, including Anandur's inappropriate comment about the happy dung fly.

Kian continued before things could further escalate between them. "I bet that you are dying to see Gabi, and if you drop the charade, I will take you to see her."

Aru let out a breath. "I guess that the cat is out of the hat, or the rabbit is out of the cage, or whatever the saying is. I would very much like to see Gabriella. I've been very worried about her."

The truth was that Kian wasn't even upset about Aru's subterfuge. He would have done the same thing if he was in the god's shoes. What made him angry was that they had somehow missed the spy bug, which meant that the team and Julian had been sloppy.

Who knows what they had talked about after they were convinced that they were bug-free? They could have talked about Annani for all he knew. He would have to question them thoroughly about every word they'd said.

"How much do you know about Gabi's condition?" Turner asked Aru.

"I know that she's transitioning into immortality, but I don't know what that entails. Is she in danger?"

"The transition is not without risks, but Gabi is doing better than most." Kian pushed to his feet. "Come. I'll take you to her."

As Negal and Dagor rose to join Aru, Kian put up a hand. "Only Aru can come. You need to stay here."

Negal looked at his team leader with worry in his eyes. "We shouldn't separate."

"It's okay." Aru motioned for him to sit back down. "If they wanted to harm us, they would have done it already. They need us as much as we need them."

Kian wasn't sure what the gods could do for him and the clan, but evidently Aru had something to offer.

As Anandur and Brundar followed them out of the penthouse, Aru raised a brow. "Why do they get to come? I trusted you not to harm me, and you should have trusted me in return."

Right, as if he was any match for the god. The guy could thrall him to do whatever he pleased, and Kian would happily comply.

"It's protocol." He put his thumb on the elevator button. "Their job is to protect me at all times."

"Aren't you the boss?" Aru asked. "Don't you make the rules?"

The guy was sharp, and Kian made a mental note to be more careful with what he said to him from now on.

"I answer to a council. The clan is not an autocracy."

"Is it a democracy?" The god followed him into the elevator, and the brothers entered after him.

"It is, and it is not. All major decisions have to be put to a vote. Some do not merit the full assembly, and the council vote is enough, but some require the vote of every clan member. Still, I have a lot of autonomy to run things as I see fit."

"But not regarding the twenty-four-seven guards," Aru said.

"No. I can't defy the rules on that."

Aru

Aru's heart was thrumming with excitement mixed with trepidation. He would finally meet Gabi as himself, not as Uriel—his borrowed identity.

He'd been lucky that a name close to his real one had been available for purchase, and it had made it a little easier to use it and hear it on Gabi's lips, especially when she was climaxing.

He'd never expected her to learn that he was a god, and the fact that the Fates had made it so spoke volumes about their plans.

Was Gabriella Emerson his one and only?

Would she forgive him for the lies?

He had no choice; surely she would understand that?

"How did you smuggle the bug past all of our precautions?" Kian asked. "Were my people sloppy?"

They had been, but it wouldn't have made a difference if they had been more diligent.

"It's very small, undetectable by human devices, and we can control it remotely. We just kept moving it from person to person."

Kian frowned. "Our hearing and eyesight are nearly as good as yours. How is it possible that they didn't hear or see it? How small is that thing? The size of a mote of dust?"

"A little larger than that." Aru watched the numbers on the elevator display change from positive to negative. "How deep into the ground are we going?"

"Pretty deep. After this episode is over, we are going to collapse the passages and block all entrances to the underground. Regrettably, this location is compromised beyond salvation."

As the elevator doors opened, Kian motioned for Aru to step out first; his bodyguards followed, and he was the last to exit, but as they started walking, the brothers fell a few steps behind to give them privacy.

Aru could feel the cold gaze of the blond guard, freezing a hole in his back.

"What's wrong?" Kian asked.

He must have shivered. "I like Anandur." Aru glanced over his shoulder, and sure enough, the blond's hard eyes were boring holes into him. "But the other one gives me the creeps, as the humans like to say." He'd spoken quietly enough so only Kian could hear him.

Kian laughed and clapped him on the back. "You've got good instincts, Aru. Brundar is the one you should be wary of."

Surprised by the familiar gesture, Aru realized that Kian's presence hadn't evoked the prickly response that encountering an unfamiliar god or immortal usually did. "I wonder why the back of my neck didn't prickle even once. It should have."

Kian shrugged. "Not necessarily. You knew that you were meeting an immortal. In my experience, the prickling gives you a warning when you don't realize that you are in the presence of a competing immortal, or in your case, a god."

"That wasn't my experience, but then we are separated by seven thousand years of genetic tinkering, so things might be different for me."

"Yeah, I guess so. Is that why you and your friends don't glow?"

Aru stopped walking. "Only members of the royal family glow."

Were the gods living among the immortal descendants of Ahn or his two siblings? Otherwise, how would Kian know about the glow?

"Oh, really?" Kian affected a surprised tone. "Jade must have mentioned something about the gods glowing.

Perhaps she didn't know that commoner gods didn't glow."

"Perhaps." Aru resumed walking.

Kian had remarked about Aru's lack of a poker face, but Kian wasn't a good liar either. If he'd learned about the gods having a glow from Jade and the ones living in his community didn't have it, he would have wondered why they didn't. But since he wondered why Aru and his teammates didn't glow, the ones in his village most likely did.

Should he reveal that he already knew about the surviving gods?

Kian would find out soon enough, so perhaps it was a good idea to build a better rapport with him before it happened and reassure him that he had nothing to fear from Aru and his teammates.

"You shouldn't abandon this great building and its underground compound just because my teammates and I followed the signals here. We will never disclose this location. Your secret is safe with us."

"Even if you mean what you say, you and your friends have implanted trackers, and your movements are recorded. Your commander and his superiors will know that you were here."

Aru shrugged. "So what? We've visited thousands of locations, and we will visit many more over the next century. No one will pay attention to our short sojourn here."

"What about the old trackers? The ones we took out of Igor and several others when we thought that he was the only threat? Their movements were recorded as well."

"Don't worry about that. No one other than us follows those."

Kian sighed. "Even if I trusted you and your friends to keep quiet about us and this location, which I don't, because I'm too paranoid to trust strangers, especially gods, the information could be compelled out of you, right?"

"Yeah, but why would anyone bother? We are not important. We are just what the humans refer to as foot soldiers."

He happened to be more than that, but it was thanks to his unique talent, which was a secret he and Aria guarded zealously.

Kian stopped and turned to him. "The only way the information will be safe is if they can't find you. We can take the trackers out of you the same way we did for the Kra-ell, and we can stage a plane crash to explain your demise." He grimaced. "My wife won't like the idea, but we could put your trackers inside gerbils and put those gerbils on a private plane that will crash into the ocean. It would be very convincing, especially if you notify your commander that you are chartering a private jet for some important mission."

Kian must have spent some time thinking about that, or else he had staged someone's fake death before. In either case, it was a tempting proposition, and Aru wished he could accept it.

"Thank you for the offer, but we can't do that. We have families that depend on us, and if we disappear, they will suffer."

"If you and your friends die in an accident, there will be no retribution against your loved ones back home. Are there financial consequences?"

"Not really, but we wouldn't want to cause our families the anguish of believing we've died." He smiled. "Eternal life is a blessing and a curse, and living forever with the pain of losing a child is not something I want to subject my parents to."

Kian nodded. "I can understand that."

"I'm not dismissing your idea out of hand, though. Let's revisit it in a hundred years. In a century, our circumstances might change dramatically."

"Indeed." Kian stopped in front of a door marked as a clinic. "Where is your bug now? I assume that when you heard about Gabi, you attached it to Julian?"

"Correct. And then we moved it to Gilbert because he promised Gabi that he wouldn't leave her side."

"Does your bug need a live host like the trackers?"

"No, but it's easiest to hide it on a person. It has a very limited range, and its charge doesn't last long. The less we move it around, the longer it can broadcast."

"I appreciate your candor." Kian put his hand on the door handle. "I would also appreciate you removing it from Gilbert and handing it over to me."

Kian

"I'm sorry, but I can't do that," the god said.

Kian removed his hand from the handle. "Perhaps you would like to rethink your answer?"

Aru was taken aback. "What I meant was that I couldn't hand the bug over because we are running low on the spy drones, and we can't resupply, but if you allow me free access to Gabi, I'll gladly remove the bug and show it to you if you'd like. The technology is so far superior to anything humans can currently produce that it won't do you any good to take it apart."

After William's unsuccessful experience with trying to take apart the trackers, which were supposed to be old technology, it hadn't even crossed Kian's mind to suggest that William try to reverse engineer the bug. What he was concerned with was that there was more than one, and more specifically, where the others were deployed.

Thankfully, no one who had been in contact with the gods had returned to the village, so the location hadn't been compromised, but Kian had no desire to spend the night in the keep, especially since he planned to offer Aru and his friends the penthouse.

"How many more bugs did you attach to my people?"

"That's the only one."

"I doubt it."

As Kian put his hand back on the door handle, he could hear Aru's heart thundering in his chest. The god was anxious to get inside the clinic and see Gabi, which meant that he was primed to make concessions to make it happen, especially since the object of his desire was right there behind the door, and Kian was the only thing stopping him from entering.

"I swear on my honor, that's the only one," Aru said. "Well, the only one left. Before entering the building, we swept it with several bugs, but we didn't make it all the way to the penthouse or down to the underground levels, so we didn't find anything of use and retrieved them before they ran out of power. We are very frugal with how we use the drones we have left. They need to last us over a hundred years, and we've already used up a third monitoring the Kra-ell."

Kian believed him, but he wasn't done with his interrogation. "You no longer need to monitor the Kra-ell, and human technology will catch up at some point, so you will be able to replenish your supplies."

Aru groaned. "There is only one drone in here, and it's perched on Gilbert's shoulder. I would like to take it back, but if you want it that much, you can have it."

Kian still didn't depress the handle. "I'll make you a deal. You'll tell me how I can locate and identify these drones, and I'll let you have it back."

"You don't have the necessary technology."

Kian smiled. "Then you'll have to provide it."

If Aru was human, he would have popped a vein by now. "I can't. If I do, you will be able to see everything our drones see."

Kian's smile broadened. "I don't see a problem with that. For the next hundred years or so, all you can spy on is us, the Kra-ell, and various humans. Sharing the information with us does not present a conflict of interest for you."

Letting out a breath, Aru closed his eyes. "If I agree, Dagor and Negal will remove me from my post and keep me under house arrest until the ship returns for us."

"So, it's a yes?"

"You don't leave me much choice."

"No, I don't, but I'll sweeten the deal for you. For as long as Gabi is transitioning, you can stay in the penthouse we've just come from and see her whenever you want. I'll add your thumbprint to the elevator's database so you can use it to travel freely between the penthouse and the clinic."

Aru looked surprised. "Isn't that your place?"

"It belongs to me, and I used to live there, but I live else-where now, and I rent out the penthouse. The previous renter moved out not long ago, and I haven't found a replacement yet, so you and your friends can use it. There are three bedrooms, each with its own bathroom, and a gorgeous terrace that includes a swimming pool. It even comes with a concierge service. Whenever you are hungry, you can call the security desk downstairs, and they will arrange for a delivery."

The god regarded him with amusement in his dark eyes. "Are you sweetening the deal for me or for you?"

"I think it's a win-win, which is what great deals are all about. I get to keep an eye on you, and you get to see Gabi whenever you want."

"Not to mention Jade and Morgada and the two immortal males who are staying in the penthouse across the vestibule."

"Indeed."

Aru must have learned that from eavesdropping on the team's conversations through the spy drone, but the team wasn't going to stay in the other penthouse for long.

Once the god showed him how to identify and locate the bugs and agreed to stay in the keep, Kian was going to lift the lockdown and allow the team to return home.

His main motivation was that he wanted to return to the village, and it wouldn't be fair to do so while the others were stranded in the keep.

"How long is Gabi's transition going to last?" Aru asked.

"About six months." When the god's face fell, Kian chuckled. "But she's not going to be in the clinic for the entire time. The first stage is the most difficult, and it lasts anywhere between a few days and several weeks."

"You scared me." Aru let out a breath. "I thought that Gabi would be bedridden for half a year."

Aru

If Kian didn't open the door in the next two seconds, Aru was going to shove him aside and barge in, consequences be damned.

The invitation to enjoy the penthouse was a honey trap, but he had a feeling that if he declined, he wouldn't get to see Gabi at all. Especially after Kian learned what he'd heard thanks to the spy drone.

Aru had no doubt that Kian would interrogate every member of the team he had sent the day before, the doctor and Gilbert, and when they recounted everything that had been said, he would realize that the genie was out of the bottle or the lamp, or whatever it was that genies were usually trapped in, and that Aru knew about the gods living in Kian's community.

"We can continue our talk later." Kian finally opened the door to the waiting room.

The doctor greeted them with a smile. "Hello, Aru. Can I call you Aru?" He offered his hand.

"What else would you call me?" He shook the immortal's hand.

The doctor was another example of an immortal who could have passed for a god.

It made sense to him now. Some of these immortals were the descendants of the royals, and therefore possessed a more godly appearance than those who were the descendants of commoner gods.

"Do gods have last names?" Julian asked.

Kian chuckled. "Given that there are three trillion of them on Anumati, I'm sure they do. How many individual names could they have come up with?"

"We are usually referred to as the son or daughter of, fill in the mother and father's name. And if that's not enough to distinguish who we are, we can include the maternal and paternal grandparents' names. Familial connections are more important to us than our ancestors' place of origin or their occupation, which is what most human surnames are based on."

"We are the same," the doctor said. "But we have to adopt fake last names when dealing with humans. You did so as well."

"I did." Aru darted his eyes toward the door standing between him and Gabi. "Can I please see Gabriella now?"

"Regrettably, she's not awake at the moment." The doctor walked over to the door. "But given her pattern so far, she will wake up soon. In the meantime, you can chat with her brother."

Aru wasn't looking forward to that. Gilbert was not his fan at the moment, and Aru expected some posturing on the brother's part.

Julian opened the door and poked his head inside. "Can we come in? Aru and Kian are here." He glanced at them over his shoulder. "Brundar and Anandur will have to stay in the waiting room."

Anandur nodded. "That's okay as long as the door stays open."

"That's doable." Julian stepped aside. "You can go in."

Aru didn't wait for Kian to let him pass. Instead, he surged forward, entered the room, and went straight to the hospital bed.

"Oh, Gabi." He took hold of her small limp hand and brought it to his cheek. "I'm so sorry."

"Sorry for what?" her brother asked. "For inducing her transition? For lying to her? For planning to abandon her? You need to be more specific."

"All of the above," Aru murmured against Gabi's soft palm.

"That's not what I want to hear," Gilbert said.

Kian cleared his throat. "Since Gabi is asleep, we can take care of the spy drone business. Where is it?"

With a sigh, Aru put Gabi's hand down and turned around to look at her brother. There was some familial resemblance, but even though the brother had claimed to have been induced by a god, he still looked human.

"What are you talking about?" Gilbert frowned. "What spy drone? Ours?"

"No, his." Kian pointed with a tilt of his head.

So much of what had bothered Gabi about her family's uncharacteristic behavior made sense to Aru now, but he didn't have time to think about it. Perhaps later, they would leave him alone with her so he could gather his thoughts.

Pushing away from the bed, he walked over to Gilbert and extended his hand. "May I touch your shoulder? You have a little something there."

"What is it?" Gilbert turned his head, trying to see what was there, but the bug was too close to his neck for him to see.

Aru gently lifted the tiny device and put it on his fingertip. "This is it. The mighty spy."

Gilbert's eyes bugged out. "That's a drone? It's the size of a flea."

"It's a little larger than that." Kian leaned over to take a closer look. "But not by much. It's the size of a small mosquito. How does that thing see and hear and transmit information?"

"How does a real mosquito do that?" Aru retorted. "Much of our technology is based on genetics and is built from biological components." He smiled. "That's the extent of my technical acumen, so don't expect me to explain more."

"How long has this thing been on my shoulder?" Gilbert asked.

"It arrived with Julian," Kian said. "And since Aru was mostly interested in how Gabi was doing, he kept the drone in this room."

"Crap," Gilbert muttered. "I might have said things to Gabi that he shouldn't know."

Kian frowned. "Like what?"

"I'd rather not repeat them in case he missed it."

"I didn't miss it." Aru turned to Kian. "Let's step outside. I don't want any negative energy around Gabi."

Kian

nger mixed with worry had Kian flexing his hands. "Why should the energy turn negative? We are all civilized people here. What have you heard?"

Aru cast the brother an apologetic look. "Gilbert told Gabi that she doesn't have exclusive bragging rights to having been induced by a god because he had been induced by one as well."

Kian swallowed a vile curse. "What else?"

"Gabi said that she was under the impression that all the gods were gone and only their immortal descendants remained. Gilbert told her that the surviving gods are the clan's most guarded secret."

Fuck! If Gilbert had said anything about Annani, he was going to throttle him.

"What else?" Kian demanded.

"That's it." Aru shrugged as if he hadn't just learned the clan's most guarded secret. "Then he talked about me and what I was supposedly capable of and why I was dangerous to immortals."

"Was I wrong?" Gilbert asked.

"I don't know." Aru rubbed the back of his neck. "I've never tried to thrall any of you, so I don't know if I can. I know that the Kra-ell's minds are not susceptible to manipulation, but human minds are, so perhaps I can thrall those who are half human and half something else."

Thank the merciful Fates Gilbert hadn't said more. Perhaps the situation was still salvageable.

Kian liked Aru, and he really didn't want to kill him and the other two or force them into stasis, but if they learned about Annani, he would have no choice. Toven was less problematic because he wasn't a direct heir to the Anumati throne, but it was better if the gods didn't know who the survivors were.

It would be a damn shame to have to get rid of them, because the clan and humans needed them.

If taking down the Eternal King was the only way to save the human race, Kian would need access to the resistance, and that meant he needed the three rebel gods alive and well and not in stasis.

Aru took a deep breath and then looked at Kian. "Gilbert didn't say more, but I've deduced a few things from clues you provided."

Kian was afraid of that. "That's not a conversation we should have while standing in the waiting room of the clinic. We should move it to my office." He started toward the door.

Aru didn't follow. "I want to stay with Gabi."

"She's asleep. You'll get to talk to her when she's awake."

The god arched a brow. "Will I?"

Evidently, he was afraid that after learning what he had deduced, Kian would retract his offer to stay in the penthouse and see Gabi whenever he pleased.

"Don't worry. Everything I promised you still stands. I'm not the kind of guy who goes back on his word. I want us to go to my office because this is not the kind of conversation that should be conducted while standing next to a woman in a hospital bed who needs peace and tranquility."

Aru cracked a smile. "Wasn't that what I said a moment ago?"

"Come on, wise guy. My old office is just around the corner."

"Is it really?"

"No, it's one level up."

When Aru still hesitated, Kian shook his head. "I give you my word that you'll get to spend as much time with Gabi as she will allow you, which might not be much after she learns of your deceit. But in my experience, women are merciful, and if you grovel enough, she might forgive you. My offer of free use of the penthouse still stands as well."

Casting one more longing look behind him, Aru let out a sigh and followed him out of the clinic.

Thankfully, Gilbert got the hint that he wasn't invited and stayed behind, or maybe he just didn't want to leave his sister.

Kian waited with his questions until the four of them reached his old office and took seats around the conference table. It wasn't that he feared someone might overhear them on the way, but the subject was too grave to discuss casually.

He also needed time to think, but the short walk hadn't been long enough to come up with a solution for the conundrum he found himself faced with.

"So, what did you deduce from what I've told you?" he asked.

Aru cast a glance at Anandur and Brundar. "My teammates don't know any of this. I watched the feed from the drone alone in my room, and I deleted the relevant footage. If they ask about the missing time, I'll say that the doctor was examining Gabi and that I didn't want them to see that."

Obviously, Aru was hinting that the confidential nature of what he was about to reveal might not be appropriate for the ears of Kian's bodyguards.

"You can say anything in front of Anandur and Brundar. I have no secrets from them. "

The god nodded. "You asked me why my teammates and I don't have a glow. I concluded from your question that the gods living in your village have it. Since only those of royal descent glow, your gods are the descendants of the Eternal King's children."

The blood chilled in Kian's veins.

If Aru was not who he claimed to be, and he was one more assassin the Eternal King had sent to eliminate any potential heirs, Kian would really have no choice but to kill him or force him into stasis.

Then again, if Aru was an assassin, he wouldn't have revealed what he'd figured out.

Why was he doing that? Was it an attempt to gain Kian's trust?

And how come his mother had never mentioned gods with no glow?

Could it be that Aru was fishing for information?

That would be a clever way to get Kian to admit that descendants of the Eternal King were living in his community.

He wasn't going to fall into that trap.

"According to our legends, all gods were luminous. That was how humans identified them. Some might have been brighter than others, and there were stories about gods who had lost their glow after losing a truelove mate or suffering some other calamity, but there was no mention of any gods that were born without a glow."

Aru

~~~

Was Kian weaving tales of radiant gods to conceal the presence of the Eternal King's descendants in his community?

Or were his tales true, and all the exiled gods had been luminous?

Much had changed over the seven millennia since the rebels had been exiled. Gods born post-rebellion might have been designed without the radiant glow. Yet, the majority of Anumati's population was ancient, predating the rebellion, and save for those with royal lineage, they were not luminous.

It wasn't likely that they had all undergone procedures to remove their glow, but perhaps there was an elixir that could create or enhance luminosity or, conversely, one that muted it.

Was it possible that the rebels had striven to equalize things in more ways than anyone had suspected?

In their quest for equality, they might have found a way to make everyone in their community glow, at least a little. It could have been achieved with simple measures like rubbing oil infused with gold on their skin or by more complicated methods that involved genetic alterations.

As far as Aru knew, the rebels hadn't been equipped with what was needed to conduct genetic experiments and alterations, but it was possible that some equipment and instructions had survived from the original creation of humans, which had happened two million years ago.

It was hard to believe that any tools had remained hidden for so long, and the technology must have been primitive compared to what the gods could do now, but perhaps it had been enough to make everyone luminous to some degree.

"The division is very clear on Anumati," he said. "Those of royal descent glow, and everyone else does not. There are several royal lines, their descendants are numerous, and they possess different degrees of radiance. Those closest to the original royals naturally are the brightest. It makes it very easy to differentiate between the aristocracy and the commoners."

"How do you explain our legends then?" Anandur asked. "They were very clear about all the gods being luminous creatures. That's how they appear in human legends as well."

Aru shrugged. "It's just a thought, but maybe there was a way to enhance or subdue the glow with chemicals. The rebels were all about equality, so they might have wanted every god in their new utopia to be equally luminous."

Kian looked skeptical. "I doubt that's what happened. The gods could suppress their glow at will. Maybe the Eternal King decreed at some point that all the non-royals had to stop glowing. The old gods were forced to suppress it, and the young gods were genetically altered so they no longer had the ability."

Again, Kian surprised Aru with insight into the way the Eternal King might have thought and operated that would have never occurred to him. "You might be right about that. When I get back to Anumati, I'll try to find some old gods who are not the Eternal King's supporters and who are willing to tell me the truth."

Perhaps the Supreme would answer that question if he asked very politely and explained what had prompted his inquiry.

Tonight, Aru would contact Aria and tell her what he had found out. He had no doubt that the Supreme would be delighted by his discovery and would want him to find out more.

He might have no choice but to enter one of the immortals' minds to get the answers the Supreme would demand.

Kian regarded him with a frown. "Do you still think that you are going back to Anumati? With what you know, I can't let you leave."

"I'm on your side, Kian. I'm not a threat to you, your people, or the gods living among you, whether they are the descendants of the Eternal King's rebellious children or just common gods. I'm part of the resistance, and admitting that to you was a risk I took because I knew that you needed me as much as I needed you."

Kian leaned back in his chair. "What exactly do you need me for? What can a bunch of immortals do to help free a trillion gods from the rule of the Eternal King? We are utterly insignificant."

Kian

Did Kian even want to help free the gods?

The Eternal King was a piece of work, but he kept the gods in check, and he at least cared about public opinion, which limited to some extent what he could get away with.

Whoever replaced him might be worse.

"Of course, you are significant," Aru said. "Every person, every mind is important, and every day more minds join the resistance. Your advantage is that you don't exist as far as the king is concerned. He doesn't know about you, and I would like to keep it that way. The problem is that I need to keep reporting about the Kra-ell. I can say that they rebelled against Igor, overthrew him, and took out their trackers, but then I will have to supply their new location, and that's where you live. I hate to say it, but your communities will have to separate, and it's better to do it now than to wait a century, when the integration will be so complete that it would be too painful to do so."

Kian had no intention of doing that, and not only because he now felt like he needed the might of the Kra-ell more than ever. He liked the idea of their integrated community.

The worst thing for immortals was stagnation and boredom, and the Kra-ell infused the village with new interest —even if not all of it was positive.

Kian shook his head. "There is no need for that. You can claim to have lost track of them because they removed the trackers. What else are you supposed to do during your tour of duty on Earth?"

"After we found out about the settler ship's arrival and we discovered the surviving Kra-ell, we were tasked with finding the missing pods and either verifying that their occupants had perished or reviving those who are still in stasis."

"Your job was to find the royal twins," Kian stated.

He had no doubt that he was right, and Aru didn't try to deny it.

The god nodded. "Yes, that too."

It hadn't occurred to Kian before, but it was likely that the twins were also luminous, which might explain why they had always been veiled. Maybe they couldn't manage their glow as adeptly as his mother and Toven could. The ability to control it might come with age, and they had been young when their mother had smuggled them onto the settler ship.

It was a question he should address to Annani and perhaps also Toven.

Toven had been so good at suppressing his glow and had done it for so long that he had lost the ability, and according to Annani, her half-sister's luminosity had also been lost or greatly diminished after her first mate had been killed.

Come to think of it, Areana and Toven had both been suffering from depression when they lost their glow, and Toven had regained his after finding happiness with Mia, so perhaps there was a connection.

Bridget would say that a test sample of two was not good science, but Kian didn't need to prove anything to anyone, and two was good enough for a hunch.

Leaning back, he crossed his arms over his chest and leveled his gaze at Aru. "What exactly are you expecting us to help you with?"

"I'm not sure yet." Aru mimicked Kian's pose. "But if you believe in the Fates, then you must suspect that they brought us together for a reason."

"I knew it," Anandur muttered under his breath. "This is a bad bromance."

Shaking his head, Kian ignored the fatuous comment. "My belief in the Fates does not influence my decision-making, especially when the safety of my people is at stake. The Fates might have orchestrated your meeting with Gabi, but that's as far as my belief in supernatural forces can stretch. Even those who believe in them wholeheartedly accept that the Fates are not supposed to get involved in the greater design of nations."

Aru nodded. "You are right. Forget I said that. We can't rely on supernatural beings who are known to be capricious to guide us, but everything else I said about the Eternal King and the resistance is true. A cooperation could be beneficial to both of us." He smiled. "We have similar goals, but the most important one for now is staying alive and protecting the lives of those we care about."

"Who am I supposed to cooperate with? I can accept that you are a member of the resistance, but you are not its leader, nor do you even have access to whoever is running the show."

"You don't know much about me. What are you basing your assumptions on?"

Could he have been wrong about the god? Was there more to him than being the leader of an insignificant team investigating an insignificant planet?

Perhaps he was the son or nephew of someone who was close to the resistance leadership?

"All I can base my assumptions on is what you have told me. Did you lie about who you are?"

"I did not." Aru uncrossed his arms and leaned forward. "This information has to stay between us." He looked at Brundar and Anandur and then back at Kian. "I need the three of you to vow that what I'm about to tell you doesn't leave this room."

Kian uncrossed his arms as well. "I can give you my vow, but since I'm not Kra-ell, how can you trust it? The same is true for Anandur and Brundar. I can vouch for their trustworthiness and honor, but how can you be sure that I'm not lying?"

"Sometimes, a gut feeling is all we have." The god's eyes bored into Kian's. "If we want to move this to the next level, I have to trust my instincts about you and take a risk, and the same is true for you. Otherwise, we will just keep dancing around each other and make no progress."

That was true, and they each had leverage over the other. Kian had Gabi, who seemed to be Aru's truelove mate, even if the god hadn't realized that yet, and that made her the most precious person in the universe to him. He would never do anything to endanger her, her family, or anyone she cared about.

Also, Aru and his teammates were currently isolated on Earth, and Kian had the means to force them into stasis or kill them. Other than inborn immunity, there was no defense against the gods' thrall, but he was lucky to have the Kra-ell on his side. The purebloods were immune to thralling and could easily overtake the gods.

Aru's leverage was obvious. He knew about the immortal community, and now he also knew about the gods being part of it and suspected they were of royal descent.

"I give you my word that what you are about to tell us will not leave this room unless you later give me permission to share it with my council and the leaders of the other branches of our community when the time comes for decision-making. I'm not an absolute ruler, and important decisions have to be approved by the council." And also by his mother.

"That's acceptable." Aru shifted his gaze to the brothers. "I need to hear you say it."

After both of them gave him their word, Aru let out a breath. "I have a way to communicate with the resistance leadership. My teammates don't know about it, and neither does anyone on the patrol ship, and I need it to stay that way. That's why it can't leave this room."

Kian frowned. "How? You said that you can't communicate with Anumati unless the signal goes to the patrol ship first and is then redirected from there."

"I have a way, but I'm not going to disclose it."

Kian had an inkling about the method Aru was using to communicate with Anumati, and it was the same one he had suspected Igor of employing but couldn't prove.

"Fair enough. So, what's the next step?"

"I have to ask for instructions. I suspect that the resistance will find it very advantageous to have a base of operation on the forbidden planet, and they will appreciate your help establishing it."

"I'm not sure that's something I want." Kian leaned back. "As you have said, the human race might already be a target for the Eternal King just because of how populous it has become and how technologically advanced it is.

Why would I want to add rebel sympathizers to that and ensure this planet's annihilation?"

His words didn't seem to have the impact he'd hoped for.

The god regarded him with his dark, focused gaze. "The resistance can give you and your people a fighting chance. The alternative is to submit and helplessly watch the end. The Eternal King will not stop at culling the human population. He deems hybrids of all kinds abominations, which is ironic because all the created species have some godly genes in them, but he would order your annihilation nonetheless."

Turner

✦

Ever since Aru had left with Kian and the brothers, Turner had been trying to get information out of Negal and Dagor, but so far, they hadn't said much about anything of consequence. If they weren't stuffing their mouths with the little sandwiches Okidu kept bringing out or sipping on their coffee, they were expertly avoiding answering his questions about the resistance.

Turner suspected that they had centuries' worth of experience talking in circles about important issues and not saying much. They were supposedly young gods, but what was considered young on Anumati?

Anyone under a thousand years old?

These two were either born politicians or had been trained to avoid answering questions without appearing rude.

Usually Turner was a great interrogator, walking a fine line between befriending his subjects and intimidating them, but evidently gods were not easily intimidated by immortals, and rightly so.

The two seemed more wary of the Odu than of him or Magnus, so maybe he should let Okidu conduct the interrogation.

Well, that was an idea. Perhaps the subject of the Odus would be a good one to get them talking. The Odus were ancient history to these gods, so discussing them shouldn't be a problem, and once Negal and Dagor loosened up, they might reveal a thing or two that was useful.

After Okidu had refilled their coffee cups and returned to the kitchen, Turner leaned back. "So, there are no more Odus on Anumati?"

Jade had told them that they had been replaced with simpler versions of household robots, but he could pretend not to know that.

"Not this model," Negal said. "The new models look more like machines, and their learning ability is greatly curtailed." He glanced in the direction of the kitchen. "The old model is so lifelike that it's disturbing. It's difficult to think of him as anything other than a person, but that wasn't why they were banned."

"It was because of the back door to their programming," Dagor said. "They could easily be turned into killing machines. The new ones have brains that are solid core.

You can't tamper with those without destroying them, so the way they come out of the assembly line is the way they stay. All our technology is like that now, and it's a pain in the ass because we can't fix anything. Once it's broken, it has to be discarded."

That was progress. He might have just learned something useful.

"It makes sense." Turner rubbed a hand over his jaw. "I assume that production is closely monitored and regulated, and when the product leaves the factory, it can't be altered in any way. That ensures that no new monstrosities can be built."

Dagor grimaced. "Everything that's made on Anumati has to have the king's stamp of approval. Which makes it very difficult for the resistance to come up with creative solutions for encrypted communication. The only way to transfer information so it doesn't fall into the wrong hands is in person, and even that is problematic because the king employs telepaths. They can't read what you are thinking, but they can sense that you are not happy and plotting something, and then they send the interrogators after you."

"No wonder the resistance has to work at a cosmic snail's pace," Magnus said.

That was so terrifying and disturbing that Turner had to suppress a shiver, which was rare for him. He'd seen and experienced too much to get easily rattled, but what Dagor described was hell disguised as utopia.

Turner suspected that drug use was rampant on Anumati. If people had to be happy to avoid interrogation, they needed something to help them achieve that state. Happiness was doable in short bursts but wasn't sustainable over time.

"Are any of the products used by the gods manufactured in the colonies?"

Negal shook his head. "The colonies supply raw materials. Whatever they make is for internal consumption."

"Yeah, because it's crap," Dagor said. "Even if it was allowed, no one would buy stuff made off planet."

"What about food?" Magnus asked. "Is that brought into Anumati from the colonies?"

Negal cast him a condescending look. "It makes absolutely no sense to use interstellar ships to transport food. It makes much more sense to transport those who need the food to the colonies than the other way around."

So that was why the gods were colonizing. It wasn't only to collect raw materials and experiment with creating new species. They needed to offload chunks of their population repeatedly, but since gods didn't like to work hard, they created servants from local species. It was much cheaper and less complicated than building factories and producing robots or cyborgs to do the work.

Not a bad system.

Turner took a sip from his coffee and put the cup down on the table. "The Eternal King might be a cold bastard, but he's found a way to keep the population well fed and occupied. Boredom is probably the most difficult problem for gods. If they are not kept busy with interesting and creative endeavors, they will go insane or choose to go into stasis."

Negal nodded. "Many of the wealthy old gods choose to sleep for thousands of years. It solves both of the problems you mentioned. Food and boredom."

"That's a clever solution," Magnus said. "It seems like the king has everything running as well as can be expected, and I wonder why people are rebelling. Is it still about the Kra-ell and their quest for equal rights?"

"It started with the Kra-ell struggle for equality," Negal said. "But it didn't end there. The rebellion gave the king the perfect excuse to tighten his control over the population and further reduce individual freedoms. Most people accepted the new reality, but some didn't. Every day, more and more realize how little freedom they really have and that everything in their lives is predetermined, including what traits they and their children possess. Those born with traits the king doesn't want and can't control are discriminated against. Immunes, in particular, have been targeted until there are practically none left on Anumati. Those unlucky enough to be born like that do their best to hide their immunity to compulsion. Getting off planet and settling in one of the colonies is usually their best option. That way, they can at least choose where to go and not get sent to a dangerous place."

Turner lifted his coffee cup. "Not to mention that being off planet means that they can allow themselves the luxury of not feeling happy every minute of the day."

"What other traits are discriminated against?" Magnus asked.

"Telepaths, seers, remote viewers," Negal said. "All of them threaten the Eternal King's control because they can pierce the veil of his propaganda."

Turner tilted his head. "Aru mentioned something about the king pretending to have learned about his children's demise from the oracle. Isn't the oracle a seer?"

Negal snorted. "He doesn't kill them off. He gathers them around him so he can control which of their predictions see the light of day. Seers are either employed in the service of the crown or sent away to remote planets with volatile populations where they are not likely to survive."

"Clever bastard," Turner muttered. "I just wonder what will happen once he's removed. Whoever replaces him might not be as capable and cause more harm than good."

Turner had seen that happen too many times on Earth. Eliminating despicable rulers did not guarantee a better life for their populations. More often than not, the replacement turned out even worse.

Negal surprised him by nodding. "That's why the resistance is not in a rush to remove him anytime soon. We are taking it slow, so when the time comes, we will not ruin our civilization while trying to make it better."

Aru

Aru had hyperbolized the consequences of Kian and his clan refusing to assist the resistance, but he had a good reason.

He had done it to drive the point home.

Nothing was immediate. They had one hundred and fifteen years before his team could no longer hide what they had found, and when they did and the news got to the king, he wouldn't respond right away. When he finally turned his sights on Earth, it would take a ship another hundred years or so to get there, or perhaps a little less if the king only sent a group of scientists with a pathogen on a small ship that was faster.

According to this calculation, Kian had between three to five hundred years to come up with a solution. Hopefully, humans would not develop interstellar travel ability in the interim, or the grace period would be severely shortened.

But even if they had the full five centuries until the arrival of the Eternal King's forces, the resistance might not yet be ready to help.

Humans were most likely doomed with or without the resistance, and Kian probably knew it.

What Aru was offering him was a sliver of hope.

There was nothing worse than hopelessness and helplessness, and those could only be alleviated with action. Waiting for the inevitable disaster without doing anything to prevent it, even if the chances of success were low, would destroy Kian and everyone he shared the dire news with.

That was no way to live, and Aru was sure that despite Kian's reservations, he would grasp at the proverbial straw he'd been offered.

Briefly closing his eyes, Kian took a deep breath and nodded. "You are right. I'd rather go down fighting. In a hundred years or so, we might be able to make all humans immune to disease or even turn them immortal, but that won't save them, nor would it save us. The king will just use some different means to decimate or annihilate the population. It could be done by introducing a pathogen that will kill crops worldwide and cause mass starvation or by detonating EMPs in Earth's atmosphere and frying our electrical grids and means of transportation. Our existence is so fragile, so perilous, and so easily extinguished." He waved his hand. "We live with a false sense of security that is born of ignorance, or maybe the ostrich syndrome. We bury our heads in the sand and convince ourselves that nothing is going to happen to us."

Aru was still stuck on Kian's remark about his clan's ability to turn humans immune to disease or even immortal.

Was the clan privy to the gods' secrets of genetic engineering?

"I don't know what ostrich syndrome is, and I'm not well versed in the state of human scientific research, but I was under the impression that they are far from being able to eradicate all diseases. Does your clan have proprietary knowledge that the rest of your world does not?"

Kian's pinched expression relaxed. "A hundred years is a long time, and scientific research has gotten a boost from artificial intelligence. I'm told that experiments that would have taken years to run can be simulated in minutes. AI even makes suggestions for new treatments."

Aru doubted Kian was telling him the entire truth.

He had said 'we' might be able to make humans immune to disease, and Kian didn't bundle his people together with humans. He definitely had been referring to his clan's ability to do so, and not to human science.

Aru smiled. "Nice try, but I know that you are not relying on humans to find the solution."

Kian didn't deny it, but the small lift of one corner of his mouth indicated that he wasn't angry about Aru being able to deduce the truth once again.

"I need to watch myself with you, Aru. You are cleverer than you appear. No wonder you were chosen to lead the team and to communicate with the resistance."

"Thank you." Aru dipped his head.

He had been chosen because of his ability to telepathically communicate with his sister regardless of distance, but he also needed to watch what he said to Kian. The guy was watchful, intelligent, and paranoid. He didn't miss much.

Pushing his chair back, Kian got to his feet. "Since you need to get instructions before we can continue our talks, let's get back to the clinic and see whether Gabriella is awake."

Finally.

Aru was out of his chair so fast that the thing toppled on its back.

Anandur chuckled as he lifted the chair. "Someone is anxious to get to his mate."

Glaring at Aru, Brundar re-sheathed the dagger he'd pulled out. "No more sudden movements, please."

"Noted."

Gabi

Gabi was lost.

She'd been walking for hours, searching the deserted streets of downtown Los Angeles, but she didn't know what she was looking for.

Perhaps when she saw it, she would recognize it.

Night was falling, and her legs were hurting badly, but she couldn't stop. If it was the normal pinching of shoes that got too tight after a long day, she wouldn't have been worried, but it was an all-over ache, the type she usually experienced when having the flu, just ten times worse.

She had to keep going, though. She couldn't stop.

What was she searching for?

Was she trying to find her way home?

Where was home?

She had a vague memory of a contemporary-looking townhouse, but she hadn't been there in so long that it couldn't be her home.

Gilbert would know where she needed to be.

She should call him. He would come to get her and drive her home, wherever it was. Her brother was always there for her when she needed him, and she needed him now.

"Gilbert," she murmured. "Come get me."

As a large hand clasped hers, she smiled, thinking that her wish was answered, but there was no one with her on the street. She was still alone. Was it a phantom touch?

"It's me, Gabi. Can you open your eyes?"

The voice sounded familiar, but it didn't belong to her brother. She had mixed feelings about it. She was excited to hear it and also aggravated by it, but she didn't know why.

"Can you wake up, Gabi?" the voice insisted. "I don't know how long they will let me stay here. Gilbert agreed to leave you alone with me, but he is in the waiting room, so if you wish, I can ask him to come in."

Was the voice part of the dream?

If she was sleeping and dreaming, then walking on the streets of Los Angeles didn't make sense, so that part belonged in the dream world, and the phantom voice was real.

She also realized that she knew whom the voice belonged to.

Uriel.

The guy who hadn't answered her text and left her stranded in that horrible hospital.

"Good of you to finally show up. Are you going to get me out of here?" She still didn't open her eyes, not because she didn't want to, but because her eyelids refused to obey her command. "Why can't I open my eyes?"

"I'll get the doctor." Sounding alarmed, he let go of her hand.

"No. Stay." She lifted her hand, hoping he would take it again because she missed his touch. "Just give me a moment."

She heard him exhale, and then he took her hand, lifted it, and kissed her palm. "I'm so sorry. I should have been there for you."

"Why weren't you?" She finally managed to force her eyelids to part, but her vision was blurry. "Did you get my text?"

"I did, but I was in the middle of something very important that I couldn't get out of, and I couldn't come to you." He chuckled. "In the end, it's good that I didn't because I wouldn't have been able to find you if I hadn't sent a spy drone after Magnus, who talked about you with Julian, who said that he was going to take care of you. I moved the spy from Magnus's shoulder to Julian's, and that's how I knew that your brother was with you and that you were taken care of. I also knew where they had taken you, so if Kian hadn't offered to bring me to you, I would have infiltrated the place no matter what it would have cost me."

Her vision finally clearing, Gabi narrowed her eyes at Uriel. "I have no idea what you are talking about. Who is Magnus? And who is Julian? And where am I?"

He frowned. "You shouldn't be so confused. Orion released you from the compulsion to forget things around me, and you should remember everything you were told. I need to get the doctor in here."

The door opened a moment later, and the handsome doctor walked in. "I heard you through the camera." He pointed at a cylinder that was attached to the wall near the ceiling and then looked at her. "Do you remember me?"

She smiled. "How could I forget a face like yours? You are the doctor."

"What's my name?"

"Julian?"

Uriel had said that someone named Magnus had talked with Julian, who had said that he was going to take care of her, so it was logical to assume that the doctor's name was Julian.

"What's wrong with Gabi?" Uriel asked. "Is it my presence that's causing the memory problem?"

"It might be." The doctor checked her pupils. "Let's put it to the test. Can you step outside for a moment?"

"Of course." Uriel cast her one more worried look before letting go of her hand. "I'm not going anywhere. I'll be just outside the door."

Lifting a feeble hand, Gabi pointed a finger at him. "Don't you dare disappear on me again."

"I won't. I promise."

When the door closed behind Uriel, the doctor asked, "Do you know why you are here?"

"I'm transitioning into immortality," she said quietly as the memories rushed back in. "I was in a hospital. Gilbert came to get me with you and a couple of other guys. Then you brought me here." She looked at the closed door and shook her head. "I must have dreamt the part about Uriel being a god and his real name being Aru." A snort escaped her throat. "He's a god in bed, that's for sure. That was probably what prompted the crazy dream."

"It wasn't a dream." Julian didn't look amused. "I hope the confusion is temporary and that it will clear up. Otherwise, we might have a problem."

"What do you mean? What problem?"

"Your mind might have been permanently affected by the yo-yoing of memories. I hope it wasn't, and that the transition will clear it up, but you might need rehabilitation after the critical stage of your transition is over."

Aru

"What's going on?" Gilbert asked as Aru walked out of Gabi's room.

"She has issues with her memory. It seems that my presence triggers Orion's compulsion to forget what she knows about immortals. She thought that she was still in the human hospital and didn't remember that you took her out of there."

"That's not good." Gilbert rubbed a hand over his mouth. "What does Julian think?"

"He's checking whether her memories will return in my absence."

"What if they don't?"

"I don't know. I know nothing about any of this, and I feel so damn helpless. There is nothing worse than the inability to do anything."

Gilbert regarded him with curiosity in his eyes. "You really care about her."

"Of course, I do."

"It's not at all obvious. You two had a fling, you accidentally induced her transition, and now she's becoming immortal. You have no obligation to her. You can walk away, and Gabi will find a nice immortal dude to settle down with. There are plenty of them in the village who would do anything for a chance to score an immortal mate."

The growl that rose from deep in Aru's throat had Gilbert take a step back.

He lifted his hands. "No need to growl, buddy. I was just checking to see how serious you are about my baby sister. She's been hurt before, and I vowed to do everything in my power to never let it happen again."

"I understand." Aru let out a breath. "I have a sister, too, and if anyone ever hurt her, I would tear his insides out with my fangs."

The look Gilbert gave him was far from horrified. In fact, he seemed satisfied. "I assume that your sister is still single?"

"Yes."

"Younger? Older?"

Aru had never told anyone that Aria was his twin. He'd emerged from their mother's womb first so he could claim to be older.

"Aria is younger. We are very close, or we used to be, before I was drafted to the service."

"Drafted?" Gilbert raised a brow. "Is that a thing in your world?"

"Yes. All young gods have to serve in one capacity or another."

"Do the gods have enemies?"

Aru smiled. "Not officially, but occasionally, there are uprisings or revolts on planets controlled by the gods. Some of the created species are not as grateful as others for being created and shaped in the image of the gods. That's what the official statements usually say, but I assume that they are particularly opposed to paying tribute. They want to do their own thing, and they don't want to part with a large chunk of their resources. One of the tasks of the patrol ships is collecting a portion of the tributes for Anumati. Most of it is symbolic, though, and useless to us. I guess it's meant to habituate the created species to the custom, so when they have something of real value, they will know that some of it should be put aside for the gods."

Gilbert nodded. "Gold used to be a tribute to the gods."

"Precisely."

"So, you are tax collectors?"

Surprisingly, Gilbert had arrived at the same conclusion as Kian. Perhaps it had to do with the way humans interacted and governed themselves. Taxes were an integral part of their lives, while the concept didn't exist on Anumati.

Gods did not pay tribute or taxes, and massive projects were funded by crowd-sourcing that was supposedly voluntary. The prominent families had pet projects that they supported. The rest was financed by the tribute collected from all over the galaxy.

"Only some of us are involved in collecting tribute," Aru said. "Most of the drafted gods are tasked with seeding planets, creating new species, and helping them evolve. A small portion is trained in weapons and assigned patrol duties."

Gilbert opened his mouth, no doubt to ask more questions about life on Anumati, but as the door opened and Julian stepped out of Gabi's room, he turned to the doctor. "What's going on with my sister?"

"After Aru left the room, Gabi's recall improved, so there is definitely a connection. The vestiges of Orion's compulsion are probably the culprit, and I believe that they will clear up in time. Don't forget that she's spending more time unconscious than conscious, and each time she wakes up, she has to reconstruct what she'd learned before. That on its own can create confusion."

Gilbert bobbed his head, accepting the doctor's authority, and Aru should have done the same, but he'd always had trouble with accepting things at face value.

"Don't you think that Orion needs to come over and reinforce the undoing of what he has done in person?"

Julian shook his head. "I don't think his compulsion is still in effect. At this point, Gabi's mind is working autonomously, but it's following the rules it has been given by Orion. It will take time to reset itself." He looked at Gilbert. "I'll call Vanessa and ask her opinion. She's better equipped than me to deal with problems that have to do with the mind."

So, the doctor was not as sure as he'd pretended to be about Gabi's mind returning to normal without assistance.

That helpless feeling washed over Aru again, making him suddenly sweat even though the clinic's air conditioning was working just fine.

"Who's Vanessa?" he asked.

"The clan psychologist." Julian quirked a smile. "She's mated to one of the Kra-ell purebloods."

The lack of concern in the doctor's voice eased some of Aru's worry. Perhaps Julian had decided to consult with the psychologist just as an afterthought.

"Which Kra-ell is she mated to?" Aru asked.

"Mo-red."

"He's a good guy."

Listening to the spy drones, Aru had never heard Mo-red being rude or berating anyone, which wasn't true of most of the purebloods.

"Yeah. Surprisingly so," Julian said. "He was one of Igor's pod members, and he stood trial with the others, but Vanessa and Lusha got him and the others off with just community service." He chuckled. "With how blood-thirsty the Kra-ell are, the outcome of the trial surprised me."

That was a fascinating story, and Aru wanted to hear more about the trial, but right now, he wanted to see Gabi more than he wanted anything else.

"Can I go back in there?" He waved a hand at the door.

Hopefully, the doctor wouldn't tell him that she needed to rest and he couldn't see her.

Could he thrall the guy to let him in?

Perhaps he could do that like he did with humans, and Julian wouldn't even know that he'd been thralled.

"Yes. Definitely. She will wring my neck if I don't get you back in there." He smiled at Gilbert. "I thought that you were overbearing, but you're easy compared to your sister. She's a ballbuster."

A proud grin spread over Gilbert's face. "I taught her not to take shit from anyone."

If Aru wasn't confusing idioms, calling a person a ball-buster, especially a woman, was not a compliment. Why would Gilbert be proud of that?

"Excuse me, but Gabi is nothing of the sort. She's kind, accommodating, and sweet. She's a lovely lady any male would be proud to call his mate."

Julian and Gilbert exchanged amused glances.

"I applaud women who are assertive and don't take bull from anyone, so it wasn't meant as an insult." Julian put his hand on Aru's shoulder. "It was a compliment. Come on. We don't want to keep your lovely lady waiting."

Aru frowned at him. "Why do I have a feeling that you are mocking me?"

"I'm not. If I look amused, it is because I know what it's like to fall in love, and it makes me happy to see another male as besotted as I was. Still am." He paused at the door. "I'm not embarrassed to admit that I fell for my mate just from gazing at her picture."

"Is she a ballbuster?"

The doctor chuckled. "Ella can definitely rise to the occasion."

Gabi

The doctor had promised to keep Uriel in the waiting room for a few minutes so Gabi could sort herself out, not that she could do much while confined to the hospital bed and attached to a catheter and an IV bag.

She wished she could take a shower, do her hair, and put on makeup, but none of that was an option.

For some reason, when she'd asked Julian for her bag, he had given her a half-mumbled excuse and left the room, so she didn't have a brush or a mirror and had to untangle her hair with her fingers. He had left some mints on her bedside table, though, so at least she wouldn't have a stinky mouth when she berated Uriel.

Aru. His name is Aru.

Why was it so difficult to hold on to her memories? They were like beads and pebbles in a kaleidoscope, creating different random patterns every time she woke up, and her mind went into another mental spin.

As the door opened and Julian ushered Aru in, Gabi couldn't decide whether she should smile or glare at him. She was happy he was there, but she was also mad at him.

"Look who's back," Julian said. "Do you know who he is?"

She nodded.

"Do you remember his name?"

"Which one? Uriel Delgado or Aru?"

"Fantastic." Julian clapped Aru on his back. "I told you that Gabi's mind will sort itself out. I'll leave the two of you alone now." He glanced at the camera and winked. "I promise not to peek."

Gabi rolled her eyes. "As if. Why are males so obtuse? You're a doctor. You should know better."

Grinning, he looked at Aru. "What did I say? She's a ballbuster."

"I'm not." Gabi groaned.

Even if she was willing to forgive Aru, and even if she was in the mood for some hanky-panky, which she wasn't, she was too weak to move, every bone and muscle in her body ached, and she was hooked up to a catheter and an IV.

When the door closed behind Julian, Aru pulled the rolling stool Gilbert had used out from under the counter and rolled it over to her bedside. "Julian is a strange guy." He straddled the small stool, dwarfing it with his bulk. "Are all doctors like that?"

She frowned at him. "I don't want to do small talk. I want to know who you are, why you lied to me, and what you were thinking having unprotected sex with me when you knew you could induce me?"

"I didn't know that I could do that, and since disease and pregnancy were not an issue, I had no reason to be concerned. I had no idea that you were a Dormant or even what Dormants were, and I didn't know that I could induce a Dormant's transition. The world of the immortals is as new to me as it is to you."

Well, that took care of at least half of her ire. He hadn't known.

"What does it mean to be a god? Do you have special powers?"

"I have mind control powers that work on most species but not on other gods. I can thrall, which is a form of hypnosis, for lack of a better description. It's not what Orion did to you. That was compulsion, and it works differently." He raked his fingers through his hair. "Compulsion is supposed to be less dangerous than thralling, but perhaps my information was wrong. Or maybe the combination of my thralling with Orion's compulsion was what got you in trouble. But I used so little. It shouldn't have had an adverse effect on you."

Aru was rambling, which was kind of cute. He was nervous and unsure, which meant that he cared about her and wanted her to think well of him, but he'd also admitted that he'd hypnotized her, and that wasn't okay.

"When did you thrall me?"

He lifted his eyes to her. "I thought you knew. The fact that you are transitioning should be clue enough. You wouldn't be if I hadn't bitten you. Do you remember me doing that?"

"I don't." She lifted her hand to her neck. "I thought that you bit me here, but there was no mark the next morning, so I thought that I dreamt it."

"My saliva has healing properties, and so does the venom. That's why there was no mark. But if I hadn't thralled you to forget the bite, you would have remembered it." He took a deep breath. "I also thralled you to ignore my fangs and glowing eyes. They would have terrified you and given me away. I couldn't allow that to happen."

Gabi nodded. "That makes sense."

If she hadn't fainted on sight, she would have definitely run away screaming. Eric had shown her his fangs during the welcome dinner, and they were monstrous. Later, she'd learned that his fangs weren't even fully grown yet, so Aru's were probably the size of a saber-toothed tiger's.

"Am I forgiven?" Aru's eyes pleaded with her to say yes.

"For what exactly should I forgive you?"

"For not telling you the truth about who I was, for inadvertently inducing your transition, and for not rushing to your side when you asked me to come get you from the hospital."

Yeah, it was all of the above, and it didn't help that she understood why he had done all those things. It hurt that she hadn't been his first priority.

Gilbert had begged Kian to let him out of the locked-down village to come to her aid. That was what people who cared for each other did.

But to Aru, she had been just another inconsequential human female he was having a good time with.

Gabi sighed. "Tell me the truth, Aru. Throughout our time together, did you think of me as just another random hookup? Or did you feel that there was something different about me? Something more?"

Aru

Aru rose to his feet, sat on the bed next to Gabi, and took her hand. "You were not a random hookup." When she arched an eyebrow, he chuckled. "Well, maybe at first. But no, not even then. From the first moment I saw you in the airport lounge, I knew that there was something special about you. Something that called to me, but I didn't know what it was. I just assumed that I was attracted to a beautiful, intriguing woman. But then we were seated next to each other on the plane, and I got to know you a little, and you enchanted me."

Gabi snorted. "You were enamored by my irrational fear of flying?"

"I was impressed with your bravery. You were worried about your family, and you overcame your crippling fear of flying to check on them. I think I started falling for you right then."

Her eyes widened. "Don't say the L word."

He lifted her hand and kissed the tips of her fingers with their dainty, red-painted nails. "I'll save it for last, then."

"Don't make false promises just because you feel sorry or guilty or anything like that. It's not fair to me or to you."

"I'm not making any promises because I'm not talking about the future. I'm still talking about the past."

"Fine." She gave him a half-hearted smile. "So, what else did you like so much about me on the plane? Was it how I was crushing your hand the entire five hours? Or was it my endless prattle about my family?"

"Both." He smiled behind her fingers. "I loved it that you found solace in my touch." He closed his eyes. "I'm sorry. I forgot that the L-word is disallowed. It made me feel good that you relied on me for comfort, and it felt good to hold your hand and distract you from your fear. It was also nice to hear about your family and how close you were to your brothers and your nieces and nephews. The way a person interacts with their family says a lot about them, and your heart is full of the L-word for your brothers, their children, and their mates." He glanced toward the door. "I like Gilbert. He's very protective of you."

Gabi's eyes misted with tears. "Gilbert is my rock. I don't know what I would have done without him."

Damn, hearing her say that chafed.

He wanted to be Gabi's rock, the one she could count on to come to her aid whenever she needed anything, be it rescue from a clinic where she didn't feel comfortable or emotional support when she felt overwhelmed or scared and needed someone's hand to hold on to.

Except, he couldn't be that male for her, not in the long run, so it was good that she had Gilbert, and they were both immortal. Well, Gilbert was, but Gabi was on her way to becoming so as well.

Come to think of it, Gilbert hadn't triggered Aru's alarm. He must already consider him family because he was Gabi's protector.

"Yeah, your brother is a good guy. He's also smart and insightful."

The mist evaporated from Gabi's eyes. "I'm glad that was the impression he left on you. He's such a goofball that sometimes people don't take him seriously, but on the inside, he's a very serious guy. After our parents died, he had to support two depressed teenagers financially and emotionally. I guess that's when he developed his sarcastic humor. It was a survival mechanism." She stopped and pursed her lips. "You wouldn't know anything about it, would you?"

"About sarcasm? I think I do."

"I mean about dealing with death. You're a god. Your loved ones don't die."

"Hopefully, they don't, but there are many things that can kill gods and immortals. Anything that is flesh and blood can be killed. It's just harder to do."

Her cheeks pinked. "Thank goodness. When Gilbert told me that you were a god, I thought that maybe you could become incorporeal or corporeal on demand." She lifted her other hand and rubbed her temple. "I might have had a few creative dreams about it."

Her words, combined with the deepening color of her cheeks, made him harden in an instant. "Might have? You either did or didn't."

"I did." She looked at him from under lowered lashes. "They were very...interesting."

"I would love to hear all about them." He glanced at the camera mounted on the wall. "But perhaps not here."

She laughed. "Julian said that he muted the sound, but since I'm not in a state to do anything other than talk, perhaps I should save my sexy dreams for when we can actually do something about the side effects of my story-telling."

Unable to help himself, he leaned over and kissed her cheek. "I can't wait."

"Yeah, neither can I." She lowered her eyes. "Are you going to stick around? Or do you still plan on leaving as soon as your negotiations are done?"

"You know that I wasn't negotiating flea-market finds, right?"

Gabi nodded. "You were negotiating with Kian, but I don't know what about or why. Gilbert doesn't know what's going on. He knows you and your friends are gods, but he doesn't know why you are here or what you want. Or maybe I just haven't been awake long enough for him to tell me."

He stroked her hair. "I want to tell you everything, but Julian warned me not to overtax you. How are you feeling?"

She smiled. "Not sleepy. I think I'm getting better." She glanced at the IV bag. "I told Julian that I was aching all over, so he put something in the bag to help with the pain, and it was such a wonderful relief. I think that the aches sapped my energy and made me sleepy, and now that it's gone, I can stay awake longer."

There was a difference between falling asleep and losing consciousness, but Aru wasn't sure what it was. That being said, he suspected that bodily aches didn't cause the loss of consciousness.

"Is it normal for the transition to be painful?"

Gabi smiled sheepishly. "Julian said that I might be growing taller. He didn't take my measurements before it started, so he can't say for sure, but he says that all the transitioning Dormants who had similar complaints grew a little taller. I wouldn't mind gaining an inch or two."

"You are perfect the way you are. I don't want you to change."

She pouted. "A couple of inches wouldn't change what I look like or my personality but becoming immortal might. I already feel different."

Gabi

Aru or Uriel, god or human, it didn't really change anything. He was still the same guy, and the more they talked, the more comfortable Gabi was with him.

It was like nothing had changed when everything had.

She was turning immortal, and he was a god, and she didn't really know what it meant for their future. They had so much to talk about, but she would probably slip away again, and the fear that he wouldn't be there when she woke up was enough for her to cling to consciousness for as long as she could.

Aru frowned. "In what way does turning immortal make you feel different? Is your eyesight better or your hearing?"

Males were so literal.

"I think that the biggest change is knowing that Gilbert and Eric and the rest of my family are immortals or on

141

the way to becoming immortal. It makes me less fearful, so maybe the next time I need to fly across the country, I won't be as terrified."

Aru kissed the tips of her fingers again, which she really liked. It was as if he couldn't keep his hands and lips off her, but since she wasn't well, he only allowed himself to touch and kiss her fingertips.

It was so sweet.

His dark brows turned down in a deep V. "If immortals possess the same healing abilities as gods, surviving a plane crash is possible, but it's not guaranteed. That being said, commercial flights are extremely safe, much safer than driving a car or taking the train."

She rolled her eyes. "I know that. But phobias are not rational. Knowing that my family is more resilient than ever and that I don't need to stay awake at night worrying about them eases me in ways I couldn't imagine. It's such a liberating feeling."

"I'm glad." He turned her hand palm up and kissed it.

Gabi chuckled. "Do the gods practice Vulcan lovemaking customs? For them, it's all about touching hands."

"I've never heard of the Vulcans. Is there a country or a people by that name?"

"Yes, but they are fictional." She glanced at the television screen across from her bed. "If you stay with me, we can watch old episodes of *Star Trek* together. It was such a fun show, and I know how much you like watching television."

"What is it about?"

"It's about humans going where no one has gone before, meaning the stars, and meeting all kinds of interesting aliens. Hey, maybe the creator was one of your people who somehow got stranded on Earth and fed the imaginations of millions, preparing us for possible future contact with extraterrestrials."

"Not likely. The previous team was picked up in its entirety, and none of the other teams reported missing a member."

"It was just a joke, Uriel. I mean Aru." Gabi shook her head. "It's all so confusing, but it shouldn't be. I knew very little about you before, and now I know a little bit more than just your last name and that you are from Portugal, but then that's all fake." She shook her head. "Now that you don't have to go anywhere, and you don't need to keep secrets from me either, you can finally open up and tell me everything."

Given his frown, that was a no.

"How did you know that my fake last name was Delgado? Or that I was supposedly from Portugal. I never told you that."

"Oops." She lifted a hand to her lips. "I thought you knew that we knew. Well, I didn't remember that when I was with you, but I remembered it when I was alone. I thought that Delgado sounded sexy, and it suited you so well. It's a shame that it was fake."

He shook his head. "Was there an answer somewhere in there that I missed?"

Gabi smiled sheepishly. "On the day of my arrival, when I had dinner with my family, they introduced me to Orion and Onegus—two gorgeous immortal males. I told them that the guy I met on the plane was just as gorgeous as they were, and Onegus got suspicious, so he asked the clan's hacker to check your background. The hacker found out your name and that you were living in Portugal. Your fake identity must have been really good, because they concluded that you were just a handsome human who didn't warrant further investigation. They probably didn't bother to dig too deeply because I wasn't anyone important, so it didn't matter who I was dating. But just in case, Orion compelled me to forget everything I was told when I was around strangers, including you."

Gabi had expected Aru to be angry about the hacker investigating him, but the only part of her story that seemed to bother him was Onegus's decision not to continue the investigation.

"I haven't met Onegus yet, and I don't know who he is, but he should have done a better job checking up on my fake background. The guy who sold me the fake identity promised that it was a hundred percent legit and that it would pass every inspection, but I was sure he exaggerated just so he could charge the obscene amount that he did."

"So, you're not mad that they investigated you?"

"Why would I be mad? I'm just stunned that a series of coincidences could have potentially derailed my mission. I don't know what would have happened if the clan had trapped me while I was with you. Dagor and Negal would have tried to free me, the clan would have retaliated, and things might have ended badly." He let out a breath. "I'm so glad that I decided to splurge on the best fake identity money could buy. It helped us avoid a disaster."

That didn't sound good. What the heck was Aru's deal, and what did he want from the clan?

Gabi pulled her hand out of Aru's grasp. "Tell me why you are here and what you hope to achieve from your negotiations with the clan."

He sighed. "It's a long story."

"Are you in a big rush to leave?"

"No. I'm staying with you even if I have to sleep on the floor. Your brother might have an issue with that, but I'll just have to explain that from now on, I am your rock and that he can return to his family."

Aru

As soon as Aru had uttered the words, he regretted saying them. He wanted them to be true. He wanted to be Gabi's rock, the one she turned to when she needed anything, big or small. Not her brother.

Except, he hadn't told her the truth.

In a perfect world, nothing would have made him happier than becoming Gabi's rock, but the world was far from perfect, and he was committed to a cause that had the fate of trillions on the line. He had to go wherever the Supreme sent him to be the eyes and ears of the rebellion and report his findings.

Gabi regarded him with a penetrating look. "Can you be my rock, Aru? Because you don't look sure about it."

"I want to be with you." He squeezed her hand.

"But you can't."

"I can, but not forever."

"How long?"

"A hundred and fifteen years, give or take a couple. That's when my patrol ship returns."

She laughed. "That's long enough. Let's see if you can survive one month with me first, and then we can talk about a century."

It was a relief to realize that Gabi didn't think of him in the same terms he thought of her. If she did, she would be talking about forever.

Aru forced a smile. "Is that a challenge?"

Did she even know about truelove mates?

If she didn't, he wasn't going to tell her. His feelings for her ran deeper than any he'd had for any female before her, but that didn't mean that she was his one and only.

Could she even be his truelove mate?

Gabi was a hybrid, half human and half goddess, or rather mostly human, with just a little bit of godly genes, making her immortal.

According to the lore, she couldn't be his truelove mate, but then the lore was as much part of the propaganda as everything else on Anumati.

Her smile turned into a frown. "No, it's not a challenge. I would never want you to stay even a minute longer than you want to. If you stay, it will be because you want to be with me and not because you want to win a bet. That's a terrible reason to be with someone. We should be together only as long as we make each other happy, whether it's a week, a month, or a year. I don't want to be stuck in a relationship that doesn't work."

It was such a human thing to say that it pained him.

Even gods who had their mating arranged by their families, and did it out of convenience and not love, stayed together. They might have enjoyed scores of paramours, but the family unit stayed intact. The union was sacred whether they loved each other or not and whether they had children together or not.

So yeah, it was mostly about politics, forging alliances, and uniting with other families, but the system worked. Separations were incredibly rare, and when they happened, it was usually because one of the partners found his or her truelove mate, and no one dared to stand in the way of Fate.

It was considered bad luck.

Gabi's forehead furrowed. "You don't seem to agree with me."

"I don't agree with the way humans take their mating commitments lightly. Things are different on Anumati."

"Of course, they are." She waved a dismissive hand. "If they are anything like the immortals, they are all mated to their truelove mates and can't think of being with anyone else."

So, Gabi knew about that and apparently didn't consider him a worthy candidate for being her one and only.

Aru laughed without mirth. "Nothing could be farther from the truth. Truelove matches are extremely rare, and arranged matings are the norm, as is sleeping around. We are a promiscuous bunch."

She recoiled as if he had slapped her. "I will never tolerate infidelity, not even in a casual relationship. If that's how you are, how you conduct yourself, you'd better leave now. There is no future for us. Not even for a day."

Damn, he should have remembered that she'd been badly hurt by her ex's infidelity. Hell, he should have remembered how angry hearing about it had made him.

"I apologize. That was incredibly insensitive of me." He reached for her hand, but she pulled it away, and his heart squeezed painfully. "I was just describing things as they are for Anumati's upper class, but that doesn't mean that everyone is like that. I am not. I'm not interested in sleeping around. In fact, being a commoner affords me the freedom of not having my mating arranged, and I promised myself that I would not mate anyone unless she was my one and only. I just never expected to find her, and certainly not on Earth, so I resolved to remain a bachelor, which is very upsetting to my parents. Especially my mother. She hopes for a grandchild."

Gabi

Aru's words reverberated in Gabi's head—"I promised myself that I would not mate anyone unless she was my one and only. I've just never expected to find her, and certainly not on Earth."

Her heart thundered in her chest, and it was a wonder that Aru didn't hear it with his godly ears, or maybe he did, and he thought that the sound was coming from the medical equipment.

Thank goodness for that.

Had he just told her, in so many words, that she was his truelove mate?

Maybe she misunderstood?

No, she couldn't have.

"Aru." She touched his hand. "Look at me."

He lifted a pair of haunted eyes to her. "I'm sorry. I must make no sense to you."

"You just said that you didn't expect to find your truelove mate on Earth. Does that mean that you found her?"

A small smile bloomed on his handsome face. "Did I?"

"Don't do that." She wanted to slap his arm but regrettably wasn't strong enough to do that. "Don't you dare answer my question with a question. Is it yes or no?"

"Maybe? I've never felt this way before about anyone. Does wanting to be with you every minute of the day mean that you are my truelove mate? Does the fact that seeing you makes my heart soar mean that you are my one and only?"

She shook her head. "That's how I felt when I was dating Dylan, but that could be simple love or infatuation, and there is nothing mystical about it. I don't know how a truelove mate is different from someone you just love."

His eyes looked tormented. "Do you feel for me the same way you felt for your ex? Do you love me?"

She swallowed. "I don't feel about you the same way I did about Dylan. I was a kid when I fell for the most popular guy in school, and it might not have been real love. I'm older and smarter now, and I acknowledge that I don't know you well enough to love you. But I do want to be with you every minute of the day, and seeing you does make me happy, at least most of the time. Does that mean that you are my one and only?"

He arched a brow. "Most of the time, but not all?"

"Sometimes I'm mad at you or frustrated with you, but I'm still happy to see you."

His smile was brilliant. "Then you love me."

Damn, it was so difficult to admit it, and it made no sense to be in love with a guy that she'd just met, but he was a god, and the rules were different with him. Heck, there were no rules.

"I might be in love with you," she admitted. "But who wouldn't be?" She waved a hand over his face. "You are a god. So gorgeous that you're blinding. And you're also charming and attentive. What's not to love except for your fear of commitment and your evasiveness?"

"I don't have a fear of commitment. I just can't commit for more than a hundred and fifteen years."

He'd said that before, and she'd laughed, but that was before he'd told her that he had found his truelove on Earth.

"Why do you need to go? Can't you quit?"

Aru shook his head. "I wish I could, but the fate of Anumati is more important than what I want, and I made a commitment I can't back out of no matter what it costs me."

"Then can I come with you?"

Aru's eyes widened. "You can't. No one back home knows that there are immortals on Earth—" He stopped mid-sentence. "But I'll have to report it so they will know." He swallowed. "I can't report it." He raked his fingers through his hair. "I don't know what to do."

He looked so lost, and she didn't know what to say to make it better for him. The only comfort she could offer him was the warmth of her embrace.

"Come here." She scooted aside to make room for him. "Lie down next to me."

He looked with longing in his eyes at the sliver of space she'd created. "Are you sure it's okay? You have wires and tubes attached to you."

"Then you will have to be careful around them."

Moving with the speed of a god, he kicked his boots off and climbed on the bed so carefully that it barely moved under his weight.

Lying on his side, most of his body must have been hanging over the side of the bed because it wasn't touching hers, but Gabi would have none of that. "Come closer." She also turned on her side and put her hand on his shoulder, which was as far as it would go, given the limitations.

Aru scooted a little closer, his chest lightly touching hers, and put his arm gently around her. He kept the bulk of his body away from hers, which was probably smart given all the wires attached to her chest and other things she didn't want to think about, like the fact that there was no female nurse on site, which meant that Julian had put the catheter in.

Talk about embarrassing.

Whatever. He was a doctor, and he had probably done that a thousand times to scores of female patients.

Aru closed his eyes. "It pains me to see you like this. I want you out of the hospital bed, out of the clinic, and out of the underground."

She snorted. "You and me both. But on the bright side, I haven't lost consciousness yet, which is probably the longest stretch since I started transitioning. That's a good sign." She lifted her hand off his shoulder and cupped his cheek. "Maybe your presence makes me stronger."

He leaned into her hand and closed his eyes. "I hope so. I only want to bring you happiness and joy, but instead, I'm the harbinger of doom."

"What are you talking about? My transition? It's not a bad thing. It's a good thing. You turned on my immortal genes, and I'm grateful for that."

"Thank the merciful Fates for that and for making your transition relatively easy. I was told that it's much tougher for some." He turned his face, so his lips were at her palm, and he kissed it. "If you'll have me, I will gladly spend the next hundred and fifteen years with you. That's more than I ever hoped for."

Aru

When Gabi fell asleep, Aru wasn't sure whether she'd lost consciousness or was just dozing off, but since no alarms went off and the doctor hadn't rushed in, he assumed that everything was okay.

Sliding his arm gently off her, he shifted back and lowered his feet to the floor.

The effort at stealth was probably unnecessary, but Gabi needed her rest, and if she was sleeping, not unconscious, he didn't want to wake her up.

Aru would have loved nothing more than to stay with her and hold her until the next time she opened her eyes so they could talk some more, but he had promised Kian to tell him how to identify the spy bugs, and the immortal was probably waiting for him to do so before going home.

They had only touched the tip of the iceberg, and there was so much more Aru could learn from the immortals, provided that they agreed to share things with him.

Holding his boots in his hand, he tiptoed to the door and opened it.

Outside, he found Gilbert in the waiting room, but Kian was gone. Not that it surprised him. The leader of the immortals had better things to do than wait around for him. What did surprise him was that no one had knocked on the door to remind him that Kian was waiting.

"Where is Kian?" he asked Gilbert after closing the door.

"Got tired of waiting for you and went back upstairs. He said to send you up when you emerge."

Aru dropped his boots on the floor and pushed his feet into them.

"I hope you don't mind." Gilbert didn't wait for Aru to answer before pulling out his phone and snapping a picture of him. "My better half wants to see what you look like."

Aru shrugged. "You could have asked the security people to supply you with a portrait from the surveillance feed."

"Nah, I doubt the surveillance cameras caught your best side. By the way, what do the gods wear on Anumati? I keep imagining them in white togas and gold sandals."

"You're not that far off. Anumati is hot and humid despite being dark, and clothing tends to be airy."

Gilbert grinned. "I'll be damned. So, the Greeks and the Romans were imitating godly fashion?"

"Perhaps." Aru headed for the door. "Or maybe similar climates prompted similar fashion." He opened the door and then stopped. "How does Kian expect me to get back to the penthouse when I can't activate the elevator?"

"Anandur is on his way to get you," the doctor called from the open door to his office. "I notified Kian as soon as you came out."

That made sense. Neither Gilbert nor Julian had asked him how Gabi was doing because they didn't need to. The doctor could see everything that was happening in her room, as well as the readouts from the monitoring equipment.

Turning around, Aru walked into the tiny office. "Gabi said that it was the longest stretch of wakefulness she'd had since her transition started. That's a good sign, right?"

Julian nodded. "She's doing remarkably well. You have nothing to worry about."

"She also said that my presence makes her feel stronger. Do you think it's true, or did she imagine it because my presence lifted her mood?"

The doctor lifted his hands. "The mind and body are interconnected, and positive feelings have a positive impact on the body. That's one explanation. The other could be that you release some pheromones that are beneficial to your mate. There isn't much known about the gods' physiology." He chuckled. "Contrary to popular belief, doctors don't know everything, and we are often stumped by what human bodies can do, let alone the bodies of gods."

"What popular belief?" Anandur poked his head into Julian's office. "No one thinks that doctors know everything other than the doctors themselves. You are the only doctor I know who admits to being stumped."

Far from looking offended, Julian lifted one brow. "How many doctors do you know that you are entitled to an opinion about my entire profession?"

"I know three." Anandur smiled. "Four, if you include Vanessa. She's my favorite, by the way." He turned to Aru. "Let's go, buddy. Kian is impatiently waiting."

With a nod goodbye to Julian and Gilbert, Aru walked out of the doctor's office. "Someone should have knocked on the door to remind me that Kian was waiting. I forgot all about it until Gabi fell asleep."

"And interrupt a mates' reunion?" The big redhead draped his muscular arm around Aru's shoulders. "Even the mighty Kian wouldn't dare to intrude on that. The Fates wouldn't be happy."

It was reassuring to find out that the immortals shared the gods' belief in the Fates. Any commonality was welcome, making conversations flow more naturally without having to explain the foundation of their belief system and how it affected their actions. So much of the gods' culture was influenced by their belief in the Fates, the oracles, and the one force in charge of everything.

"I don't know whether Gabi and I are fated to be together," Aru said, even though deep down he knew that they were. "Everything happened so fast. We barely know each other."

The guard summoned the elevator, which must have been idling at the clinic level because its doors opened immediately.

"After you." He motioned for Aru to go in. "I have a little test that might help you determine whether or not Gabriella is your one and only."

"You do?"

Anandur frowned. "I wouldn't have said that I have it if I didn't. So here is the test. Think of the sexiest, most desirable movie star or celebrity on Anumati or here on Earth, someone whom you fantasized about hooking up with. Is there someone like that?"

"There is," Aru admitted with a sheepish smile. "There is a famous singer on Anumati who is one of the most beautiful goddesses ever born, but that's not why I was attracted to her. It was that damn voice. I got hard every time I heard her sing."

"Excellent." Anandur rubbed his hands in glee. "Try to recreate her singing voice in your head."

Closing his eyes, Aru imagined listening to one of his favorite songs by Alva, and he felt his lips curving in a smile.

"Are you thinking about the song?" Anandur asked.

Aru opened his eyes. "I'm already on the third verse."

"Congratulations." Anandur clapped him on the back. "You passed the test. You didn't get aroused, which means that no one other than Gabi can elicit a sexual response from you, which means that she's your one and only."

Kian

"I'm so glad it's finally over that I'm going to invite the family for dinner tonight." Syssi's grinning face filled Kian's laptop screen. "That way, you can tell everyone at once about the gods."

"You don't have Okidu."

"I don't mind cooking for a change." She let out a breath. "I didn't expect to feel so cooped up after only a few days, but I can't wait to be back at the university." She leaned on her elbows and looked into the camera of her phone, which she'd propped on her cappuccino cup. "Hanging around the students makes me feel young."

He chuckled. "You are young."

Kian rarely left the village, and he had no problem with that. In fact, he avoided mingling with humans as much as possible. He hated the attention he got—the looks, some ogling, some envious, and some hostile, but rarely friendly.

His godly heritage had gifted him with nearly godly looks, and humans were attracted to beauty regardless of sexual interest. Even small children liked the pretty teachers better. Come to think of it, perhaps humans had been preprogrammed by the gods to give beautiful people preferential treatment to enhance willing compliance. But despite their preference for beauty, they resented those whom they considered better looking than themselves.

Syssi smiled. "Compared to you, nearly everyone is young. So, when are you lifting the lockdown?"

"You want out of the village, and I can't wait to be back, which is my main motivation for lifting it this evening. I can't return to the village while the others are stuck here, so I need to allow everyone aside from the Guardians stationed at the keep to return home. In the meantime, though, I'm stuck in the penthouse, waiting for Aru to finish snuggling with Gabi. I can't lift the lockdown until I'm assured that there are no more spy drones following our people back to the village."

Syssi groaned. "I thought that it was a done deal. Don't tell me that you might not lift the lockdown after all. What if Aru can't prove to you that there are no more bugs? We can't stay locked down forever. I'm getting island fever."

"Don't worry. I'm holding the female he loves. Aru will bend over backward to please me so I will allow him to keep seeing her."

"The Fates are amazing." Syssi sighed. "Who could have ever imagined an encounter like Gabi and Aru's? And the consequences are just mind-boggling. Gabi was the necessary ingredient to make this cooperation work."

"Indeed. From all the pairings the Fates have orchestrated so far, this one must be the most daring. They might get in trouble for that."

"Why? And from whom? Aren't they the ultimate force in the universe?"

"According to our lore, even the Fates have to obey the rules governing them. Their job is to help individuals fulfill their potential and to arrange love matings for the worthy, but they have to do it in a way that seems plausibly coincidental. If they break the rules, they are sent to purgatory by some larger force."

"God?"

Kian snorted. "We have a good reason not to use the term God in reference to the unspecified all-encompassing universal law that has no name."

"How about the Architect? I like that one."

"Of course, you do. You are an architect."

"That's what my diploma says, but the only thing I've designed in recent years was the addition to our old home. I also offered a few suggestions to Gavin when he was designing phase three."

"You forget the Perfect Match environments. Yours are the most imaginative."

She chuckled. "That's because they probably don't come from my imagination but from precognition, like the Krall environment. Perhaps there is an underwater city somewhere like the one I created for the Mer adventure. Maybe even on Earth. We still don't have access to the deepest parts of the oceans."

"That would be nice." Kian got distracted as he saw the elevator door open on the small window in the corner of his laptop screen. A moment later, Anandur walked out with Aru at his side. "Aru is back. I'll call you later."

"Take a picture of him and his friends for me. I'm curious to see how closely they resemble my vision."

"Will do. Goodbye, my love." He blew her a kiss before ending the call.

Turner was in the living room, getting as much information out of the two other gods as he could, but they were well trained and said very little.

Kian closed the laptop, lifted it off the desk, and tucked it under his arm. Using the room that used to be his old office evoked some nostalgic feelings, but the truth was that he didn't miss the penthouse. The only fond memories he had from the place had been after Syssi moved in with him. All the years he had lived there as a bachelor were one big blur of days indistinguishable from one another.

Being alone sucked.

With a sigh, he opened the door and walked to the living room.

Aru nodded in greeting. "I apologize for keeping you waiting. I was so immersed in my reunion with Gabi that all other thoughts and considerations were pushed aside."

Kian cast him what he hoped was an understanding look. "I know how precious it is to find your one and only. Nothing in the world seems to matter apart from her."

Aru's face fell. "I wish I had the luxury of dedicating the rest of my life to Gabi, but I have duties that I cannot abdicate." He glanced at his two teammates. "Are you okay?"

Negal nodded. "Turner gave us what the humans call the third degree, but we didn't tell him anything that he wasn't supposed to know." He smiled at Turner. "But you got some insight into life on Anumati and the reasons for the unrest, right?"

Turner nodded. "It was a fascinating conversation. The Eternal King is a genius, and I doubt the rebels can find someone to replace him who's as capable but is honest and transparent. No one can hold so much power and be in charge of so many people and not become corrupt."

"Power corrupts, and absolute power corrupts absolutely," Kian quoted.

"We will find a suitable replacement." Aru walked over to Dagor and took his laptop. "As part of our negotiations, I promised Kian access to the software that's monitoring our spy drones so he can be assured that we have no more drones following his people."

Dagor's fangs punched out over his lower lip. "Why would you do that? What is he giving you in exchange other than access to your human?"

"My human is turning immortal, and as important as she is to me, there is much more at stake here." He shifted his gaze to Kian's laptop. "I see that you come suitably equipped. You can download the software we are using to monitor the drones. Do you have my little spy?"

Kian pulled a ring box out of his pocket. He had placed the tiny thing in an old box the previous renters had left behind so it wouldn't get squashed. He'd also sent pictures to William, but that had been an exercise in futility because looking at the device told William nothing about how it worked.

"Let's do this in my office." Kian turned back toward the hallway.

"How many offices do you have?" Aru asked.

"Too many. I have one in every residence, past or current, and in every office building my clan owns."

"I think you work too hard."

Kian snorted. "Tell me something I don't know."

"There are many things I can tell you that you don't know." Aru waited for Kian to open the door.

"I can't wait to hear them." Kian motioned for the god to go in. "But we both have mates we are eager to return to, and I also have a young daughter who wants her daddy to play with her before her bedtime, so we will have to continue our talks tomorrow."

Also, the family was coming over for dinner so he could give everybody an update in one go, but that wasn't something he wanted to share with the god.

He would still need to update the council, but they could wait until he had something more concrete to tell them.

Aru

"How old is your daughter?" Aru asked Kian.

It was difficult to reconcile the gruff leader with a loving mate and the father of a small child, but the way his harsh face softened and the crease between his brows smoothed out told a story of a very different male when he was off the clock, as the humans referred to leisure time.

Aru had a feeling that Kian didn't get to spend much time with his family and that he had to fight for every minute he could salvage to be with them.

"Allegra is almost ten months old going on twenty."

"That must be one of those idioms I haven't grasped yet. What does it mean that she's going on twenty?"

Kian smiled, his whole face brightening. "It means that she acts much older than her actual age. Allegra is very smart, and she knows how to communicate with us even when she doesn't have the words to express herself yet.

Slight changes in tonality convey her meaning as well as if she articulated it, or better. All parents think that their child is special, but I know that mine is."

"Of course. I would love to meet her."

Kian regarded him with a guarded look. "Perhaps one day we can meet up in a restaurant in the city or here, but I can't invite you to my home if that is what you were suggesting."

"It wasn't. I would rather not know where your village is so no one can compel me to reveal your location. I'm just curious to meet your wife and daughter."

Kian nodded. "Let's leave the social interactions for the future. Right now, I need to make sure that no spy drone is following me or my people home."

"Naturally." Aru put the laptop on the desk and flipped it open. "This is the software that monitors the drones." He opened the ring box and gently picked up the miniature device. "It's low on energy, so I can't fly it. I'm just going to put it on your shoulder and show you what it sees."

"How do you charge it?"

"I have a charger back in my hotel room."

"I can have someone pick up your things and bring them over."

Nice try. As if he was going to let the immortals go through his stuff and discover the other gadgets his team had. The landing pod didn't have much space, so they could bring only a limited number of things with them, and they couldn't afford to part with any of it.

"I'll send Negal to do that later." Aru opened the application and showed the screen to Kian. "All these squares represent spy drones. The ones that are grayed out are those we've lost. They ran out of juice before we could collect them, and there was no way to find them. When they stop emitting, that's it."

"It seems to me like a flawed design."

"As with everything else, something had to be sacrificed to make the drones nearly soundless and invisible. What we used them for in Gor's compound was not what they were designed for, but it worked great for our purposes. We would get the drone to land on the clothing of one of the guards that were stationed at the entrances to the tunnels, and it would hitch a ride with him into the compound. That's how we got to see and hear what was going on. If we were lucky, we managed to move the spy to the guard that was stationed outside the compound the next day so the spy could hitch a ride back with him, and we could fly it a few meters out and collect it from a branch or a bush. But most times, that wasn't possible, and we just collected the information it transmitted until it died, and that was it."

"I see." Kian leaned toward the screen. "I guess the yellow squares represent the active drones."

"They represent the drones that are fully charged and ready to deploy, but look what happens when I click on one of these squares. The crossed-out eye means that they are not active." He moved the cursor to the only green square. "That's the one on your shoulder."

As he clicked it, the office and his face filled the screen. He smiled and waved.

Kian still looked skeptical. "Can I click on all the yellow squares?"

"Go ahead." Aru slid the laptop toward him.

Kian clicked through twenty or so before he was reassured that the rest would show him the same thing.

"How do you activate the other drones?"

"They need to be out of their box, and then I double-click on the yellow square until it turns green. It's not going to turn green unless the drone is detached from its carrier case."

The case was in the car, but Kian didn't need to know that. As far as he was concerned, it was in their hotel room.

"I want you to activate the other drones for a few seconds each. I want to see their squares turn green when they are on. I want to see what they see."

"But I don't have them with me."

"Then send Negal to collect your things. I'll wait until he returns with the drones."

The guy was paranoid, but Aru could understand that. If he was protecting his mate and daughter, he would have been just as diligent.

"Very well. Our hotel is not far from here, so it shouldn't take long, but before he goes, I need some reassurances from you."

Kian nodded. "What do you need?"

"We didn't bring a lot of equipment with us, but we can't allow what we have to fall into the wrong hands. I want your word that our things won't be searched and that we are not under surveillance while we are your guests in this penthouse."

It was a leap of faith to trust Kian to answer him truthfully, but Aru's gut said to trust the guy, and it wasn't as if he had much choice. Either way, Kian's answer would reveal what kind of person he was and if there was a future for their cooperation.

"There is one surveillance camera outside the door, so security knows when everyone who stays here comes and goes. There are also two cameras on the terrace, and their job is to warn against burglars and assassins. There are no cameras or listening devices inside the penthouse, and I'm willing to bring in a bug detector to prove it to you. As to your things, I need to know that none of them are weapons that could be used against my people. If you have defensive weapons, I can understand your need for them, but I don't want them up here in the penthouse. You will have to leave them in one of the lockers downstairs. You'll have the code, and I can give you access to the security camera feed that monitors the locker room so you'll know that no one is taking your things out, but you should know that security will alert me the moment you take them out."

Aru shook his head. "You could alter the feed so it will run in a loop, showing that there is no one in the locker room. We need to come up with another solution."

Kian rubbed his chin. "What if we put one of your bugs in there? I don't know how to tamper with your technology, so you'll know when and if anyone tries to get your stuff, and my surveillance will tell me if you are attempting to get your weapons out without notifying me."

"The spy drones are not built for long-term surveillance. It will run out of juice in a couple of days, and I don't know how long it will take Gabi to transition. I'm not leaving until she is out of the clinic."

"I get it. Can you put the bug there along with its charger, so it doesn't run out of juice?"

"That's not a bad idea. If the bug doesn't need to be hidden, that's not an issue. And you will know that I'm not using it or any of the others to spy on you or your people because I'm giving you access to the monitoring software."

Kian

Kian frowned. "It just occurred to me that you are using a human-made laptop. If your bosses back home didn't know about the progress humans have made, they couldn't have expected you to get what you needed to monitor the spy drones on Earth."

"That's very astute of you, Kian, and you are absolutely right." Aru reached into his pocket and pulled out a device that looked like a cell phone. "This is the device we use to communicate between ourselves and to monitor the drones and many other things. For some reason, that specific application doesn't work, and the way our devices are built, it's impossible to fix a problem. Luckily, Dagor knows a thing or two about programming, and he found a way to duplicate the application using human-made resources."

That sounded way too convenient, but Kian couldn't detect deceit in Aru's scent or tone. "I find it hard to believe that all of your devices malfunctioned at the same time and with the same application. Also, our programming language is not compatible with yours. I'm not an expert on those kinds of things, but if the same apps need different programming to run on an Apple or an Android device, I assume that god-made devices and their applications cannot run on human-made laptops."

"Our devices are synchronized, so if there was a problem with one, the others get it too, but I'm not an expert, and we should ask Dagor. He will probably be able to explain this better than I can, and in the meantime, Negal can bring our things from the hotel. Where is that locker room you were talking about?"

"It's in the lobby." Kian pushed his laptop closer to Aru. "First, though, load the application onto my laptop."

Despite Aru's reassurances, Kian had an uncomfortable feeling in the pit of his stomach. His paranoia didn't need much fuel to flare up, and now it was burning hot.

He'd given Aru a clean laptop that wasn't connected to any of the clan servers. The god might have a bug capable of decrypting even William's state-of-the-art encryption.

It took longer than he'd expected to copy the application, and when it was done, Aru checked that everything was working correctly. "Here you go." He pushed the laptop over to Kian. "We've just made one more step in our complicated courtship dance."

Kian chuckled. "Which one of us is the skittish bride?"

"You, of course. I'm the one doing the courting, and you are the one pushing back."

"Simple," Dagor said. "I had to write the program from scratch, using an application that can write other applications. I can show you the YouTube video that taught me how to do it. It's easy when you know the basics."

Kian still wasn't convinced. "What went wrong with your devices? Why couldn't they monitor the drones?"

Dagor grimaced. "Do you think that only humans produce subpar glitchy products? Someone in acquisitions must have gotten a hefty kickback from the supplier of these spy drones. They are cheap garbage."

If that was garbage, Kian wondered what quality products looked like on Anumati.

"They are not that bad," Aru said. "But you are probably right about the kickback. The Borvod conglomerate got the contract for all the military surveillance equipment, and they are big supporters of the Eternal King, so of course they get the lucrative contract even though their products are not as good as their competitors'. That's how things work on Anumati."

"It would seem that's the way things work everywhere." Kian chuckled. "If the gods only knew how similar they are to the humans they created, they would think twice before looking down their noses at humans and referring to them as a lesser species."

"Created species," Aru corrected him. "It's considered rude to call them lesser."

"Of course." Kian smiled. "I wouldn't want to be rude. I just hope that nepotism isn't used when building interstellar ships. That could be dangerous."

"The king is not stupid," Dagor said. "Although he might have realized that it was a bad idea to award ship-building contracts to his supporters only after the settler ship got lost. Maybe it had a subpar onboard computer and communication system."

"Possibly." Aru rose to his feet. "Can we wait for Negal in the lobby? I want to store our things in the locker and go back to the clinic. I don't want Gabi to wake up without me there. I promised that I would stay with her so her brother could go back to his family."

"What about the demonstration?" Kian asked. "I want you to activate the drones so I can make sure that I can monitor their activity on my laptop."

"Dagor can probably do a better job with that than I can."

Turner followed the god up. "I don't know about you, but I want to head back home. Is that okay with you?"

Kian stifled a snort. "You are the security expert. You tell me if that's okay."

"I think it is." He looked at Aru. "You really want this alliance, don't you? And not just because you found your mate among our people."

Kian had a feeling that Turner was asking the question for his benefit and not because he expected an answer from Aru. He had already arrived at the conclusion that Aru wanted to establish cooperation.

The god nodded. "I do."

"And you are not going to do anything to jeopardize it, right?"

Again, this was meant for Kian's ears.

"Not if I can help it." Aru shifted his gaze to Kian. "But if you try to stop me from seeing Gabi, I will not be as agreeable as I am now."

"As long as we are on friendly terms, and I don't deem you a threat to her or any of my people, I will never use your visiting privileges for leverage."

He'd planned on doing that before, but Aru was honorable and making good on every promise, so it would be uncalled for.

"Good." Aru offered him his hand. "Thank you for being reasonable."

Kian shook what he'd been offered. "Thank you for being reasonable as well. Today, we've planted the first seeds of future cooperation. I hope they will grow into a mighty tree."

Beside him, Turner murmured, "Let's hope that the Eternal King doesn't discover it and chop it down."

Aru

"Gabi hasn't woken up since you left." The doctor's expression was indulgent as he regarded Aru. "She fought hard for every waking moment with you, and it has taken a toll on her body. She's compensating for the lost hours of rest."

"So, she's well?"

"Yes." Julian waved him off. "Go on. She's bound to wake up soon."

"Thank you."

Aru turned around and headed to Gabi's room. If she was still out, there was no point in knocking, so he just opened the door and walked in, startling her brother.

"You could've knocked." Gilbert held a hand to his chest in a dramatic parody of fright. "You scared me."

Ignoring the theatrics, Aru walked over to the bed and moved a stray curl away from Gabi's forehead. "My apologies. I didn't know that you were still here."

The guy lifted a brow. "Where else would I be?"

"You should've gone home to your family. I told you that I will be staying with Gabi from now on."

"Oh yeah? Where have you been for the past three and a half hours?"

Gilbert was right about that.

"Kian needed lots of assurances that I don't have any more spy drones following his people. Your leader is very thorough, and he doesn't take shortcuts or trust anyone's word when it comes to his clan's safety."

"That's good. I appreciate him keeping my family safe." Gilbert didn't get up from the stool, forcing Aru to remain standing.

His only other option was to sit on Gabi's bed, and he didn't want to do that with her brother in the room.

"But sometimes his paranoia is a pain in the rear," Gilbert continued. "I have a business to run, and from time to time, I need to visit it in person, but even if that wasn't an issue, I work from home, which is really a pain when my three little ones are there because my mate can't take them to preschool or the babysitter's."

"Well, I'm here now, so you can go home."

"Oh yeah? What if you need to leave again? Who is going to keep an eye on Gabi?"

"I'm done for tonight. My teammate brought our things here, and we are staying in Kian's old penthouse, so if I need to grab a quick shower or change clothes, it's only going to take me a few minutes. I also have access to the elevator now, so I don't need to wait for one of the guards to escort me."

Gilbert didn't look convinced and remained seated. "Are your friends going to come down here to visit Gabi as well?"

Aru shook his head. "Kian only allows me to come down here."

That was actually good because it had given him an opportunity to talk to Kian privately without Negal and Dagor around, and tomorrow, they would probably continue their talk away from others as well. The problem would be leaving Gabi alone. When she was asleep or unconscious, the doctor was good enough, but when she was awake, she should have someone who cared about her for company.

"Smart guy," Gilbert said. "I don't want strangers around my sister."

"I'm a stranger to you as much as my teammates."

That got a smile out of the guy. "But you are not a stranger to Gabi, and she likes having you around. Your buddies, on the other hand, are not welcome here. She wouldn't appreciate them coming in and out of her room." Gilbert cast a fond smile at his sister. "Gabi has always hated being sick, and she would absolutely hate it if strange men saw her in this weakened state. She can barely tolerate Julian taking care of her. She would much prefer a female doctor. Although to be fair to Julian, Gabi likes him much more than the female doctor who took care of her in the human hospital." When Aru bared his fangs, Gilbert lifted his hands. "Julian is happily mated, and he's giving Gabi all of his attention because she's his only patient. The doctor in the hospital was probably overworked and had no time for Gabi. Just keep your buddies away from her until she's back to her normal self."

"That's a given. I would never allow anyone in this room other than the doctor or a family member."

"Good." Gilbert rose to his feet. "I'll take a break for a few hours, visit the family, help Karen put the little ones to sleep, and I'll come back. I don't want Gabi to be alone even for a moment."

"She's never alone. The doctor is here, and when she's asleep, she doesn't need anyone to keep her company."

"Maybe." Gilbert stopped at the door. "But there is a change of guard. Julian is going home, and Merlin is taking the night shift."

The way Gilbert had said the other doctor's name raised Aru's hackles. "What's wrong with the other doctor?"

"He's a bit strange. You'll see what I mean when he gets here."

That was unacceptable. "Does he know how to take care of Gabi?"

"He's a real doctor with the right schooling and a degree, but he's eccentric. He makes fertility potions in his house. Who does that in the twenty-first century?"

That didn't sound so bad.

Aru didn't have a problem with someone experimenting with things, especially since he came from a place that regulated everything and didn't allow private innovation.

As a knock sounded on the open door, Aru and Gilbert both turned their heads toward the sound.

"Hi there." A male with white hair and a long white beard walked into the room. "I'm Doctor Merlin." He offered his hand to Aru. "And you must be the god who induced Gabriella."

The guy's eyes were smart, with a hint of mischief crinkling their corners, but the rest of his appearance didn't inspire confidence. His white coat was stained, and he was wearing red sports shoes with purple pants.

"My name is Aru." He shook the guy's slender hand. "I understand that you are replacing Julian."

"Only for tonight. The young man misses his mate, and he asked me to take over for him. Caring for transitioning Dormants is not my usual thing, but I'm doing him a favor." The doctor must have caught Aru's appraising look because he waved a hand over his colorful attire. "Excuse my unprofessional appearance. I was supposed to be here earlier, but as usual, I lost track of time working on an experiment, and when I realized how late it was, I didn't have time to change. I hope Julian has a clean coat I can borrow."

Great. Someone with an iffy grasp on the concept of time and no experience caring for transitioning Dormants was going to be in charge of Gabi's life for the next twelve hours or so.

"Excuse me for a moment." Aru rushed out of the room and walked into the doctor's office.

Thankfully, Julian was still there, collecting his things into a brown leather satchel.

"Are you sure it's okay to leave Gabi in the hands of a doctor who has no experience with transitioning Dormants?"

"I'm sure." Julian cast him a smile. "And not just because I can't spend another night away from my mate. Gabi is not in danger, and Merlin is a capable and experienced doctor. He was treating humans a century before I was born." Julian slung the strap of his satchel over his shoulder. "Don't let Merlin's clownish appearance fool you. He's a far more accomplished physician than I am."

Syssi

"Let me help you." Alena walked into the kitchen. "You've been slaving in here for hours."

"I underestimated how long everything takes." Syssi handed Alena a bowl of potato salad. "But I'm so glad that the lockdown is finally over. Kian thinks that I'm organizing this dinner so he can give the entire family an update about the new gods all at once, but the truth is that I'm celebrating the end of being stuck in the village."

Okidu had been with Kian the entire afternoon, and Syssi hadn't wanted to ask Amanda or Alena to loan her their Odus. But it had been a long time since she'd cooked anything elaborate, and she'd forgotten how much work went into preparing a meal for a large family.

She'd thought it would be fun to have the kitchen at her disposal without Okidu wringing his hands and telling her to be careful because the kitchen was full of dangers, but halfway through it, she'd wished he was there to do the cleanup.

Alena had been watching Allegra and couldn't help in the kitchen until Annani had arrived and taken over babysitting her granddaughter.

"When is it officially happening?" Alena returned to take another dish to the dining room. "Can we leave now?"

"I'm not sure, but I think so. In any case, Kian's return to the village will signal the end of the lockdown." She cast her sister-in-law a smile. "Can't wait to get out, can you?"

Alena shrugged. "I'm used to being cooped up in the sanctuary for weeks and sometimes months at a time. The village is much larger than the sanctuary, and there are more people to interact with, so I'm good, but Orion is going nuts. He can't wait to get out."

Syssi glanced in the direction of the playroom, where Annani was entertaining Allegra, or perhaps the other way around. "Are you planning on going back there?"

"To visit, for sure. To live, I'm not so sure. I'm working on convincing my mother to permanently relocate to the village and have the sanctuary residents elect a council to run the place."

"Maybe some of them will want to join us in the village as well?" Syssi finished arranging the imitation-meat pie slices on the tray and handed it to Alena. "Can you put this in the warming drawer?"

Would anyone notice that the meat inside the pie wasn't real?

She could have made two separate dishes, one with the imitation ground beef and one with the real thing, but she had no real ground beef in the freezer and no time to get some.

Alena looked around the kitchen until she found the bank of warming drawers. "Most will probably want to stay in the sanctuary, but perhaps some will want to leave and settle here or in Scotland. I also expect some of the village and castle residents to join the Alaskan community. It's a great place for recluses who don't enjoy interacting with humans. I think we should open the sanctuary to whoever wants time out from the world."

"That's not a new idea." Syssi handed her another tray to put away. "Turning the sanctuary into a retreat for clan members has come up several times, but somehow it never gets done."

"It won't happen until Annani officially declares her intentions." Alena put the tray of sliced potatoes in one of the drawers. "As long as the sanctuary is her home, it's going to remain restricted to members by invitation only."

Syssi gasped. "Why didn't I think of it before? I should have asked Gerard to cater this dinner. He wasn't stuck in the village, and he could have delivered it ready."

"As if that was an option. First of all, you decided to have this dinner a few hours ago, and if you called Gerard about it, he would have laughed in your ear and hung up on you. Secondly, I offered to help, and you said that you were looking forward to cooking because you never get the chance with Okidu around."

Syssi sighed. "I forgot how much work it is. I'm just glad that Okidu is returning home with Kian so he can serve dinner and clean up afterward."

"Indeed." Alena laughed, the sound nearly as ethereal as her mother's, only several decibels louder. "What would we do without our Odus?"

Wiping her hand on a dish towel, Syssi turned around and leaned against the counter. "Pretty soon, we will have an Odu for every household. Kaia and William say that they have deciphered enough of the journals to build a basic house servant who can perform all the simple tasks of cleaning, cooking, gardening, etc. It's not going to be an Odu, and it won't be able to babysit or look human, but perhaps it's for the better."

"I don't know." Alena scrunched her nose. "I'm very fond of my Odu, and he's a lot more to me than a servant, even though he hasn't been rebooted yet, so he doesn't exhibit the same sentience as Okidu and Onidu. I don't want a glorified Roomba cooking in my kitchen. I want someone I can talk to."

"If we can talk to Siri and the Google Assistant, I'm sure we will be able to talk to the new breed of servants."

"Not a new breed," Alena corrected. "A new model."

"Right."

As the front door opened and Allegra squealed in happiness, Syssi pushed away from the counter. "Kian is home, and so is Okidu. My kitchen duty is over."

Kian

As the family gathered around the dining table, Kian took Syssi's hand and kissed her knuckles. "Thank you for preparing this amazing meal for us."

"That's sweet of you to say, but dinner hasn't been served yet, so you can't comment on it being amazing. I'll settle for edible." Syssi smiled apologetically at his mother. "I'm so out of practice that I had forgotten the recipes I used to make all the time. I had to look them up online."

Kian didn't let go of her hand. "It must have been difficult without Okidu's help."

"It was, and it reminded me how much I appreciate having him around. By the way, how did the gods react to him?"

"They recoiled," Kian said. "Aru quickly got over his initial reaction, though. He explained that they were taught the Odus were monsters, or rather that they were turned into monsters, but what was not written in the history books was that they were altered at the command of the Eternal King. Since then, the king has gone as far as changing the entire manufacturing process on Anumati. Everything they make is solid state, meaning that they can't take things apart to fix them or alter them in any way. The official position is that it was done to prevent turning devices into weapons, which they were never intended to be. What it means for the resistance is that they cannot alter communication devices, and the only way they can transmit information is in person, which severely limits what they can do."

Aru hadn't revealed his secret communication method, and Kian wasn't expecting him to ever disclose it, but he had guessed it. He was communicating telepathically with someone on Anumati, and that person was either part of the resistance leadership or had personal contact with someone who was.

Kian was betting on the sister Aru had mentioned.

The sample he was basing his assumptions on was too small and had only two members, Vivian and Ella, but since they were mother and daughter and the only ones in the clan who could actually converse with each other in their minds, it made sense to him that only people who were closely related could communicate that way.

He'd promised Aru to keep it a secret, so he wasn't going to say anything about it to his family, not even to Syssi. Although, for once, he was actually hoping that she could get into her receptive state and see who Aru's contact was on Anumati.

Could it be the brightly luminous goddess Syssi had seen in a vision? Or maybe the servant?

Syssi hadn't planned on telling him about the vision but had thankfully changed her mind and had also asserted her will about inducing future visions.

She was right about him having no right to limit her access to her Fates' given talent. Now that she wasn't pregnant, passing out or losing consciousness for a few moments wasn't dangerous to her.

After all, she was an immortal.

Still, he was uncomfortable with her doing it while alone because she often passed out, and he got her to promise him that she wouldn't induce visions unless there was someone in the house with her who was aware of what she was doing and when and could rush in to help her if needed.

"What about the other two gods?" Orion asked. "How did they react to Okidu?"

"More or less the same as Aru. They didn't run away screaming, but they were uncomfortable around him." Kian chuckled. "That didn't stop them from consuming the appetizers he served them. When I took Aru to see Gabi, Turner managed to get them to talk a little about life on Anumati and tell him why people were unhappy."

Annani put down her glass of sparkling water. "I would like to hear what they said."

On the way back to the village, Turner had updated him about his conversation with the two gods, and Kian did his best to recount what Negal and Dagor had told Turner, as well as what he had learned from Aru.

When he was done, silence stretched across the dining table.

"This is a major conundrum," Annani said. "It must be terrible for those who do not agree with the king. I cannot imagine needing to censor my thoughts for fear of someone invading my mind, deciding that I am up to no good, and calling in the inquisitors. But taking down the king might do more damage than good. I do not know how the resistance is going to achieve that, and I cannot concern myself with the future of Anumati's monarchy when humanity's fate and our clan's fate are at stake. We need to find a way to protect Earth." She turned a pair of worried eyes on Kian. "After all the talk of me moving to your village, I think we need to consider moving the entire clan to my sanctuary. Naturally, it will need to be expanded to accommodate so many people, but it is the most secure location we have. It is the best hidden."

Kian leaned over and patted his mother's hand. "Nothing is imminent. We have many years to build a new shelter if we so desire. Most of our people will not want to live in Alaska under a glass dome that is buried deep under the snow."

"Survival is paramount, my son. Personal preferences are secondary. Until now, we were worried about the Doomers doing away with us. Now we are facing a much bigger threat." She rearranged the folds of her silk gown. "I need to tell Areana about the Eternal King. The Brotherhood needs to prepare as well."

Amanda huffed out a breath. "The Eternal King can have Navuh and his bunch of hoodlums. But we need to get Areana out. We also need to get Sari on a video call so she can be part of this discussion. This affects all of us."

"Good idea." Kian pushed to his feet. "I can cast the call on the television screen so we can all see her."

"We can't let the king get Navuh and his so-called hoodlums," Kalugal said. "If the king finds any of the hybrid descendants of the rebel gods, he will either destroy the entire planet to make sure that all the abominations are gone, or he will comb Earth until the last one of us is hunted down." He turned to Amanda. "Like it or not, we need to warn the Brotherhood."

She arched a brow. "How do you propose to do that? Expose Areana or Lokan? Or maybe we should just send Navuh a letter?"

"We can figure out the logistics later," Kalugal said. "First, we need to decide whether to do it and when. As Kian said, nothing is happening anytime soon, but we need to prepare."

"Hello, family." Sari appeared on the screen. "What a nice surprise."

Annani

At first, when Aru had told them about the Eternal King's possible displeasure with the rapid increase in the number of Earth's inhabitants and their technological advancement, Annani had not been overly worried.

The growth rate was slowing, and as far as she knew, no one had come up with a way for humans to travel faster than light even in theory, so the king's two major concerns were taken care of.

If he still wanted to cull the human population by introducing a pathogen, though, finding a way to make every person on the planet immune to disease seemed to be more easily achievable than interstellar travel, and a hundred or so years was probably long enough to make that a reality.

But Aru had delivered another warning, which Kian had either failed to mention before or only found out about today.

The Eternal King deemed all hybrids abominations, and if he ever found out about their existence, he would destroy them. That threat hit much closer to home, and Annani's worry intensified tenfold.

They all had to hide, and a secret village in the Malibu mountains was not a good enough hiding place from the might of the Eternal King.

"Good evening, Mother," Sari said from the television screen, and as David joined her on the couch, he dipped his head and repeated the greeting.

Annani forced a smile. "I do not know whether I should greet you with goodnight or good morning. It is three o'clock in the morning in Scotland. Did we wake you up?"

"We were both awake," Sari said. "We were watching the telly."

"So, that's what it's called in Scotland," Amanda said. "TV watching."

Sari glared at her sister while David blushed, proving Amanda right.

As everyone waved their hellos, she smiled. "I wish I was there with you. It's not Friday yet in Los Angeles, though, so this is not a Friday night family dinner. Have I missed someone's birthday or anniversary? What are you celebrating?"

"Regrettably, this is not a celebration," Kian said.

"So, what is it about? Are the three new gods causing trouble?"

"They aren't," Kian said. "But what they have to say about our dear great-grandfather is most troubling. He's a threat to humanity and to us, and the resistance is not ready to take him down, nor will they be ready a hundred years from now or even a thousand. They are very limited in what they can do." He recounted what he had told the family for Sari and David's benefit. "Mother is so worried that she's suggesting we all move into her sanctuary."

Sari's eyes darted to Annani. "Seriously? You are usually the most optimistic among us. What prompted this extreme concern?"

"A gut feeling." Annani smoothed her hand over the folds of her silk gown. "It is similar to what prompted me to get into my plane and escape before Mortdh's attack. I knew that I had to act quickly or things would not end well for me. I was right then, and I am right now, but with a little less sense of urgency. We have time, but we need to use it wisely."

"I agree," Kian said. "But I don't want us to make hasty decisions born of fear either, and moving everyone into your sanctuary is exactly that."

Annani lifted her chin and looked down her nose at her son. "When Mortdh started amassing an army in the north, the council of gods deliberated for days on end on what to do about the threat. Perhaps if they had talked less and done more, they would not have all died."

"Maybe we need a new sanctuary," Syssi said. "I don't know where, though. We have a difficult time hiding from the Doomers and from humans, and their technology is nowhere near as sophisticated as what the gods have at their disposal." She chuckled. "Perhaps the underwater city I created for the mer's Perfect Match adventure was a premonition of where we are going to live in the future."

"What about the ship?" Alena asked. "The king would never think to search for us on a cruise ship."

"Not a bad idea," Amanda said. "But first, we need to get that wedding cruise underway, or you are going to deliver your baby out of wedlock just like I did." She smiled sweetly at her sister.

Alena chuckled. "I've had thirteen children without the benefit of marriage or a mate, so I win." She rubbed her protruding belly. "I can have this baby without a wedding, but Orion wants us to be married by the time it arrives. I still think we can have a modest ceremony at the village square and get it over with."

Annani glanced at Orion, who had not responded verbally to Alena's comment, but his face revealed how disappointed he was with her dismissive attitude toward their wedding.

"We should still have the wedding cruise as planned." Annani turned to Kian. "Alena and Orion are not the only ones who are waiting. The other couples are just as disappointed."

"I know." Kian sighed. "But what can I do? When we came up with the idea, and I purchased the ship, we didn't know that we would be sharing the village with the Kra-ell or that we would be visited by three gods from Anumati."

Annani put her delicate hand over his. "You have a knack for overcomplicating things because you seek perfection. Things become much easier when you are willing to compromise. As much as I would have liked every resident of the village to join the celebration, that is not possible. The Kra-ell will have to stay behind to safeguard it, and Kalugal's men will remain with them." She smiled at her nephew. "You can bring Shamash to help with Darius, and Rufsur will want to accompany Edna, but Phinas can stay behind and help Jade hold the fort, so to speak. Also, Vrog and Aliya should come because Vlad and Wendy are one of the couples who want me to marry them on the cruise ship."

"What about the new gods?" Toven asked. "What will we do with them while we are merrily sailing on the boat?"

"They can continue to be our guests at the penthouse," Annani said. "Aru will be busy taking care of Gabriella following her transition, and we will be back before she is well enough to be moved."

"I want to meet these gods." Toven turned to Kian. "Can you arrange a meeting?"

Kian shook his head. "I don't want them to see you or Annani. As it is, they already suspect that you are the descendants of the Eternal King's children."

Annani frowned. "How and why? Did anyone say something they should not have?"

Kian grimaced. "I did."

Kian

"I asked Aru why he and his friends didn't glow."

Kian hadn't wanted to bring up the glow question in front of the entire family, and he would have preferred to do that privately with his mother and Toven, but he couldn't explain why Aru suspected that without telling them the entire sequence of blunders, first with the spy drone that had gotten past all of their careful prep work, to Gilbert telling Gabi what he shouldn't have, and then Kian's own slip-up.

"They do not glow at all?" Annani looked surprised. "They must be suppressing their luminescence."

"They aren't," Kian said.

"Oh," Syssi exclaimed. "You promised me a picture of Aru and his friends. I bet everyone wants to see what he looks like."

"I've sent it to you already." Kian waved a hand. "Check your messages."

Syssi's cheeks pinked. "Oops. I was cooking and didn't check my messages. I don't have my phone with me either."

She started to rise when Okidu rushed over. "Here is your phone, mistress."

"Thank you, Okidu." Syssi opened the messages application. "Oh, wow. He's even more handsome than he was in my vision." She handed the phone to Annani. "Right? Look at those cheekbones. So chiseled."

Kian gritted his teeth. "Aru doesn't look like a god. In fact, he looks like he has Kra-ell blood in him, but that's not possible given the taboo they have on intermixing."

His mother was still looking at the photo. "Not all gods were fair skinned like me." She lifted her eyes to Toven. "Toven and Mortdh were darker, and so was Ekin. My father was very fair, though, and his hair was nearly white. My mother was a redhead like me."

"I wonder what the Eternal King looks like." Alena took the phone from Amanda.

"Very luminous," Kian said. "According to Aru, royals glow and commoners do not, but there are thousands of royals. Not that thousands out of three trillion is a lot, but it's still pretty rare." He turned to Toven. "Do you remember any gods who had no glow?"

Toven shook his head. "Some were more radiant than others, and I remember Ahn as being very luminous, but I can't think of anyone who had none whatsoever." He tilted his head. "As you know, with practice, gods can control their glow. We can diminish it, extinguish it, or enhance it. Maybe commoners on Anumati are not allowed to be luminous and are taught at a young age to stifle it."

"That's another issue I wanted to address with you," Kian said. "Since Ahn was the father of the Kra-ell royal twins, they probably were radiant as well, and that might have been another reason for them to be veiled at all times. Maybe their control over their glow wasn't good. At what age do the gods start to glow, and at what age can they control the level of luminosity?"

"That's a good question." Amanda looked at their mother. "Did you glow as a child? Or did you develop it later?"

Annani pursed her lips. "I do not remember ever being without it. Even some of the immortal children were born luminous, and as to the issue of control, it takes practice. I was able to control it by the time I was eleven years old, but only for short periods of time. I did not gain full control of it until I was sixteen, and even then, I had slip-ups when I got emotional." She smiled wistfully. "I was willful and impulsive, so that happened quite often."

"Well, that sucks." Amanda crossed her arms over her chest. "Why have none of us inherited your glow?"

"I do not know." Annani smiled apologetically. "I was never good at science. Maybe luminosity is a recessive gene."

"It probably is," Amanda said. "It's also not beneficial to earthlings who don't live underground. Being luminous makes it difficult to hide."

"That is why it is important to learn to suppress it." Annani waved a hand. "If only the royals glow, I do not understand how all the gods I remember were luminous to at least some degree. I know for a fact that not all of them were of royal blood." She looked at Toven. "Am I right?"

He nodded. "Your mother was a commoner before she mated your father, and she was quite luminous."

"Aru could have been lying," Sari suggested via the video feed. "He might have made up the claim that only gods of royal descent glow, knowing that it would trick you into revealing that you had seen gods and knew that they were radiant."

Kian shook his head. "He already knew that gods were living among us. Gilbert told Gabi that she didn't have exclusive bragging rights for being induced by a god and that he had been induced by a god as well. He didn't know that he had a tiny spy drone on him and that everything he was saying to his sister was being heard by her inducer."

"That's most unfortunate," Kalugal said with a smug smile. "Someone got sloppy and allowed a bug to infiltrate the keep."

"It's not detectable by our technology," Kian defended the team.

"How big is it?" Alena asked.

"A little larger than a flea and smaller than a mosquito."

Kalugal snorted. "That's still big enough to see with the naked eye. If your people were more diligent about security, they would have noticed it."

Kian narrowed his eyes at his cousin. "Is that how you learned about all the things you were not supposed to? Did one of your startups develop a tiny spy drone?"

Kalugal lifted his hands in mock surrender. "I don't have tiny spy drones, and I never did."

Behind him, Darius uttered a little whimper in his stroller, and Kalugal turned to pick up his son. "Hey, sweetie. There is no reason to get upset." He kissed the baby's cheek before cradling him in his arms. "No one is angry at anyone. Uncle Kian and your daddy just enjoy teasing each other, but we are the best of friends."

As the baby settled in his arms, Jacki let out a breath. "Kalugal has the magic touch. Somehow, he always manages to calm Darius down."

Annani regarded Kalugal and his infant son fondly. "He is a sensitive little fellow."

"I know," Kalugal murmured. "He doesn't like it when people argue." He kissed the top of Darius's head.

"So, what's the verdict?" Amanda said. "Was Aru lying, or is there another explanation for the discrepancy?"

"Maybe there was a way to create the glow artificially," Kian said. "The rebels were all about equality, and they didn't want to recreate Anumati's class system in their community. Perhaps one of their doctors came up with a way to chemically induce luminescence, or maybe they stumbled upon a way to activate the gene responsible for it."

"It might not have been about equality," Annani said quietly. "It might have been about hiding the royal descendants by making everyone luminous. Perhaps my father knew that the Eternal King would one day send assassins to kill him, his siblings, and their children, and he wanted to protect the next generation by making them indistinguishable from the other gods."

Alena shook her head. "Forgive me, Mother, but that doesn't make sense. You all knew how to suppress your glow. All your father had to do was to decree that glowing was disallowed, and everyone needed to suppress it."

"That is true," Annani conceded. "But the young gods could not have obeyed his command. They did not have the control needed to do that."

"Perhaps we should consult Okidu's journals," Syssi suggested. "Maybe the answer to this riddle is hidden between their pages."

Aru

Aru sat on the little swivel stool that Gilbert had vacated and looked at the bed longingly. He wanted to lie down next to Gabi, but the bed was narrow, and he was afraid she wouldn't be comfortable.

Julian had said that she needed her rest, and Merlin had repeated the same instructions, so it was best if Aru didn't disturb her regenerative sleep for his own selfish reasons. He worried about her despite both doctors reassuring him that she was doing splendidly.

Through the eyes of the spy drone, he'd seen Gilbert lying down on a field cot last night, but he must have removed it from the room in the morning.

It wasn't important. He could lean his head on the bed and catch a few minutes of sleep until Gabi woke up, which would hopefully be soon.

With a sigh, Aru put his arm on the bed and rested his forehead on it. From this angle, he spotted something that he hadn't noticed before. A little corner of a canvas fabric that was the same color as the clinic's floor protruded from under the hospital bed, and as he dropped down to his knees and leaned down to pull it out, he was happy to discover a folded bundle of tubes that were connected to the cream-colored canvas fabric with cords threaded through loops.

So, that was where the cot disappeared to during the day.

As Aru spread it out next to Gabi's bed, he made a mental note to purchase three of those for his team. The cot wasn't heavy, so it wouldn't add too much weight to their backpacks as they hiked through Tibet in search of more Kra-ell pods, but it would make camping during the night much more comfortable.

But wait, what about Gabi?

Would she want to join them on their quest?

He had to convince her to come with them because he couldn't conceive of leaving her, and he couldn't just stay idle for the next century until the patrol ship arrived.

Fates, what a mess.

Lying down on the cot, Aru let his booted feet dangle over the end and draped an arm over his eyes.

"How am I going to solve this puzzle?" he murmured quietly. "Is there a solution?"

If anyone could figure it out, it would be Aria. His sister was brilliant and an expert solver of complicated puzzles. She was the reason that he'd joined the resistance, but even before that, she'd always been a source of guidance and advice.

Taking a few long breaths, Aru quieted his mind and reached through the ether to his sister.

Can you talk?

Yes. Her mental voice sounded joyful. *How have you been, Aru?*

I'm well. I've met the leader of the immortals, and I think we can rely on him and his people. But before we talk about that, there is something more important I want to tell you about.

What can be more important than the rebellion?

My truelove mate. I found her, Aria.

There was a long moment of silence on their mental connection before Aria's mental voice sounded in his head. *You said that there are no gods left on Earth.*

I was mistaken. I have reason to believe that some are living among the immortals. Perhaps they are the children of the rebel gods who were born on Earth, so they have no trackers in them and don't show up on our tracking systems.

Did you meet those gods or not?

I did not.

So, who is your truelove mate? Did you fall in love with a human?

The incredulity in her tone was ironic. Aria was a rebel through and through, and she abhorred the discrimination against the Kra-ell and the other created species, and yet she sounded shocked that he might have fallen in love with one of them.

Gabriella is not human. She is immortal or about to become one. She is in the process of transitioning into immortality. He explained the what and the how as best he could, given the limited knowledge he had received on dormant carriers of godly genes and the way they were activated.

When he was done explaining, Aria asked, *How do you know that she is the one?*

I feel no desire for anyone else, not even for Alva. And you know how obsessed I am with her. I want to be with Gabi, and I can't imagine being without her. I just don't know how I'm going to accomplish the tasks I still have to complete while being with her. She will be nearly as strong and as resilient as a goddess when her transition is complete, but I do not know whether she would want to travel with me and my team to remote corners of this planet. Most of our travels involve long hikes and sleeping on the hard ground in the cold and in the heat. That is not the lifestyle I want for my mate. I want her to be comfortable, pampered, and have all the luxuries this planet has to offer.

The sound of Aria's laugh stopped his ramblings. *What is so funny?*

When you informed me and our parents that you would never take a mate unless she was your one and only, I lost hope of you ever finding happiness with a worthy female. But here you are, completely besotted with a hybrid, half-human half-goddess. When Mother and Father learn of your choice, they will don their mourning garb.

Their parents were not part of the resistance, and even though they had been shipped off planet to one of the less hospitable colonies, they still believed in most of the propaganda. They would consider Gabi an abomination.

I do not intend to tell them.

The only way he could communicate with his parents was through the patrol ship, and anyone who thought the connection was private was a fool.

Neither would I, Aria said.

She couldn't even if she was so inclined. Their parents did not know about his and Aria's mental connection, and they could never find out.

But you will have to tell them when you return with your mate.

Aru let out a mental sigh. *Think about what you just said. How can I return with my hybrid mate? I cannot take her with me on the ship.*

That is right. You cannot. Aria sounded as despondent as he felt.

I need you to use that brilliant brain of yours and come up with a solution.

You ask too much of me, Aru. This is a puzzle that even I cannot solve.

Give it a try. Perhaps the Supreme will inspire you with an idea.

Aru entertained a slim hope that the Supreme would relieve him from his duties and arrange for a permanent posting on Earth for him. But the truth was that his and Aria's connection was too valuable to waste, and although the Supreme might be sympathetic, a discharge was not in the cards.

Do you really want me to tell the Supreme about your half-human mate?

We hide nothing from the Supreme. He sighed. *Genetically, my mate is mostly human and has only a little bit of godly genes in her, but she is more perfect to me than any goddess could ever be.*

Annani

While the discussion about Okidu's journals and the possibility of future robotic servants continued throughout dinner, Amanda did not take part in it. Instead, she leaned back with a contemplative look on her lovely face and barely touched her food.

Annani waited for a lull in the conversation to ask, "What is on your mind, daughter of mine?"

Amanda shrugged. "Nothing that's important to what we were talking about, although it is related."

"Let's hear it," Kian said. "You have a knack for thinking outside the box."

Amanda rewarded her brother with a brilliant smile. "Thank you, Kian. Usually, you refer to my unorthodox ideas in less complimentary terms."

He let out a long-suffering sigh. "Because many of them are hare-brained and don't bring the results we hoped for, like the paranormal conventions you and Syssi organized or publishing Eva's book in the hopes of the story attracting Dormants, but once in a while, you have a good one."

She rolled her eyes. "That's how it works, Kian. If you try a hundred things and one of them pans out, consider yourself lucky, but if you don't try any, you won't get the one that does."

Kian cast her a fond look. "With that out of the way, please share your thoughts with us." There had been only a trace of sarcasm in his tone.

"Fine. I was thinking about Aru's claim that only the gods with royal blood glow and commoners do not, and it occurred to me that the gods might have experimented with the created species, using royal genetics to enhance some and commoner genetics to enhance others. There might be created species out there who glow. Then, another thought crossed my mind. What if the glow was connected to metabolic function? What if the food on Earth activated the glow gene for all the gods and not just the royals? What if that was one of the reasons Earth was declared a forbidden planet?"

"Oh, wow." Syssi put a hand on her chest. "That could totally be the reason. The royals on Anumati wouldn't have wanted the commoners to discover how to get the glow and lose their exclusive luminous status as a result."

"I find it hard to believe," Annani said. "If the food on Earth enabled common gods to have a glow, it would have been discovered eons before the rebels were exiled to

Earth. According to the myths, the gods created humans, and we know that humans existed on Earth long before the rebels were forced to make Earth their permanent residence. The information would have found its way back to Anumati."

"Not necessarily." Amanda tapped her lower lip with her finger. "It might have been a more recent development. Perhaps a new food was introduced. Beer, for example, was created by the goddess Ninkasi. It didn't exist on Earth prior to the rebels' arrival. It could have activated the glow gene."

"Then how come we don't glow?" Kian waved a hand over himself. "With how much beer I consume, I should be as luminous as Mother, and Anandur should glow like a supernova."

As everyone laughed, Amanda pouted. "I used beer only as an example of a newly introduced dietary consumable. It was one of many new foods that were introduced during that era. The rebel gods jump-started human civilization, and one of the ways they did it was by introducing innovative agricultural systems and cultivation of plants."

Annani smiled. "I remember learning about that. My father hired Khiann to teach me about commerce, trade, and the different methods of shipping goods from faraway places." She chuckled. "Now I wish I had paid more attention to what he was actually trying to teach me rather than flirting with my future husband."

She had done more than flirting during those precious days, but even though her children were all adults and immortals were not shy about their sexuality, there were some things a mother did not discuss with her children.

Amanda smiled at her sadly. "I'm glad that you enjoyed every moment you had with Khiann. Your time was better spent flirting than learning about commerce."

Taking a fortifying breath, Annani nodded. "I agree. But back to our discussion. Let us assume that you are right, and a certain food activated the commoner gods' glow genes. We need to find out what it was. Perhaps Bridget and Kaia can take a sample from me or Toven and find the gene responsible for our glow."

Next to her, Kian stiffened. "We have not analyzed your blood for a reason, Mother. This needs to remain a mystery."

Annani shook her head. "We had our reasons before, but perhaps it is time to take the next step in our quest for answers."

Kian glared at her. "We are not going to learn anything helpful from analyzing your blood, Mother. I can tell Aru that we suspect Earth's food is the activator and send him on a quest to find which one it is." He chuckled. "Maybe that was what Gilgamesh was trying to find."

"Grapes?" Syssi suggested. "How old are they?"

"We can easily find out." Amanda pulled out her phone and looked to Annani for permission. "May I?"

The dinner table was not the place for phones or tablets. It was a time for family and friends to come together and enjoy each other's company, face to face with lively conversation. But dinner was over, coffee and tea had been served along with dessert, and the evening was winding down.

Annani nodded. "Yes, you may, but please read to us what you find out so we are all part of your discovery."

"Thank you, Mother." Amanda got busy typing on the screen.

Aru

After Aru had exhausted all the amorous words that he knew in his native language to sing Gabi's praises, he hoped he would be able to translate them into English so he could tell her all the things he'd told Aria about her.

His sister had patiently listened to him describing the way he and Gabi had met, and how he was convinced that their encounter had been fated, and how Gabi's connection to the clan of immortals couldn't have been coincidental either.

Oh, Aru. It gladdens my heart that you are so deeply in love, and that your connection to Gabriella opened up an opportunity for the resistance to establish a base on the forgotten planet, but I worry about your mate's perilous condition. Perhaps you should aid her transformation to ensure her survival.

Aru frowned. *How can I aid her? I'm not a healer.*

His sister laughed. *You do not need to be a healer to aid one of the created species. Your blood is a potent medicine to them, and your mate can benefit from a small transfusion.*

Aria had studied to become a healer before she had been offered a position in the service of the Supreme, so he didn't doubt her knowledge, but he had to wonder why none of the troopers tasked with monitoring the created species had been told about such an important remedy.

That should have been a crucial piece of information in the Watchers' training. Why have we not been told about our blood's curative abilities? Is it a closely guarded secret that only healers are privy to?

Most of the gods on Anumati will never encounter a member of the created species, so there is no need for this to be common knowledge, and the Watcher troops are supposed to watch and squash uprisings when needed, not to interact with the locals. The healers, on the other hand, are expected to be shipped off to distant colonies and help the ruling gods there. Can you think of a better way to gain the population's gratitude than to offer miraculous heal-ings to its leaders? Mostly, it is achieved with our genetics-altering equipment, but in an emergency, when nothing else is available, our blood can be used instead.

That makes sense, but it would have been good to know, nonetheless. Aru opened his eyes and glanced at Gabi, who was still sleeping soundly. *How much should I administer, and are you sure it is safe?*

Very little, Aria said. *The quantity should be the size of the tip of your little finger, and it is perfectly safe. A good spot to take the blood from is the bend of your arm, and to administer, use the vein on the back of your mate's hand. If you lick the spot first, it is not going to hurt when you put the needle in. Do you know where you can find a syringe?*

I am in a well-equipped clinic. They have syringes here.

He had been updating Aria about the state of human progress ever since he had landed on Earth five years ago, including what he had learned from watching shows about doctors and hospitals. She knew it wasn't the primitive place it used to be only a few centuries ago, and so did the Supreme, who had informed him through Aria that he should not report the full extent of human progress to his commander even though the god was part of the resistance.

Still, it was not possible to report nothing. The patrol ship had noted the human-made satellites and other signs of progress, and some of it must have already reached the Eternal King.

Excellent, Aria said. *So, it should not be a problem. Do you know how to use it?*

I can find an instruction vid, but I'm afraid of administering the transfusion and doing something wrong. Perhaps I should thrall the doctor to do it for me.

That might be a good idea. But make sure that the healer doesn't remember it. The created species shouldn't know about this method, or the gods among them will be in danger.

These are immortals. They don't get sick, and they don't need our blood's help. The transition is a rare occurrence for adults. Usually, the induction is done at puberty when the risks are so minimal that they are negligible.

It took a moment for Aria to respond, and Aru imagined her looking up as she examined the information from all angles.

The question is how good these immortals are at keeping secrets. If they are closely involved with humans whom they care about, they might reveal your secret.

Could their blood work as well as ours? Aru asked.

Not likely. You should proceed with caution. Have you thralled any of the immortals yet?

Not yet. Thralling the doctor will serve two purposes. I will find out whether I can thrall immortals, and I will get a trained healer to administer the transfusion instead of doing it myself and risking hurting Gabi.

Good luck, Aru. Tell me how it goes.

Hold on, we are not done yet. I also need you to consult with the Supreme about what I should tell the leader of the immortals.

He could sense the tension coming from Aria even without her verbalizing it.

What did you tell the leader? she asked.

I didn't tell him about our method of communication, only that I have a way to get in touch with the resistance leaders.

What if he figures out how you are doing it?

Aru turned on his side and propped his head on his hand. *He won't. Not unless he knows someone who can do what we can, and that is impossible. Our ability is extremely rare.*

Aria sighed. *It is rare now, but it might not have been over seven thousand Earth years ago when the original rebels were exiled to Earth. Some of them might have been strong telepaths.*

Not much was known about the group of the original rebels. The three known names were the king's children —his two sons and a daughter. The rest were only mentioned as rebels, and no names were provided, supposedly to save their families the shame.

However, the problem with a society of people who live forever was that someone always remembered what really happened and who had been involved, but the king knew how to deal with that as well. Not everyone choosing to enter stasis and sleep through several hundreds or thousands of years did so because they were going insane from boredom. Some were coerced, some were bribed, and some did it to save themselves the trouble of dealing with the king's secret army of informants.

Turning on his back, Aru stared at the ceiling. *It would be a very unlikely coincidence if there were telepaths like us among the immortals, especially given their diluted godly genes.*

Aria sighed. *I hope that you get invited to their community soon so you can find out what talents these immortals have.*

That wasn't going to happen. He and Kian had both agreed on that, but Aru could find out about the different talents from Merlin. The doctor was a talkative fellow, and it wouldn't be difficult to get him to list all the various talents the immortals had.

I might have another way of finding out that does not involve visiting their secret location. I have a tracker embedded in my flesh, and I don't want to expose them unnecessarily.

I forgot about that, Aria said. *Luckily, I got recruited for this job before I was implanted with a tracker. However, given how paranoid our ruler is, he will soon have every god implanted even if they have no plans of ever leaving the planet. He just wants to know where everyone is and what they are doing.*

Aru let out a mental breath. *On Anumati, he does not need trackers to follow every citizen. Surveillance is everywhere.* Supposedly, it was to prevent unlawful or unkind behavior, but it was about so much more than that.

That is why we are building the resistance, Aru. We are fighting for our freedom while the noose is tightening around our necks. Tell me all you have learned about these immortals so far, so I can give the Supreme all the pertinent information about them. We should welcome any help we can get in moving the rebellion forward.

Syssi

Grapes had turned out to be older than they had suspected. They'd been cultivated for over eight thousand years, and other crops had conflicting cultivating times on the web.

Syssi had been ecstatic to discover that coffee had been used to brew beverages in Ethiopia over five thousand years ago, but the date was quoted only by one website, and its claim was disputed by several others that reported a much later date.

That was very disappointing. She would have loved for coffee to be the gods' glow activator.

"It seems that Amanda's first guess about beer was the most likely," Kian said. "But the problem with that hypothesis is that Aru likes beer, which means that he drank it during his five years on Earth. If that was the activator, he would have developed a glow by now. That being said, he's not much of a drinker, so maybe larger quantities and a more prolonged consumption are needed to make a difference."

"I wonder if they make beer on Anumati," Annani said. "Ninkasi must have brought the knowledge of how to brew beer from home. Otherwise, how would she have come up with the idea?"

"Beer can be produced from more than just barley," Syssi remembered Jacob telling her about it.

He'd wanted to start a home brewery and had done all the research, but then his life had ended needlessly.

He could have lived forever.

As a wave of sadness threatened to swallow her, she shook her head and continued, "Wheat, corn, rice, and oats can also be used to make beer. The fermentation of the starch sugars in the wort produces ethanol and carbonation to make beer. What I'm trying to say is that beer on Anumati could be made from other grains that don't have the same effect as the one made from barley."

"It's very unlikely that beer is the activator," Kian said. "It was just a shot in the dark."

"It was an idea." Amanda shrugged and went back to reading on her phone. "Listen to this. Bioluminescence is not exclusive to sea creatures that glow in the dark. According to research that was done at the Tohoku Institute of Technology in Japan, humans have it as well, just at very low levels, and it has to do with metabolism. Free radicals interact with lipids and proteins, which sometimes contain fluorophores, a fluorescent chemical compound that can produce photons of light." She lifted her eyes to their mother. "It looks like I was right, and humans were created with the help of royal godly genes." She smiled. "I wonder if they were someone's pet project."

Kian chuckled. "Perhaps humans are the Eternal King's pet project, and he has a soft spot for his creations, so he will not do away with them when he finds out how successful his experiment has become."

"You might be onto something. Maybe humans were the king's pets," Annani said. "Maybe we have misinterpreted everything, and he sent his rebellious children to Earth to make a new start away from Anumati. Perhaps he made Earth a forbidden planet so no one could interfere with their new world."

Amanda leaned over and took their mother's hand. "That's wishful thinking, Mother, and you know that. I would like to believe that great granddaddy is a nice guy too, but we've heard enough to know better."

Annani sighed. "Spreading propaganda can go both ways. What if his enemies are spreading lies about him?"

Kian had a feeling that their mother knew very well that her grandfather was not a good guy and was just entertaining what-if thoughts to lift everyone's mood.

"There is more." Amanda went back to her phone. "The glow is most pronounced in the early afternoon when human metabolism is the most active. The glow is mainly concentrated in the cheeks, forehead, and neck." She looked up and grinned. "Those are precisely the spots that get red when someone gets drunk. Coincidence? Maybe not."

"As fascinating as this is, that is not how my glow works." Annani intensified her luminance until it was difficult to look at her. "We glow all over, and we don't need to eat a big meal to do so." She looked at Toven. "Am I right?"

He dipped his head. "Naturally, but I can't make mine as bright as yours. I couldn't do that even when I was in my prime."

Mia elbowed him. "Don't talk like that was in the past. You are still very much in your prime."

"Thanks to you." He leaned toward her and kissed her cheek.

It suddenly dawned on Syssi that her vision of a brightly shining goddess must have been of a royal, and since it seemed like the more royal blood one had, the more intense the glow, perhaps the goddess she'd seen in her vision was the queen? Annani's grandmother?

As a shiver ran down her spine at the thought, she resolved to induce another vision about the goddess.

Turning to Kian, she reached for his hand. "Aru told you that there are many royals, right?"

"Yes, thousands. There is more than one royal family."

"Then the Eternal King is not really eternal," Dalhu said. "For there to be other royal families, there must have been other monarchs before him."

"Good observation," Kian said. "I should make a list of questions for Aru and his friends. As long as Gabi is transitioning, he will be more inclined to answer them."

Dalhu's comment must have distracted Kian because he hadn't noticed Syssi squeezing his hand. Usually, she and Kian were so in tune that he could guess her intent from the subtlest clues, but not this time. He hadn't gotten the hint when she'd asked him about the royals on Anumati.

Amanda knew about the vision as well, but she hadn't connected the dots either.

Perhaps it was better that way.

Syssi wasn't ready to share her vision with Annani before she knew more. Her mother-in-law might get excited for nothing.

"I have a question," Jacki said. "Is what causes humans to glow the same as what makes bioluminescent creatures emit light?"

Amanda shook her head. "Deep-sea fish, fireflies, and most other light emitting creatures have luciferin, which means light bringer in Latin."

Jacki's eyes widened. "Is that what Lucifer means? A light bringer? Why would the devil bring light?"

Amanda laughed. "Religions have a way of distorting the meaning of words for no good reason. Lucifer is the

Latin name for Venus, as it appears in the morning. Therefore, it is the light bringer. Since Venus is also the goddess of love, my take on it is that it was a malicious attempt to attribute carnal love to the devil and, by association, portray all women as devilish."

Aru

As Aru's mental conversation with Aria continued, he kept glancing at Gabi, hoping to see her make the slightest of moves or sounds, anything to indicate that she wasn't unconscious and only resting, but so far, she hadn't stirred even once.

Was it normal?

Would Merlin know?

Despite Julian's assurances about Merlin's competence as a healer, Aru still didn't trust the guy.

Thank you for all the information, Aria said. *I will relay it to the Supreme at the first opportunity I have.*

Aru put his legs over the side of the cot and sat up. *Please let me know as soon as you have instructions for me.*

I will. Good luck with the transfusion operation.

Thank you. Be well, Aria.

You too, Aru.

As the mental channel closed, Aru pushed to his feet and walked over to Gabi. Her breathing seemed normal, and so was her heartbeat, and the monitors were humming away as they had been doing when he'd returned.

There had been no change.

Turning around, he walked to the door, opened it only as much as he needed to slip through so the bright light of the waiting room didn't disturb Gabi, and stepped out while leaving the door slightly ajar.

The office door on the other side of the waiting room was open, and through it, Aru could see Merlin sitting in the swivel chair with his back to the desk, his red-clad feet propped on the file cabinet that stood against the wall, and a phone pressed to his ear.

"Don't you go baking in the middle of the night, love," Merlin said. "I know you miss me, but you don't need to make me cookies for when I return tomorrow morning. You should take a relaxing bubble bath or watch a movie with Lisa."

"She's not home," the woman on the other side said. "Supposedly, she's studying for a test with Parker."

"Oh, so that's what they are calling it these days, studying."

The woman laughed. "Cheryl is with them as well as Jade's daughter. Parker is an immortal with the stamina to match, but I doubt he has the chutzpah to flirt with three girls at once."

"Not with Drova, he doesn't, that's for sure. That girl is almost as intimidating as her mother."

Aru smiled, happy to hear that Drova had made friends among the young immortals. From what he'd learned while spying from afar on the Kra-ell in Gor's compound, he was under the impression that the relationship between Jade and Drova was strained, and Drova hadn't had many friends.

Not wanting to eavesdrop further on Merlin's private conversation, he tiptoed down the hallway in search of the supply room.

After finding a syringe, he could wait for the doctor to be done with his phone call and thrall him to administer the transfusion, or he could do it himself.

Perhaps it was better not to chance thralling Merlin.

The immortal might be resistant, and Aru wasn't sure whether it was wise to let him in on the secret of the curative effects of the gods' blood.

Aria's warning was sound, but if these immortals had stayed hidden from humans, gods, and even other immortals, they were very good at keeping secrets, and they could probably handle this one as well.

Perhaps he could use it as leverage in future negotiations.

The gods living among them probably didn't know about it, and it was too useful a trick to leave unknown.

One day, a human leader who was essential to the immortals might be dying, and it might be that the only way to save that leader was with a god's blood.

For now, though, it would be better to do the transfusion himself and save the information for when it would come in handy in future negotiations with Kian.

Surely, there was an instructional video on YouTube on how to use syringes.

After opening a few doors Aru finally found the supply closet, but looking at the assortment of syringes, he didn't know which one to choose. Aria had said that the quantity of blood should be the size of the tip of his smallest finger, so the syringe needed for that was probably the smallest size.

Pocketing three syringes just in case he messed up the first two, he walked out of the supply room, closed the door, and tiptoed back.

Merlin was still talking to his lady, but much more quietly than before, and given his throaty chuckles, they were talking about intimate stuff.

Smiling, Aru shook his head and continued to Gabi's room.

He closed the door behind him, toed off his boots, and climbed into bed with her.

Moving her just a little to make room for himself, he lifted the additional blanket from the foot of the bed and covered them both. Anyone watching the footage from the surveillance camera would only see him cuddling with his mate, and no one would see what he was doing under the blanket.

The problem was that Aru didn't know what he was doing either.

Pulling out his phone, he brought up the YouTube application and first searched how to extract the blood from his own vein.

When he was sure that he could handle that part, he searched for how to administer the blood infusion, which was more difficult to find than the first part, but eventually, he found an instructional video from India. Fortunately, he understood enough Hindi to follow it.

Extracting his blood was surprisingly easy, but when it was time to find the vein in Gabi's hand, he got nervous. Bringing it to his lips, he kissed the spot and then laved it with his tongue to provide the healing agent, and he stopped breathing as he inserted the needle.

Thank the merciful Fates, Gabi didn't react in any way, which he took to mean that she was unconscious rather than asleep, and when all of his blood was gone from the syringe, he pulled the needle out and licked the insertion point once more.

In moments, there was no trace of what he had done.

For the next hour, Aru lay next to Gabi, enjoying her closeness and listening to her steady heartbeat and even breathing, but eventually, he got restless and decided it was time to check on Merlin again.

By now, the doctor had most likely finished his phone call, and he could answer questions about the various talents the immortals possessed. Aru needed to find out whether any of them had a telepathic connection like the one he shared with his sister.

Merlin

The god emerged once more from Gabi's room and walked over to the office. Stopping at the doorway, he leaned in. "Are you busy?"

Merlin had noticed Aru skulking around the clinic while he'd been on the phone with Ronja, probably looking for a pillow or a blanket for his cot or perhaps for something else that wasn't as innocuous as that.

Did gods do drugs?

No morphine or any of the other drugs in that class were missing, though, so perhaps Aru was just the curious type and liked to check things out.

Merlin had intended to ask him what he needed after he was done chatting with Ronja, but a glance at the monitor in Gabi's room revealed that Aru was snuggling with her, and he seemed to be asleep.

Merlin arched a brow. "Do I look busy to you?"

"You were an hour ago. How are things at home?"

"They are splendid. What can I help you with?"

The god walked in, pulled out a chair, and sat down. "I'm worried about Gabi. She's been unconscious for long hours now, and that's not the pattern she's been following previously of waking up every couple of hours and staying awake for a little while before slipping under again. Is that normal?"

Merlin shrugged. "There is no normal with transitioning Dormants. Each case is unique, but I can tell you that Gabi is doing very well, and you have nothing to worry about. Of all the cases we've seen so far, hers is one of the easiest. Eric, her other brother, took a long time to transition. Her niece breezed through it, but her actual transition took a long time, which was very frustrating to her."

Aru frowned. "What do you mean by the actual transition? What Gabi is going through is not the actual thing?"

Merlin lifted a hand with three fingers up. "There are three stages to the transition. The first one is the most traumatic because it is fast. The body is undergoing dramatic changes, so the long bouts of sleeping and even unconsciousness are good because they let the body direct all its energy toward the change. Once the initial stage is done, the Dormant is already immortal, which translates into rapid healing, better hearing and eyesight, a more acute sense of smell, etc., but the changes continue at a slower pace for about six months, sometimes longer. For males, in particular, it's a difficult time because they grow fangs and venom glands, and that's painful. Nowadays, we have painkillers that can ease them, but in the not-too-distant past, the only remedy was getting drunk." Merlin grinned. "The amounts of whiskey the lads consumed were staggering. As you know, it takes much more alcohol to get an immortal or a god drunk than it takes a human."

Aru didn't smile, which wasn't the response Merlin had been hoping for. The guy was too serious.

"I wouldn't know because I don't drink to get drunk. But back to what you said before about Gabi's niece. What did you mean by actual transition?"

"Oh, yes." Merlin smoothed his hand over his long beard. The thing needed trimming, but Ronja did not allow him to do it himself and demanded that he go to a barber, and he simply didn't have time for that.

"Merlin?" Aru reminded him that he was still waiting for an answer.

Merlin's mind tended to wander, and it often did that, even in the middle of a conversation. "Yes, yes. Where was I? Oh yes. We usually run a test once the initial stage is completed to see how fast the newly transitioned immortal heals. We make a small cut on the palm of their hand, and we time how fast it closes. Initially, Kaia took over four minutes to heal, which is considered very long. It took weeks for her healing time to go down to under a minute, which is what it should have been when she was tested the first time. That didn't happen to any of the other transitioning Dormants. I'm telling you all this so you know to expect the unexpected. Gabi still might slip into a deeper coma and not wake up for days or even weeks, but the chances of that are small."

The god shook his head. "My mind is still stuck on the barbaric test you perform. I'm sure there is a more advanced method of testing healing speed than inflicting an injury on the Dormants right after they suffered through the transition."

Merlin pursed his lips. "When you put it that way, yeah, you have a point. But you know what? They all want to do the test even if there is no need for it. It became a tradition, a rite of passage of sorts."

"Not all customs are good, and some are better done away with. I'm not allowing anyone to cut Gabi's palm."

Merlin smiled indulgently. "It's not your decision to make. It is Gabi's, and I'll bet you that she will want the test with all the pomp and ceremony that's involved."

"How do you know? You haven't even talked to her."

"That's true, but I know her brothers. And if she's anything like them, she will want exactly what they got." Merlin leaned forward. "I have a lovely mate who transitioned not too long ago, and she came with a daughter whom I adore. My mate is a very delicate lady, and yet, she wanted to do the test, and when the time comes for Lisa, I have no doubt she will want it as well."

The god leaned back in the chair and crossed his arms over his chest. "If Gabi wants to do the test, I will not stand in her way. It's not my place to make decisions for her. But I will express my opinion about the barbarity of it."

"Suit yourself. But if you want my advice, you will keep your mouth shut and say nothing. Your most important job as a mate is to support your lady in whatever she chooses to do."

Aru

The healer had turned out to be not as nutty as he appeared, and he had some strong opinions. The good news was that he didn't have a clue about the clandestine blood transfusion Aru had performed an hour ago.

If everything went well and Gabi's transition progressed faster and easier, Aru would use the knowledge in his negotiations with Kian. The immortals didn't get sick, but other transitioning Dormants could benefit from the blood of the gods residing in the immortals' village, especially those who didn't have an easy transition like Gabi's. Hopefully, she would have it even easier going forward.

"I'll take your advice under consideration." Aru unfolded his arms. "Perhaps we should move ahead and talk about what happens after the transition is complete. At what stage do the specific talents manifest, if there are any?"

Merlin frowned. "I assume that you refer to thralling and the like?"

"Thralling, compulsion, telepathy, foresight, remote viewing, and all that. Those are the most common traits for gods."

Hopefully, he had phrased it generically enough not to raise the doctor's suspicion.

"Let's see." Merlin leaned back and smoothed a hand over his white beard. "Those who transition at puberty learn to thrall with relative ease. That applies to all the clan children and also those born in the Brotherhood. Older transitioned Dormants, like Gabi and my beautiful mate, seem to have great difficulty learning to do that, and most don't bother to make the effort. The other talents you've mentioned usually manifest even before the transition, but not always. Kian's mate has had visions of the future since she was a little girl. She even predicted the discovery of the Kra-ell. Kalugal, who is Kian's cousin, is a compeller, and he had the ability since he was a little boy as well. Magnus's wife can communicate telepathically with her daughter, who is Julian's mate, and they could do that as humans years before they joined the clan and were induced. Aside from the ones I mentioned, we also have telepaths, empaths, seers, remote viewers, immunes, and compellers, all with varying degrees of ability. In addition, many clan members are creatives, and I'm sure that some of those artistic talents are supernatural as well."

Aru was only interested in the mother and daughter telepaths, and since the daughter was mated to Julian, he could ask him about her when he replaced Merlin tomorrow morning, but he couldn't wait so long to find out whether her talent was like his and Aria's, which was the ability to actually talk in each other's heads. The more common type of telepathy was receiving or transmitting limited information to anyone in the vicinity with some level of telepathic sensitivity.

"Can Julian's mate communicate with anyone other than her mother?" he asked.

Merlin lifted both white brows and pursed his lips at the same time, looking comical. "I'm not sure whether Ella can communicate with anyone other than Vivian, but I know that Vivian can only communicate with Ella. The daughter is the stronger telepath."

Aru closed his eyes and opened a channel to his sister, who surprised him by opening it on her side and letting him in. *You were right*, he said. *They have a pair like us in their village.*

Aria's answer came in the form of a laugh. *I cannot talk right now, but I am always right. Make sure the leader of the immortals doesn't connect the dots.*

"You should get some sleep, Aru," Merlin said. "You can't even keep your eyes open. Make use of the cot, though." He smiled indulgently. "I saw that you climbed in bed with Gabi before, and I didn't say anything because it was fine for a little while, but she needs her rest, and you crowding her in bed makes her sleep less restful."

"You are right." Aru pushed to his feet. "Thank you for the talk. I think I'm going to catch a couple hours of sleep. Goodnight, Merlin."

"It was nice talking to you. Goodnight, Aru."

Later, when Aru lay awake on the too-short cot in Gabi's room, he thought about ways to salvage the situation.

Perhaps he could make up a story about an illegal secret communicator that his teammates didn't know about and throw hints about communicating with a resistance base somewhere in a direct line of sight of Earth.

From there, the messages could be transmitted to the resistance leadership on Anumati.

However, he and his teammates had already told Kian and Turner about the way things were manufactured on Anumati and that devices were made in a way that didn't allow for modifications.

But then things could have been made off planet, where manufacturing was a little less regulated, especially if the products were meant for the local market and internal consumption. Dagor had said that they were crap, which was true in most cases, but even a crappy device was better than none.

Kian could demand to see the communicator, but Aru would refuse, and that would be the end of it.

Yeah, that was what he had to do.

No one other than the Supreme knew about his and Aria's ability, and it was crucial that it stay that way.

Kian

When all the guests had left, Kian pulled Syssi into his arms. "Thank you for preparing dinner. Now that I've eaten all the dishes you made, I can honestly say that it was wonderful."

"Thank you. I'm glad you liked it, even though everything tasted a little off. I'm so out of practice."

"I savored every bite." He kissed her lightly on the lips. "Now let me make it up to you for taking Okidu away when you needed him." He swung her into his arms and carried her to their bedroom—princess-style.

Winding her arms around his neck, she rested her cheek on his chest and sighed. "I'm so tired."

That was disappointing. "Too tired for bedroom fun?"

She laughed. "Not if I get to be lazy and you do all the work."

"It's a deal, and I'll even throw in a foot massage."

Leaning up, she kissed his cheek. "That's why you are such a good businessman. You make the best deals."

"Damn right, I do." Kian sat on their bedroom couch with his mate in his lap. "It's called closing." He arranged her so her back was resting against the plush arm and her feet were in his lap. "Throwing in a treat to sweeten the deal almost always leads to a signature on the dotted line."

Her short-heeled mules were easy to take off and toss on the floor, and as he started kneading the arch of one foot, Syssi closed her eyes and let out a throaty groan that went straight to his groin.

He chuckled. "Sometimes it sounds as if you are having more fun when I'm massaging your feet than when I'm making love to you."

Syssi cracked one eye open and smiled. "Do I hear a note of insecurity in the voice of the most confident male on the planet?"

He shook his head in mock affront. "And now you are insinuating that I have an overinflated ego. I get no respect in this house."

Syssi knew he was joking, and she chose to ignore his banter and submit to the pleasure his fingers were wringing out of her foot instead.

"Do you remember the vision I told you about the other day?" she murmured.

"The one you were not supposed to induce? Yeah, I remember."

She opened her eyes and glared at him. "We talked about this, Kian. I'm not carrying a baby, so even though the visions take a lot out of me, I can handle them. I promised you that I would not induce them without telling someone what I'm about to do so they could check in on me if needed, but we agreed that I would have them whenever I wanted, and you would not give me the stink eye for that."

He lifted a brow. "Stink eye, eh? A stinging bottom is more my style."

She pouted, but there was a gleam of mischief in her eyes. "You gave me both. I don't mind the second, but I do mind the first, and you promised not to do that." She lifted a finger and tapped his nose with it. "We've made a deal."

"Oh, lass, you've got me there. I can't go back on a deal, now, can I?" He let his Scottish accent come through, knowing how much it turned her on.

"No, you can't, and stop distracting me. Back to my vision. The goddess I saw must have been a royal, and if the intensity of the glow was an indicator of royal blood, she was a queen. Do you think she could have been your great-grandmother?"

"You said that her glow was so bright that you couldn't see her face, so you don't know if she looked anything like my mother or one of my sisters, which would have been a clue."

Syssi sighed. "True. The only vivid clue was that gold vase that didn't fit with the rest of the room's decor. It looked like modern art." She frowned. "That was actually a good clue. It should have made me realize that what I was seeing wasn't ancient Sumer but somewhere else entirely —like an alien planet."

Kian moved to massage Syssi's dainty toes, which she always found ticklish, but he did that gently this time so as not to distract her again. "What else do you remember from the room? Perhaps the face of the other goddess, the servant, was clearer?"

Closing her eyes tightly, Syssi let out a breath. "Nope. I don't think that I saw her face clearly either, but I noticed her dress and also the dress of the other goddess. They were both made from a silk-like fabric like the gowns your mother favors, but the royal goddess's was much more elaborate. I mean, the pattern of the fabric was. The dress itself was simple. It was like a Greek toga, and she also wore a gold necklace." Syssi frowned. "It had a medallion, and I think it had some design on it." She opened her eyes. "I need to induce another vision."

Kian had been afraid of that, but he'd made a deal with her, and he wasn't going back on his word. "Do you want to do it now?"

Syssi gaped at him. "Now? Do you want me to do it with you in the room?"

"Well, yes. That way, I can take care of you if you faint."

"I can't do it with you here because I won't be able to concentrate. Besides, I'm too tired. I will do it on Saturday."

That was in two days, and it wasn't like Syssi to postpone something she was determined to do.

"Are you going to the university tomorrow?"

She had been complaining about being cooped up in the village, so even though it was Friday tomorrow, and it would have made more sense for her to return to work on Monday, she probably couldn't wait to get out of the house.

"No. Amanda wants us to start on Monday. She convinced me to go shopping with her tomorrow instead. After that, I'll probably be too exhausted to induce a vision, which is why I'm planning to do it on Saturday."

That explained why Syssi didn't want to induce the vision tomorrow. Shopping with Amanda was probably more exhausting than running a marathon.

He was glad that she was taking time off for herself, but shopping was one of her least favorite activities. "What prompted you to humor Amanda? You order everything online."

"I do, but Amanda has been on my case for a while now to give my wardrobe a serious update. We are going to

Joann's. She's reserving the entire morning just for the two of us."

Kian grinned. "I'm glad that you are finally going to splurge on yourself a little. Are you taking Allegra with you?"

"Your mother and Alena are babysitting Evie and Allegra so Amanda and I can enjoy our shopping spree." She let out a sigh. "The last time Amanda took me to Joann's, the visit cost a small fortune. I told her that I was never going to do it again, but the truth is that I'm not the same woman I was then. I'm a little less frugal these days."

"Thank the merciful Fates." Kian lifted one small foot and kissed its arch. "You are a major stockholder in a successful enterprise, and you can afford a fancy wardrobe."

"Right." Syssi smiled. "I keep forgetting that I own a large chunk of Perfect Match. With all that has been happening lately, Toven and I have neglected the company. We are lucky to have Hunter and Gabriel still running things for us."

"Indeed." He kissed her toes. "You are better at managing your business than I am. You have capable people running it for you."

"That's because I bought an existing enterprise and hired the founders. This is their baby, and they won't let it fail if they can help it. You, on the other hand, are running numerous enterprises for the clan, some that you bought and some that you've built from the ground up. Frankly, I don't know how you manage all of them while dealing with the seemingly perpetual emergencies that threaten the clan. I would have lost my mind from anxiety."

Leaning, he kissed her forehead. "You are my counterbalance. You bring me peace, and when it seems like the giant house of cards is going to collapse, all I have to do is think of you and Allegra and I know that everything is going to be all right."

Aru

Come morning, Gabi was still asleep, or at least Aru was pretty sure that she was sleeping and not unconscious.

Throughout the night, she'd moved her hands a few times and had even tried to turn on her side but had given up, probably because of all the wires tethered to her. He'd wanted to assist her but had been afraid to wake her up.

Both healers had emphasized how important it was for Gabi to rest as much as possible. Her body was working hard on the transition, and every unnecessary movement put a strain on her limited resources and slowed the process.

As much as Aru craved the sight of her open eyes and smiling lips, he'd refrained from doing anything that might have interfered with the speedy progression of her transition.

The sacrifice was worth it if it helped speed things up.

Once Gabi was done with the first stage of her transition, she would be out of the damn hospital bed, feeling great and having the resilient body of an immortal.

Were immortals as strong as gods, though?

Last night, he'd learned from Merlin that they didn't heal as fast. If a minute was considered the average time for an immortal's body to heal a cut, then it was significantly slower than it took a god. Aru's scrapes and other small injuries healed within seconds, and if he and an immortal both sustained the same serious injury, his fast healing might save him, while the slower rate of an immortal's healing might not repair crucial organs in time to prevent them from permanently failing.

A minute could mean the difference between life and death.

Still, immortals healed much faster than humans, and Aru was grateful that Gabi would no longer be that fragile.

If he was to be her protector from now on, which he hoped to be for the next one hundred and fifteen years, he had to learn more about immortal physiology and which injuries could be catastrophic to Gabi.

Julian could probably provide him with a basic overview, and he also needed to ask the doctor about his mate's telepathic abilities.

Pushing to his feet, he leaned over the bed and kissed Gabi's cheek. "I'll be right back, my love."

Was it his imagination, or did her lips curve up a little?

Aru hadn't told her he loved her yet, and he couldn't drop the news on her as soon as she woke up, but he was going to do that as soon as he thought she could hear it and not faint from stress.

As he'd expected, Julian had returned sometime during the early morning hours, replacing Merlin.

"Good morning," the doctor welcomed him into his office. "If you want coffee, I brewed a pot in the kitchen. It's to the left of the clinic down the hallway all the way to the end."

The smell of coffee was enticing, and Aru would have loved a cup, but he didn't want to wander too far away from the clinic in case Gabi woke up.

"I'll get some later, thank you." He pulled out a chair and eyed the bowl of candy on the healer's desk. "May I?"

Aru was hungry, and candy was better than nothing.

Julian followed his gaze and chuckled. "Suit yourself, but I would check the expiration date. I don't know how long these have been out here."

"I'll chance it." Aru dipped his hand in the bowl and scooped up as many as he could. "I'm starved."

Julian frowned. "Of course, you are. You haven't eaten anything since yesterday afternoon." He picked up the receiver of his desk phone and pressed the square that had security written over it. "Hi, it's Julian. Can you get coffee and something to eat from the café for our guest? And make sure that his buddies in the penthouse are not starving either."

"They went out to eat," the guy on the other side said.

Aru shook his head. Dagor and Negal should have notified him that they were leaving, even if it was for a short excursion to get food.

"Good. I forgot that they have a car." Julian smiled at Aru.

"I'll send someone with a tray downstairs," the guy said. "Do you want anything?"

"I'm good. I ate at home. Thank you." Julian put the receiver down. "I'm so used to relying only on my mobile phone that having a desk phone feels strange." He tilted his head. "Do they have phones on Anumati, or is all communication telepathic out there?"

Aru smiled. "Funny you should ask."

"Why is that?"

"Because I wanted to ask you about your mate's telepathic ability."

Julian's mellow expression turned menacing so quickly that it startled Aru. "How do you know about my mate?"

"Merlin told me about the various talents immortals have, and he mentioned that your mate and her mother can communicate in their heads. It's a very rare ability. In fact, there hasn't been a case of a telepathic duo on Anumati for thousands of years."

Gabi

" **I** 'll be right back, my love."

It must have been part of the dream, and Gabi didn't want to wake up and discover that Uriel hadn't said those words to her. The problem was that she was itching to get up, go to the bathroom, and take a shower.

Oh, and drink coffee.

The wonderful smell was making her mouth water. How long had it been since she'd last had anything to drink or eat?

It seemed like she'd been in a hospital bed forever. It must have been days, maybe even weeks, but it was worth it. She'd never felt so good in her life.

Lifting her hand effortlessly, she smoothed it over her hair, wondering at how silky it felt despite not having been washed in a while.

But wait, had it really been that long?

Gabi had difficulty assessing the passage of time, but if every awakening marked a new morning, then she'd been here for many sunrises she hadn't gotten to see because there were no windows in the room.

Finally opening her eyes, she glanced at the monitoring equipment to see if any of the devices displayed a date or at least what day it was.

It was truly amazing how much detail she could see now. There was no date, but next to the time, it said Friday. It was Wednesday when she'd fainted on the street, so did it mean that her entire transition had taken only two days? Or was it a week and two days? Two weeks?

And where was Uriel?

Had she dreamt about him lying next to her in the hospital bed and talking with her for hours?

And had he really called her his love?

Nah, that must have been a dream.

They had talked about many things, including truelove mates and what it meant. He'd said that he had fallen for her, and she'd told him not to say the L word, and he'd said that he would save it for last, but she must have fallen asleep, and he hadn't gotten the chance to tell her that he loved her.

Warmth spreading from her heart outwards, Gabi let herself feel all the love she'd been suppressing out of fear.

It was like a balloon was inflating inside of her and making her buoyant.

What a wonderful feeling it was to love, even better than being loved, but only if it was safe to do so, and for the first time in forever, Gabi felt that it was.

She could love this male, this god, without fear of rejection, of betrayal, of abandonment—

Then she suddenly remembered the other things Aru had said that she'd conveniently forgotten because they didn't make her happy.

His time on Earth was limited, and in one hundred and fifteen years, the ship patrolling this sector of the galaxy would return to pick him up, and he couldn't take her with him because she was a hybrid—mostly human and only a little bit goddess.

Her eyes misting with tears, she draped her arm over them and sniffled. A century was a long time, longer than any humans got to enjoy their partners no matter how much in love they were. They had an expiration date, and there was nothing they could do about it.

She was lucky to get something amazing that would last so long. Besides, a lot can happen in a century, and there was no reason to mourn Aru's future departure when it might never happen.

So yeah, she was an optimist, and that had gotten her in trouble before, but it was better to live with hope than with despair. It was better to be an optimist than a pessimist.

Letting out a breath, Gabi lifted her arm off her face and patted the stand next to her for a tissue. When she found none, she lifted a corner of the sheet covering her and wiped the tears away.

The rest would have to wait until the doctor came in and gave her a tissue to blow her nose in. She had a call button she could press, and the doctor would rush in right away, but she wasn't ready to face anyone yet. She needed a few more moments to herself to calm down and put on a brave face.

Aru

"Is that so?" Julian was still glaring daggers at Aru. "I assume that there is a story associated with that last famous pair of telepaths."

Aru couldn't understand the healer's hostility.

If Merlin had talked about it so freely, his mate's ability couldn't have been such a great secret. Why was he so angry at Aru for asking about it?

His mate and her mother's situation was very different from Aru and Aria's. They didn't expect to be persecuted or exploited because of their ability.

Or maybe they did?

"There were several famous pairs of telepaths," Aru said. "There are many stories about them, most probably fictional. As you can imagine, the possible scenarios are endless."

"Oh yeah, I'm well aware of the possibilities. My mate and her mother escaped sexual slavery by a hair's breadth. If not for Turner's quick thinking and connections in the military, I would have lost my Ella, and Magnus would have lost Vivian."

Sexual slavery was a travesty that Aru couldn't comprehend. He'd heard about the abhorrent trade that some sub-humans engaged in, abducting females and forcing them into sexual slavery by means of coercion, whether drugs, threat of physical harm, or threats to their families.

"That's terrible, but how did your mate and her mother's special talent get them involved in that?"

Julian was still aggravated, but he was making an effort to calm down. "That's a long story that I'm not sure I can tell you. The gist of it was that someone wanted to kidnap them so he could use one of them to infiltrate a harem and report to the other what she saw there. In his defense, he was trying to save his mother, who was trapped there, but that didn't justify what he attempted to do."

Aru could easily conceive of people who would use a talent like his and Aria's for spying. They were perfect for the job, so limiting who knew about the ability was smart.

"How did that individual find out about your mate and her mother's telepathic ability?"

Julian grimaced. "He's a very talented guy too. He's a compeller and a dream walker. He first met Ella when she was still human, and he thralled his way into her mind. That was how he knew about her talent. Then, he pursued her by using his dream-walking ability and lured her and her mother into a trap. We knew that he was up to no good, and we planned to trap him ourselves, but he was very clever and almost outsmarted us." Julian shivered. "I can't even think of what would have happened if he had succeeded."

"Did you get the chance to avenge your mate?"

The doctor shook his head. "I don't believe in vengeance. That person apologized and repented, and that's all I'm going to say about the subject." He pinned Aru with a hard stare. "Whatever you planned on using my mate and her mother for, you can forget about it. They are never using their talent for anything other than enjoying each other's mental company."

Aru nodded. "I agree with you a hundred percent. There are too many people out there who would love to put their hands on a pair of perfect spies. My respect and appreciation for Kian increased significantly knowing that he doesn't force people in his community to use their talents for the greater good and leaves the decision up to them."

That got Julian to deflate a little, and he slumped in his chair. "Vivian and Ella will do anything for the clan, even if it means endangering themselves. But Kian doesn't like to use civilians for military operations, and especially not females." The doctor smiled. "The ladies accuse him of being a chauvinist, but as a mated guy, I applaud him. I don't want my mate recruited for dangerous tasks."

Aru reflected on his sister's recruitment and service to the Supreme. In Aria's case, she was probably the safest where she was right now. People in the service of the Supreme were untouchable.

"I agree with you, but we don't get to make decisions for our mates. All we can do is advise, right? And the same is true the other way around."

Julian laughed. "I don't dare to do anything that Ella disapproves of. Mated bliss means avoiding strife at all costs. Fortunately, we see eye to eye on most things."

"That's good." Aru raked his fingers through his messy hair. "I hope Gabi and I will get along as splendidly as you do when we are together for a while." He let out a breath. "I haven't even told her that I love her yet."

"So, what are you waiting for? Do it! We are immortal, but life is still too short to waste on insecurities."

Aru hoped that Julian would impart more advice on achieving mated bliss, but their conversation was interrupted when the clinic door opened, and a guard walked in with a cardboard tray with four coffees and a large paper bag. "I didn't know what you like to eat, so I got one of each of the sandwiches they offer. Enjoy."

"Who did you bring all these coffees for?" Julian asked.

The guard shrugged. "I ordered two, and they gave me four by mistake."

"Then why don't you take one?" Aru pulled one of the paper cups out of the tray.

"Thank you for the offer, but I'm all coffeed out." He waved a hand. "Save it for later."

"I want coffee!" Gabi called out from her room. "Please and thank you!"

Julian and Aru exchanged looks, and a moment later, they were both out of their chairs and rushing to Gabi's room.

Gabi

s Aru and Julian burst into the room, Gabi chuckled. "Hello, boys. Where is my coffee?"

She'd managed to lift the back of her bed so she was semi-reclined, and she'd popped into her mouth one of the tiny mints Julian had left on her bedside table.

"You're awake," Aru stated the obvious and turned to Julian. "How come we didn't see it on the monitors?"

The doctor smiled sheepishly. "I was distracted by what we were talking about, so I wasn't paying attention."

Aru frowned at him. "What if something went wrong?"

"The alarm would have gone off." He walked up to Gabi. "How are you feeling?"

"Wonderful." She lifted the hand with the needle stuck on the back of it. "I want this out, and also the other one." She looked down and felt herself blush. "Is there a chance you can get a female doctor or nurse to do that?"

"If it's important to you, I can ask one of the nurses to come from the village, but what makes you think that you won't slip away again?"

"I'm over the first stage. I just know it. Is there a test you can run?"

Aru stiffened, and Julian grinned.

"Yes, there is. I can make a small cut on the palm of your hand, and if the incision closes in minutes instead of how long it would have taken a human to heal it, then you are out of the first stage, and that's a reason for celebration."

"Then do it." Gabi offered him her palm.

The doctor chuckled. "Not so fast. Most transitioning Dormants prefer to have their family and friends around them when the test is performed. It's become a tradition in the village. It's like a rite of passage, but instead of passage into adulthood, it's into immortality. As I said, it's a reason for celebration."

Gabi chewed on her lower lip. "Did Gilbert and Eric have the family and their friends watch the test performed?"

Julian nodded. "The clinic was bursting at the seams with your lovely, large family."

Gabi smiled. "I would love for them to be here. But on the other hand, I don't want to wait for the removal of the IV and the other thing. I want to shower, change into something clean, do my hair, etc. Knowing Gilbert, he's going to record the testing ceremony, and I want to look good, so when I show it to our kids one day, they won't think that their mom was a mess when she transitioned." She glanced at Aru, hoping for a smile but getting a frown.

Well, so much for what she'd thought was the infamous L word and all the talk about one and only and truelove and all that.

"Oops." She lifted a hand to her lips. "Did I say too much and scare you away?"

He shook his head. "Forgive me. I'm just not on board with the test. It's primitive and unnecessary."

That was what bothered him? Not her mention of the future kids she hoped to have with him one day?

Perhaps he was still thinking about the limited time he had with her and that it was unlikely that they could conceive in that relatively short period.

One thing at a time.

First, she needed those tubes out, then she wanted the test to confirm that she was out of the first stage of transition and could get out of the clinic, and third, they needed to have THE TALK.

"I want the test, so I know for sure that I'm out of stage one, and I want my family to be here when it is done. It's a wonderful opportunity for the rest of them to meet you. Kaia and Karen are dying to see the hunk I've been telling them about, and now that they know you are a god, I bet they're triply curious." She looked around, searching for her purse. "Where is my phone? I need to start making phone calls."

Julian put a hand on Aru's shoulder. "I need to perform a few tests that do not involve cuts. Would you mind stepping out of the room for a few moments?"

Aru's frown deepened. "What are you going to do to my mate?"

"Nothing dangerous or unsavory. Given the level of energy Gabi is exhibiting, I don't think she's going to pass out again, and I can remove the tubes that are bothering her." He glanced at her. "If you don't mind me doing that. If you want to wait for the nurse to get here, that's perfectly fine with me."

Gabi was still stuck on Aru calling her his mate. Did it mean what she thought it did?

"I don't want to wait," she said before she could change her mind. "I'll just close my eyes and pretend you're a female."

"I can live with that." Julian smoothed a hand over his stubble. "The long rest must have been very beneficial to you. Yesterday, I was convinced that you would spend at least three more days in the clinic, if not more, before you were ready for the test, and look at you now. You seem to be bouncing off the walls with energy."

"I can also see from much farther away, hear better, and also smell more things, which reminds me that you have coffee in the other room. Can I please have it? I woke up dying for coffee."

Julian sighed. "Just a sip. You are not supposed to have anything other than water after waking up from a coma, and not much of it either, but I can't say no to such a heartfelt request."

"Thank you." She rewarded him with a bright smile. "You're an angel."

Aru

Aru paced the small waiting area, replaying in his head what Gabi had said.

Their future children.

He had never dreamt about being a father. He still didn't. Why bring children into a world that might get destroyed?

The threat of the Eternal King wasn't imminent in human terms, which was how these immortals perceived the passage of time, but it was real, and it was coming.

Even if the resistance managed to topple the king much sooner than estimated, it would be a disaster if they didn't have someone better to replace him with, and that was a tall order. Things could get much worse than they were, and the Eternal King wasn't the ultimate evil.

An enormous bureaucracy implemented the king's policies, and it was old and corrupt. Not to say that it was evil either, just self-serving.

Aru wasn't a brilliant strategist or a gifted philosopher. He was just a simple god who wanted to be free to choose the way he lived his life, where and how he chose to live it, and he wanted to be free to say what he wanted to say as long as it didn't incite anyone to violence against another.

He wanted freedom, and that was the one thing that the common gods on Anumati no longer had. The erosion had been so gradual that most hadn't even realized how restricted their lives had become. His parents were the perfect example of that.

Frankly, he couldn't imagine how the resistance was going to cure the bureaucracy of corruption, build a system that prevented future corruption from forming, and replace the king with someone just as capable but of better character.

Perhaps Anumati should abolish its constitutional monarchy and become a full democracy, but that was also an unrealistic goal.

He just wasn't smart enough to think of solutions to all of Anumati's problems and had to trust in the Supreme and the Fates to lead the resistance toward it.

As the door to Gabi's room opened and Julian walked out, Aru wanted to rush back in, but Julian stopped him with a hand on his chest.

"Gabi is showering, and she specifically asked that you do not come into the bathroom. I told her that you would be in the room, listening, and if she needed help, you would come in."

Aru nodded. "I'll stand guard by the door."

"Good." Julian clapped him on the back. "I really don't understand how she's doing so well. She walked to the bathroom without my aid." He started toward his office and then turned around. "I forgot to mention, but Gabi grew half an inch in the two days since her transition started."

That wasn't a big change. "Anything else?"

"Gabi says that her skin is smoother, and her eyes are brighter, but I have to take her word for it. I failed to take a close-up photo of her when we picked her up from the hospital."

"Her skin was smooth before she got here."

The doctor shrugged. "If you notice any more changes, let me know, and I will write them down. We keep records of every transition."

"Of course." Aru walked into the room and closed the door behind him.

In the bathroom, the water was running, and Gabi was humming a tune he didn't recognize. Leaning his back against the door, he crossed his arms over his chest and tried to sing along. Perhaps Gabi's jubilant mood would improve his own.

He should be happy that his blood transfusion had worked, and he was. The melancholy he felt was related to the children Gabi wanted that he didn't wish to bring into an unstable world.

Opening a channel to Aria, he wanted to tell her about Gabi's miraculous improvement, but she didn't open the channel on her end, so he couldn't share the good news with her.

Aria was probably busy at some official function with the Supreme, and she never communicated with Aru unless she was alone. He was supposed to do the same, but sometimes he cheated a little when what he needed to tell her was brief.

When Gabi turned the water off, he pushed away from the door, and when she didn't come out right away, he got worried.

"Are you okay in there?" he asked.

"Yeah, I'm great. The sticky pads left a residue that refuses to come off. I'm trying to rub it off."

"I can help. Can I come in?"

There was a moment of hesitation. "Not yet. Give me a few minutes to sort things out."

He didn't know what things she needed to sort out, but it wasn't as if he could argue. "I'm right here if you need me."

"I know. Thank you, Aru."

Gabi

G abi scrubbed off the last of the sticky residue and then stood naked in front of the bathroom mirror.

Not much had changed about her, but Julian reassured her that this was only the beginning and that her appearance would become more youthful as her transition kept progressing at a slower pace.

Her breasts were still a little saggy, but the color of her nipples was brighter, and she hadn't shed as much hair as she usually did while showering.

Supposedly, she'd grown half an inch over the past two and a half days, which was a lot for a body to do in such a short time, but she hoped she would grow some more. She'd always wanted to be taller, but that was in her silly teenage days when she'd dreamt of being a fashion model.

Now that she was older and smarter, she knew better. The world of fashion was not as glamorous as it appeared, and she wanted no part of it.

Gabi chuckled at her reflection.

Even if she wanted to become a model, she couldn't. Immortals couldn't be in the limelight. They had to disappear.

"Oh, crap. I can't go back to Cleveland."

"Gabi? Are you talking to me?"

Crappity crap, she had to stop talking to herself. "No, I just remembered that I'm supposed to be back in Cleveland on Monday, and Julian said that I can't go anywhere because he wants to keep an eye on me for a couple of weeks."

When there was silence on the other side of the door, Gabi wrapped a fluffy white towel around herself and stepped out of the bathroom.

Aru stood with a hand on his hip, the other on his jaw, looking despondent.

"What's wrong?" She lifted a hand to his unshaven cheek and cupped it.

"I thought that I could take you out of here. Are you telling me that you need to stay in this room for two more weeks?"

She laughed. "No way. After the test is done, I'm out of here. Julian said that I can stay in the penthouse with you, and he will come every other day to check up on me."

Letting out a breath, he pulled her into his arms. "I love you. I just wanted to say that before something else interfered, but if that freaks you out, forget that I said it, or put it aside for when you are ready to hear it."

Her heart melted a little just from how sweet he was.

"I love you too." She wrapped her arms around his neck and stretched on her toes to kiss him on the lips. "I am Gabriella Emerson, the brave warrior of God. I will forever stand by your side with my sword drawn and my dagger in my other hand, ready to fight off your enemies, large and small." She smiled. "Well, maybe not the large ones, but the small ones for sure." She made a slashing gesture with her hand before returning it to his nape.

He gaped at her, his eyes searching hers in an effort to understand her silly declaration.

"I spoke metaphorically, Aru. I've never held a sword in my hand, and if I picked up a dagger, I would probably injure myself with it. What I was trying to convey was that I would always have your back or that I'll have it for as long as we can be together, which I hope is forever, but I know that you can't promise me that."

Looking lost for words, Aru did the next best thing and smashed his lips over hers.

The kiss quickly turned heated, and Gabi was ready to drop the towel and have her way with Aru on the narrow hospital bed, but a knock on the door put an end to those plans.

"Is everyone decent in there?" Julian's voice sounded from the other side.

"Don't come in," Aru called back. "Gabi is getting dressed." He reached under the bed and pulled out the plastic bag with her belongings. "You can get dressed in the bathroom while I see what he wants."

Gabi was about to mention that Julian had seen everything already, so there was no point in acting modestly around him, but she had a feeling that Aru would not appreciate her honesty on that subject.

"If he needs to run any more tests on me, let me know. He said something about taking blood samples."

Aru nodded, and as she took the plastic bag and sashayed back into the bathroom, she caught sight of his arousal and licked her lips. "Soon, Aru. Very, very soon."

Aru

"This better be important," Aru murmured as he opened the door, not caring if the doctor heard him. "What is it?"

He sounded annoyed even though he'd tried to go for matter-of-fact. After Gabi's sexy taunt, a polite tone would have been too difficult to muster.

"Kian is here to continue your talks."

Talk about bad timing. "Did you tell him about Gabi being ready for the test?"

"I didn't have a chance. I got a call from Anandur asking for you to come up to the penthouse. I need to take some blood samples and measurements, but after I'm done, I can escort Gabi up to the penthouse to join you."

"Okay, that's good." He rubbed a hand over his jaw. "Let me just tell her that I have to leave."

Julian nodded. "I'll wait out here."

Smart guy.

Aru closed the door, walked up to the bathroom, and knocked on the door. "Gabi?"

"Yeah?"

"Kian is back in the penthouse and wants me to come up."

"Oh." She opened the door, wearing jeans and a tight-fitting T-shirt that barely covered her midriff. "How long will you be gone?"

His eyes were riveted to the sliver of flesh showing above her waistband. "I don't think I'm coming back." When she gasped, and her hand flew to her heart, he realized how it had sounded and reached for her. "You are coming to stay with me in the penthouse as soon as Julian is done taking blood samples and some other tests. Neither of us is coming back down here."

Gabi put her hand on his chest and leaned her forehead on his clavicle. "You scared me. Don't ever do that again."

"I won't. I promise." He rubbed soothing circles on her back. "Well, I'll try, but I can't promise I'll never again say something without thinking how it sounds."

"Good enough." She patted his chest. "Go. Don't keep Kian waiting. I've heard that he can be a grouch."

"Oh, right. You haven't met him yet. This will be your first time meeting the clan's leader."

"Supposedly, Kian's bark is worse than his bite, but I'm a scaredy cat."

"No, you're not. You are my brave warrior."

She smiled. "Nevertheless, I'm glad you will be there, so I don't have to face him alone. I've gotten the impression that he's intimidating. But his wife and his sister are very nice, so he can't be too bad, right?"

"Kian is not bad. He's intense, but I didn't find him intimidating. I actually like him. He seems like a good guy doing his best for his people or trying to."

"Is he as beautiful as his sister? I mean, Amanda is so stunning that I couldn't take my eyes off her, and I've met models and actresses before."

"Kian is very good-looking. His godly genes are probably less diluted, and so are his sister's. They are most likely direct descendants."

Gabi shrugged. "It makes sense for the direct son of a god or a goddess to be the clan's leader, right? I mean, that's how society usually works. Those at the top of the food chain get to lead, and gods are definitely up there, then the immortals, then humans, and then the rest of the animal kingdom, right?"

He chuckled. Gabi always talked up a storm when she was nervous. "There are endless varieties of species in the known universe, and gods are definitely at the top of the food chain. That's why we call ourselves gods. But there is also a hierarchy among us, with some at the top and some at the bottom."

Gabi frowned. "Where are you on that scale?"

"Somewhere in the middle. If I were human, I would call myself middle class."

"That's a good place to be." She leaned into him and kissed his neck. "I'm glad that we have this in common. We are both middle class. Other than that, though, we are literally worlds apart."

"I disagree. We have a lot in common, and I would love to stay here and show you all the ways we are alike, but I need to go." He planted a gentle kiss on her forehead. "See you in a bit."

"Yes."

It was difficult to extract himself from her arms, and Aru wished they could go up to the penthouse together, but Julian needed to run more tests on Gabi, and Kian probably wanted to talk in private.

Kian

Kian stood in front of the wall of glass that formed the entire front of his former penthouse and looked at the high rise across the street, which also belonged to the clan. In fact, most of the buildings on the block belonged to the clan, and there was a network of hidden passages beneath them.

The keep was compromised, so he would have to block all the entrances to the underground from this building, but it would still be accessible through the tunnels from the other buildings.

After all, the place also housed the crypt, and it wasn't as if he could relocate it. He'd lost count of how many Doomers were in stasis down there, their bodies preserved in the meticulously controlled environment, awaiting potential revival should the need ever arise.

Moving them was too complicated to consider.

As several cars honked at once down below, Kian stepped onto the terrace and peeked over the railing to see if anyone was hurt and needed help. When everything seemed fine, he returned to the air-conditioned interior and closed the sliding door behind him.

This time of year, downtown Los Angeles was too hot and bright for him to be comfortable outside. Perhaps he should consider his mother's suggestion to move everyone to Alaska.

At least he wouldn't have to deal with the blasted heat and glare.

Except, the weather was much nicer in the mountains of Malibu, with the elevation and the ocean breeze cooling things down and the marine layer overhead providing a reprieve from the glare. Besides, Kian really liked the location, remote and yet in the center of one of the largest metropolises in the country.

Where could they possibly hide from the Eternal King?

Even the Doomers' island wasn't safe. With the technology the gods possessed, no place was, not even Syssi's imagined underwater Poseidon City.

"Did you locate the other two stooges?" Kian sat on the couch across from Anandur.

Aru was down in the clinic, but his two friends hadn't been in the penthouse when Kian and his entourage had gotten there. The guy in security had said that they were out for breakfast, but it didn't take that long to grab a coffee and a sandwich.

"You didn't tell me that you wanted to find out where they were." Anandur opened the locations application on his phone. "Their car is still in the Starbucks parking lot." He looked up. "They might have left the car there and continued on foot or called a taxi. If I were them, I would have assumed we attached a tracker to their car."

Kian leaned back and crossed his legs at the ankles. "I get that, but what else is there for them to do? Their mission is to find the Kra-ell. They found the ones who went missing from the compound, and they still have to find the other pods. They won't find them in downtown Los Angeles."

"Maybe they went shopping?" Anandur looked at his impassive brother. "Or maybe they are searching for Dormants?"

Brundar cast him an incredulous look and went back to watching the front door of the penthouse as if he were expecting assassins to burst through it at any moment.

Kian didn't expect any trouble from the gods or anyone else, but he had brought Okidu with him just in case.

The Odu was in the kitchen, preparing assorted canapés and brewing coffee.

When the door opened, and Aru walked in, Okidu rushed forward with an affronted expression on his face. "Master Aru. You should have waited for me to open the door for you."

The god arched a brow at Kian. "I thought these were our living quarters for as long as Gabi needed to stay in the clinic. Should I knock every time I return to my temporary lodging?"

It was a polite way to tell Kian that he shouldn't have just come in and made himself at home without Aru's invitation, even though the place belonged to him, but he was going to ignore it. He was doing the guy a favor, and they both knew it had nothing to do with hospitality.

"No, you don't need to knock." He motioned for the couch. "Please, sit down. We have a lot to discuss, and the day is short. I would like to avoid Friday afternoon traffic if possible."

Aru nodded. "I would like to keep it short as well. Gabi is out of the initial stage of transition, and once Julian is done administering some tests, he will escort her here. He says that he needs to monitor her for the next two weeks. If it's okay with you, I would like to stay here until he clears Gabi to go. If it's not, I can rent another place that's conveniently located for Julian to visit. He said that he would do that every other day."

"Of course, you can stay here," Kian said absentmindedly.

He hadn't talked with Julian this morning, but he had yesterday evening, and it hadn't looked like Gabi was anywhere near ready to be done with the first stage.

Had Aru aided her transition in the same way Annani and Toven had been aiding other Dormants?

Was the knowledge about the curative properties of gods' blood common on Anumati?

"That's fantastic," Anandur said. "I thought it would take her much longer to transition. Has anyone called her family to let them know? I'm sure they all will want to be here for the test."

Kian wanted to find out whether Aru had given Gabi his blood, but he didn't want to ask him about her miraculous transition in the presence of the brothers.

"Not yet," Aru said. "Gabi will start making the calls after Julian is done taking blood samples and measurements." He looked at Kian. "Is it okay if Julian performs the test here? The clinic is too small to accommodate Gabi's large family."

Reluctantly, Kian nodded. "We can load everyone on the bus and get them here this evening after rush hour traffic is over."

Aru dipped his head. "Thank you. It will make this primitive custom more tolerable. I don't like the idea of an injury being inflicted on Gabi even if her body can heal it in seconds."

Kian smiled. "I felt the same way when my mate was tested, but it's the fastest way, and it's very visually effective. That's why it lends itself to a ceremony. Everyone can see that the Dormant has transitioned. Besides, the cut is really small." He pushed to his feet. "Let's go to my office."

When Anandur followed him up, Kian motioned for him to sit back down. "I need a few words with Aru alone, and you need to stay here for when Negal and Dagor return."

The brothers didn't look happy, but they obeyed his command without an argument for a change.

At least they knew to behave in company.

Aru

Aru followed Kian to the office and waited until the immortal closed the door behind them.

"I thought that you didn't hide anything from your bodyguards. Are you concerned about the Odu over-hearing our conversation?"

The truth was that right now, Aru would have preferred to be in the living room, eating whatever the Odu was serving and drinking coffee. He hadn't gotten a chance to consume the sandwiches the security guard had brought for him because he'd been too nervous to eat while waiting for Julian to finish removing all the wires and tubes from Gabi's body, and then he'd been summoned to the penthouse.

It still irked him that Kian had just made himself at home in the penthouse, even though it belonged to him. One did not enter the guest quarters in one's home when guests occupied them, even if those guests were not there at the moment.

Meeting in Kian's old office in the underground would have been much more appropriate.

"I'm not concerned about Okidu overhearing anything. He's like a vault." Kian motioned to one of the chairs in front of the massive desk and pulled the other one out for himself. "I need to ask you about Gabi, and I assumed you would prefer privacy for that."

Aru frowned. "What can I tell you about her that you don't already know?"

Kian's smile was suspiciously knowing. "I just find it curious how Gabi managed to leapfrog through her transition. She was unconscious through most of yesterday and the night, and then this morning, she wakes up full of energy and ready to leave the clinic?"

Aru shrugged. "Julian seemed surprised as well, but he told me that every transition is different. Some remain unconscious for weeks, while others are over it in just a couple of days. But if you think Gabi's transition is unusual, you should direct your questions to the doctor."

Kian had said that Aru shouldn't play card games because he had a terrible poker face, but he hoped he had done well enough to pass Kian's bullshit detector.

For some inexplicable reason, the immortal's smile got even broader. "As long as you keep it to yourself, it's fine with me. Don't ever reveal the truth to anyone, though, including Gabi herself."

Did he know?

Damn, there must have been a camera in the supply closet. The fact that he hadn't seen any didn't mean that there wasn't. It could have been miniature and well hidden.

Kian or Julian must have seen him take the syringes, and Kian had guessed what he'd used them for.

"How do you know about it?" he asked.

"It has been handed down through the generations, but it's a secret that only a select few are privy to. If it fell into the wrong hands, you and your friends would be hunted down, and not even your godly powers would save you. Humans can be very determined when they covet something so valuable, and they will sacrifice many to get their hands on a miracle cure."

Kian hadn't mentioned the gods' blood explicitly, but it was obvious that he knew. Still, Aru wouldn't be the first to spell it out.

"The same is true for the gods living among you. Did they use this method to aid other transitioning Dormants?"

Kian hesitated for a long moment before nodding. "Don't tell Julian or anyone else. They don't know."

Aru frowned. "You don't trust your own people?"

"It's not about trust. We have powerful enemies, and if they capture one of ours, they could torture or compel the information out of them. That's why only a few in our community know how to get into our hidden village.

Most of our members use self-driving cars that are programmed to turn their windows opaque within several miles of the entrance."

"Clever." Aru approved. "Do your enemies have compellers?"

"Their leader is a powerful compeller. That's how he controls his army of immortals."

"Is he a god?" Aru asked.

"Navuh is an immortal like me, but he inherited his power of compulsion from his godly ancestor."

Aru chuckled. "Are we back to dancing, Kian? Was one of Navuh's parents a god? Perhaps a direct descendant of the Eternal King? The most powerful compeller ever born?"

Kian

Kian considered an evasive answer or an outright lie, but he was tired of the dance as well, and it was no skin off his nose if Aru knew who Navuh's father was.

Mortdh was dead.

"His father was a god, and his mother was a human. How much do you know about the exiled gods?"

"I know about the main players. The others remained nameless, supposedly to save their families the shame."

"So, you know the names of the Eternal King's three direct descendants. The heir and his half-brother and half-sister."

Aru nodded. "Ahn was the heir, the only son of the Eternal King from his official wife. Ekin was an older son born to a concubine, and Athor was a daughter born to a concubine as well."

"Correct. Ekin didn't inherit the Eternal King's compulsion ability, but he did inherit the womanizing. He had two sons. His firstborn was a very strong compeller and a powerful god all around. Mortdh was also somewhat unhinged and had delusions of grandeur. Long story short, he fathered Navuh with a human female, and for a long time, he didn't acknowledge him as his heir because he was hoping for a pureblooded son from one of the goddesses he bedded, but after many centuries of trying, he reluctantly declared Navuh as his successor."

Aru frowned. "Why was he hoping to get a son? He could have nominated his firstborn daughter as his heir."

Kian smiled. "I don't know if he managed to produce a daughter with a goddess either, but Mortdh was the quintessential misogynist, and he wouldn't have wanted a daughter to be his successor. I don't know whether he hated women because his mother was rumored to be unhinged or maybe because a goddess had rejected him, but he detested the matrilineal ways of the gods and wanted to establish patriarchy. I don't think that he planned to ever step down, but he wanted a second-in-command, and he apparently preferred a half-breed male to a daughter. To be fair, though, even as a young immortal Navuh was more powerful than many of the gods, and his power only increased with age. If you ever find yourself in a position where you need to fight him, don't assume that you will win because you are a god."

Aru's lips curved in a barely-there smile. "What about you? Should I be worried about you besting me in a one-on-one fight for power?"

Kian didn't like the smugness on Aru's face, but regrettably, he was physically no match for a god. He could outmaneuver a bunch of them in business dealings and perhaps even in strategizing, but that was probably all.

"Regrettably, my special talent is spotting great business deals and closing them for my clan. I'm not a compeller, and Anandur can best me on the wrestling mat without even breaking a sweat."

Aru leaned back with a calculating look in his eyes. "Then why are you alone with me? I'm not a compeller either, but I can most likely thrall you, and you wouldn't even know that I was in your mind. It would definitely save me a lot of dance moves."

Kian laughed. "That is true, but you are smarter than that. You could probably overpower me either with a thrall or with your bare hands and fangs, but to what end? You can't overpower my entire clan and the Kra-ell who swore alliance to us. They are immune to your thralling and physically stronger than you."

Evidently Syssi and Turner had been right all along, and the Kra-ell were a valuable addition to the village, providing protection against powerful foes Kian couldn't have conceived of only weeks ago.

The Fates must have been at work again, and not only to arrange for Jade and Phinas's pairing. The threat of the Eternal King had been looming over humanity ever since the Industrial Revolution, and if Kian had chosen not to respond to Jade's call for help, he would have never learned about it.

The god nodded. "You are very fortunate to have gained the Kra-ell's loyalty. Your clan is better off for it."

"I know." He leveled his eyes on Aru. "Since we've got one step closer in our dance, and I told you about Mortdh's son, you need to tell me something in return."

"What would you like to know?"

"How do you communicate with the resistance?"

The god smiled. "Ask me another question."

"Have you gotten instructions from your bosses in the resistance?"

"Not yet. I will inform you as soon as I do. By the way, how did Navuh survive when his father did not? Wasn't he with him when it happened?"

Kian's hackles rose. "When what happened?"

Aru hadn't been told about the fate of the rebel gods, only that they were gone.

"Whatever it was that killed the gods."

Kian narrowed his eyes at him. "What do you know about it?"

"Not much. I assume that the Eternal King was somehow involved."

Kian grimaced. "I wish we could pin it on him, but the most likely candidate for the bombing of the assembly was Mortdh."

"Really? Why would he do such a thing?"

There was no harm in telling Aru about how the gods perished. Kian would just omit details about his mother's role in what had started the chain of events that had resulted in the eradication of the rebel gods and most of their offspring.

Gabi

"Thank you." Gabi leaned over and kissed Julian's cheek. "You've gone above and beyond the doctor's duty."

"It was my pleasure."

He'd insisted on rolling her carry-on and carrying her duffle bag to the elevator even though she was perfectly capable of doing it herself.

Heck, she was ready to do some bench presses and run a couple of miles on the treadmill, but Julian had advised against strenuous physical activities in the next couple of weeks.

We shall see about that.

She followed him inside the elevator.

There were some strenuous activities that Gabi was not going to wait two weeks for or even two hours.

Hopefully, Aru's meeting with Kian was over, or it would be soon, so she could drag him into the bedroom and tell him about the naughty dreams she'd had.

Perhaps he could re-enact some of them with his mind tricks. After all, he was a god, so even though she was an immortal now, he could still thrall her, and the best part was that it wouldn't cause her any damage.

Ah, the fun she was going to have.

Aru didn't know what he was getting himself into. He might think that gods and goddesses were a lustful bunch, but Gabi was going to prove to him that newly transitioned immortals could be just as amorous or even more so.

Julian looked at her with amusement in his eyes. "What's that smile for?"

Gabi searched her mind for a quick answer that didn't include carnal activities. "I'm so glad that my clock is no longer ticking. I can have babies whenever I want." The elevator doors opening saved her from having to say more.

"Well, that's a bit optimistic." Julian motioned for her to exit first. "As I explained, immortals have a very low fertility rate, and gods even more so. Merlin might be able to assist with his fertility potions, but you need to talk with Aru first. As gods go, he's a baby, and he's probably not ready to have kids yet."

Her eyes widened. "I didn't even ask him how old he is. Or maybe I did, and I can't remember? Do you know how old he is?"

Julian stopped at one of the double doors flanking the gorgeous vestibule. "You should ask him. I only know that he's very young. I don't know his exact age."

Was he telling her the truth?

"It doesn't matter." Gabi scanned the vestibule again, taking in the elaborate details. "This is beautiful. How much is it to buy a penthouse apartment in this building? Must be a fortune."

"It is."

As Julian lifted his hand to knock, the door opened, and an enormous redhead grinned down at her.

"Gabriella Emerson." He offered her his huge paw. "It's a pleasure to finally make your acquaintance. I'm Anandur."

"Nice to meet you, too." Hesitantly, she put her hand in his, but his grip was surprisingly gentle, and he gave it a light shake.

"Come in." He threw the door open. "Aru is still with Kian in the office, but you are more than welcome to hang out with us. Okidu made delicious canapés, and there are a few left."

"I shall make more expeditiously, mistress." An older gentleman in full butler regalia rushed out of the kitchen and bowed. "Would mistress like tea or coffee with her canapés?"

"Coffee, please." She offered him her hand. "And please, call me Gabi."

Looking horrified, the butler didn't take her hand. "Oh, no, mistress. It is most improper for me to address you by your given name." He bowed again.

Anandur leaned down, bending nearly in half to whisper in her ear. "Resistance is futile. Just go with it."

"Got it." She smiled back at the butler. "Thank you so much for the canapés. I can't wait to taste them."

His bright smile confirmed that it had been the right thing to say. "Please take a seat on the sofa, mistress. I shall bring out fresh offerings momentarily."

As she headed toward where he'd indicated, a blond angel rose to his feet and gave her the slightest of nods but didn't say a thing.

"That's my brother Brundar," Anandur said. "He's not a mute, but he pretends to be. Engaging him in conversation is as futile as trying to get Okidu to call you Gabi or to stop bowing."

She caught a barely there smile on the blond brother's lips before it disappeared, and he sat back down.

It seemed like the two enjoyed playing the good cop, bad cop game, with Anandur being the friendly, jovial one and Brundar the intimidating one. They weren't fooling her, though. The jackets they wore bulged in strategic places, indicating that they were both armed, and she had no doubt that if their boss was in danger, Anandur would drop his friendly act in the blink of an eye and become as deadly as his brother.

"Are Negal and Dagor still not back from their Starbucks excursion?" Julian asked.

"They are on their way back," Anandur said. "I asked a couple of Guardians to check whether they were actually there or gave us the slip, but they found them sitting in the coffee shop and flirting with a couple of lawyer ladies on their lunch break."

"Good for them." Julian chuckled. "Even when I was still single, I wasn't that gutsy."

"Right." Anandur nodded in agreement. "I prefer ladies that don't talk circles around me."

Julian shook his head. "I would have never thought that you would be intimidated by lawyers. Not with what your mate can do."

That got Gabi curious. "What can she do?"

"Kick mine and Brundar's butts," Anandur said with pride.

"I don't believe it." Gabi glanced at the blond brother. "Is that true?"

The guy nodded.

"Well, I'll be damned. She must be a superwoman."

Anandur grinned. "My lovely mate's name is Wonder, and it's totally a tribute to Wonder Woman."

Aru

Aru would have loved to tell Kian that Mortdh hadn't been the one who had bombed the assembly hall, but then he would have to disclose how he had found out who had probably done it, and that would blow his cover.

Besides, there was no proof, only circumstantial evidence and speculation.

Perhaps the gods had indeed been killed by Mortdh, who in a fit of rage had decided to launch a bomb from a civilian aircraft, which was all the rebel gods had been allowed to bring with them.

Had no one wondered why and how he had managed to smuggle a bomb of that kind to Earth?

It surely wasn't part of the standard equipment that had been routinely provided for gold mining or to colonists who were establishing a permanent base on a planet.

Still, it was possible that Mortdh had managed to either smuggle the weapon or make it. Ekin's elder son had been born on Anumati, and he was an adult when his father had been exiled, so he might have planned ahead and managed to smuggle some contraband, or he might have used his father's technical know-how to build a bomb from components that had been used to launch crafts with cargo and personnel from Earth to the orbiting ships.

Kian arched a brow. "No questions, Aru? I was sure you would have a thousand of them by the time I was done talking."

"I was just wondering how Mortdh got his hands on that kind of a bomb. Could it be that he built it himself? Ekin was known as a brilliant scientist, so he might have imparted some of his knowledge to his sons."

"From what I know about Mortdh, he wasn't interested in science. He wanted power." Kian crossed his arms over his chest. "The thing is, no one knows what really happened because all the witnesses died. We will probably never know for sure."

"Mortdh's son might know," Aru said. "Is there a way to ask him? Perhaps you know someone who is close to him?"

Kian regarded him with suspicion in his eyes. "That's not the kind of information I'm comfortable sharing with you. But if Navuh knew anything, he would have told the people close to him, and my spies in his camp would have brought the information to me."

Evidently, they were back to dancing around each other.

Not that he could blame Kian. They were both withholding information to protect others, and it wasn't as if Aru could even promise Kian that the information would remain between them. Everything he learned, he would report to Aria, who would report it to the Supreme, and it wasn't up to him to even know what the Supreme would do with the information.

He could share what he knew about the healing properties of gods' blood, but it seemed that Kian knew that already, so that wouldn't serve as a bargaining chip in their negotiations.

Hopefully, Aria would get back to him soon with instructions from the Supreme or the other resistance leaders.

As Aru's stomach rumbled, he put a hand over it to silence it. "Gabi should be here already." He glanced at the door. "You have very good soundproofing in here. Everywhere else I've stayed, I could hear what was going on in the adjacent rooms, but not in this building."

Kian smiled. "This place was built for immortals, and I always include the best soundproofing for our dwellings." He pushed to his feet. "It's time I was introduced to Gilbert and Eric's sister, and you need to put something in your belly. Have you eaten anything today?"

Aru shook his head. "I only had a few sips of coffee. It's been an eventful morning."

"I bet." Kian walked over to the door. "I still remember vividly how I felt when Syssi was discharged from the clinic. My sister was missing, abducted by a Doomer, so I was still frantic with worry, but I was grateful to the Fates that my mate survived the transition." Kian opened the door.

Aru followed him out of the room. "What happened to your sister?"

Chuckling, Kian stopped and turned to Aru. "That's a long story for another time, but just so you don't worry about her fate, it all ended well. My sister and the Doomer turned out to be truelove mates, he left the Brotherhood and joined the clan, and they have a little baby girl. It took me a while to get accustomed to the idea that my sister chose to mate a Doomer, but once I got my head out of my ass, I realized that he was perfect for her."

"That's one hell of a story." Aru regarded Kian with even more appreciation than before. "I don't know if I would have been able to accept a former enemy as my sister's mate. I'm very protective of her."

He would have probably shot first and asked questions later, and his sister would have hated him for the rest of their days.

Perhaps the Fates were trying to tell him something, and he should take Kian's story to heart?

"It wasn't easy." Kian cast him a wry smile. "I'm just glad that my sister is not a pushover and that she didn't let me ruin the relationship for her. She fought me tooth and nail until I had no choice but to accept that she and Dalhu were fated to be together and that I should stop trying to keep them apart or suffer the consequences."

"Like losing your sister?"

Kian nodded. "And angering the Fates."

Gabi

"Should I bring out more canapés, mistress?" The butler bowed at the waist.

Gabi looked at the half-empty tray and wondered how much of it she had demolished. The Guardian brothers had helped, but she'd consumed her fair share, devouring the small sandwiches one after the other and ignoring Julian's instructions to take it easy with food for at least twenty-four hours.

She'd been famished, Julian had left, and the brothers hadn't said a word about her not following the doctor's instructions.

"Not for me, but Aru and Kian might be hungry when they are done with their meeting."

The butler looked like she'd just given him a great gift.

"Right away, mistress." He turned on his heel and walked back into the kitchen.

"He's such a sweet old guy." Gabi snatched another tiny triangular slice covered in a delicious sauce and a slice of cucumber.

Anandur chuckled, and he looked like he was about to say something when he froze, and a smile bloomed on his handsome face. "Your mate's friends are back." He got to his feet and walked over to the front door.

She remembered Aru's friends from the lounge in the airport and the flight itself, but the truth was that she'd been so absorbed with Aru that she hadn't paid them much attention and didn't remember what they looked like other than being very handsome but not as gorgeous as Aru.

When Anandur opened the door and the two came in, she got a good look at them and had to reassess her previous opinion. They weren't as gorgeous as Aru, but they were still too beautiful to be real, like mannequins in a department store or the Ken dolls she'd played with as a kid.

What were their names? Had Uriel introduced them to her?

Gabi still wasn't sure about the soundness of her memories and what she should remember but didn't.

"Negal." Anandur offered his hand to the one with the sandy hair and blue eyes. "That was one hell of a long breakfast."

"Anandur." The guy shook what he was offered. "We didn't know that you were waiting for us." His eyes darted to her and widened. "Gabriella. Are you well?"

"I'm very well, thank you." Gabi pushed to her feet and waited for the males to approach her. "How are you doing?"

"Excellent." He shook her hand as if she was made from breakable glass.

The other guy with dark brown hair and golden eyes regarded her with a less friendly look, but he offered his hand as well. "I'm Dagor. It's my pleasure to make your acquaintance, Gabriella Emerson."

They were so formal for guys who looked so young.

She gave Dagor a bright smile. "A word of advice for when you are trying to score a hookup. Don't be so formal. You sound like someone from a previous century."

He frowned. "How should I have greeted you?"

"Hi, I'm Dagor. Nice to meet you, Gabi. I've heard a lot about you. Aru couldn't stop talking about you."

Dagor's frown deepened. "Aru didn't talk much about you at all."

"He didn't have to," Negal said. "His frantic worry for you said it all."

"Masters." Okidu emerged from the kitchen with an enormous tray. "You have returned just in time for a fresh batch of canapés."

Dagor's lips twisted in distaste. "We ate." He walked toward the sitting area without giving Okidu a second glance.

"That was rude," Gabi murmured under her breath. Out loud, she said, "Thank you, Okidu. It is so kind of you to prepare snacks for us. I can't believe how fast you are making such beautiful and precisely cut little sandwiches that are also delicious. You must show me your technique."

"With pleasure, mistress."

As he bowed to her while holding the huge tray, Gabi was sure the little sandwiches were going to slide off and fall on the floor, but the butler performed an admirable balancing act, and the tray hadn't changed its angle even by one degree.

"Wow. I'm impressed."

"Gabi!" A familiar voice diverted her attention from the butler.

"Aru!" She rushed toward him, happiness filling her heart as if she hadn't seen him in months and she missed him terribly.

She skidded to a halt when she noticed the gorgeous hunk standing next to him.

For a moment, she thought that it was another god, but then she remembered that Aru had been secluded with the clan leader in the office, so the hunk was Syssi's husband.

"Hi. You must be Kian." She offered him her hand. "I'm Gabi. Gabriella Emerson."

"I know." He took her hand and shook it firmly but gently. "Welcome to immortality, Gabi."

"She didn't have the test done yet," Anandur said from the couch. "You can't welcome her until the cut on her hand closes. That's how it's done."

Kian cast him a mock glare. "I can do whatever I please." He turned back to her. "I understand that you want your family to be here for the test."

"Of course."

He smiled. "That's quite a crowd. They won't all fit in the clinic. I told Aru that you could have it done here instead. It's not a hundred percent according to the custom, but it will be more comfortable for everyone."

That was such a generous offer.

As it turned out, Kian was generous and kind, and he wasn't intimidating at all.

"Are you sure?" Gabi looked around. "I mean, Julian will have to cut my hand, and I don't want to stain any of this beautiful furniture or carpets."

"Don't worry about it. Julian won't let a drop escape, and if he did, Okidu would take care of it." He turned to the butler. "Am I right, Okidu?"

"Yes, master." The guy dipped his head. "It would not be the first time I cleaned up blood. I remember that time outside Mistress Amanda's laboratory. That was a lot of blood to clean up. I believe that it was—"

Kian lifted a hand to stop him. "Gabi does not want to hear all the gory details. She's just left the hospital bed, and she's new to our world."

"Actually, I would love to hear that." She leaned against Aru, absorbing strength from his solid body. "I want to learn everything there is about the immortals."

Kian laughed. "It's not going to happen today, so you'd better start making a list." He looked at Aru. "I'm heading home, but I'll be back later tonight for the ceremony."

That was another pleasant surprise.

Did Kian attend every ceremony, or was he giving her special treatment because Aru was her inducer?

In either case, she was deeply honored.

"Thank you, Kian." Gabi dipped her head. "I really appreciate everything you have done for my family and me, including sending a team to get me out of the hospital and sending Julian and Merlin to take care of me. I don't want you to think that I'm taking any of that for granted. You didn't have to do any of that."

"Yes, I did. Your family is part of the clan, and so are you. We take care of our own."

Aru

Kian had gone, but he'd left the butler behind to prepare the place for the ceremony or maybe to keep an eye on Aru and his teammates. Gabi had offered to help and the Odu had declined, but she'd somehow managed to convince the cyborg to let her work with him in the kitchen.

Evidently, she didn't know that he wasn't human or immortal, but since he looked like an older human, she must have wondered what he was doing working as a butler for the leader of the immortals.

Aru wondered that as well, but for a different reason. Kian had said that the Odus had been sent to Earth by someone, crash-landed, and wandered the desert until they were found by one of the gods. He also had said that they had been in his family for many generations.

Kian hadn't told him how many Odus there were even though Aru had asked, but there couldn't be too many of them.

Had someone from the resistance sent them?

Would the Supreme know anything about it?

Was there anything the Supreme didn't know?

Aru smiled at the thought. No one made from flesh and blood was all-knowing, but the Supreme came pretty close.

Aru had forgotten to tell Aria about the Odus, and since he still had time before the guests arrived and the ceremony commenced, he could steal a few moments alone in the master bedroom.

It would have been better if he could have tempted Gabi to join him, but she was adamant about lending a hand with the preparations. The Odu had tried his best to dissuade her by pointing out the dangers of the kitchen, his worry for the safety of her delicate hands, and Julian's instruction for her to rest, but Gabi had stubbornly insisted on staying.

If the Odu couldn't convince her to get out of the kitchen, then Aru had no chance.

Well, perhaps it was worth another try.

He walked into the kitchen and wrapped his arms around her from behind. "I'm going to lie down for a few minutes." He kissed her neck. "Care to join me?"

Turning to look at him over her shoulder, she gave him a brilliant smile. "Give me five minutes to finish what I'm doing, and I'll be there. I haven't seen the master bedroom yet."

That had been surprisingly easy.

Five minutes should be enough to communicate what he needed to Aria unless the Supreme was ready to give him instructions, in which case it wouldn't be a good time. But a male had his priorities, and right now, it was getting Gabi in bed with him, even if all they did was share a few kisses.

She wasn't supposed to engage in any vigorous activity, but he could think of a few things that involved very little exertion on her part.

He would gladly do all the work.

"Hurry up, and I'll give you the grand tour." He kissed her neck again and then nibbled at it a little, making her shiver deliciously in his arms.

"You're not playing fair." She pushed her bottom out in an attempt to bump him off.

"And you are?" He gave her lush bottom a little squeeze before leaving.

"Five minutes," she called after him.

With a smile lifting his lips and a hard length filling his pants, he made his way to the primary bedroom.

Aru had already showered and changed before, so he didn't feel guilty about lying on the pristine bed fully dressed, but on second thought, perhaps he could get rid of a few items of clothing and entice Gabi with some exposed skin when she arrived in the bedroom.

In less than two seconds, he was down to his boxer briefs, and the only reason he had left them on was that he didn't feel comfortable communicating with his sister in the nude.

Closing his eyes, Aru opened the channel and asked the usual question, *Can you talk?*

I have a minute, but no more. Aria's mental voice held a note of urgency.

Is everything all right? Aru asked.

Yes, the Supreme is receiving petitioners, and I am supposed to take notes. I am doing so while talking to you.

They shouldn't communicate when in public, but this was important as it could affect the Supreme's instructions for him.

I will make it quick. Several Odus made their way to Earth and were found by one of the rebel gods. They are now the property of the immortals. I do not know how many of them there are. The leader of the immortals refused to say. I thought that the Supreme might want to know that. Perhaps they are significant in some way.

What are you thinking, Aru?

Perhaps their creator sent them to Earth to save the technology. Perhaps the Supreme would be interested in this information.

These Odus had been made before everything manufactured on Anumati was made as solid-state, so they could be used by the resistance to reverse engineer them and create more. If they were used as weapons before, they could be used as weapons again, only this time, they would work for the rebels and not against them.

I shall inform the Supreme, Aria said. *I need to go.*

Before you do, tell me, did you have a chance to discuss what I told you with the Supreme? I am still waiting for directions.

Not yet. I was only summoned now to assist with the petitioners. I hope I will have the opportunity to talk with the Supreme in private once it is done and the doors close for the night.

I hope so, too. Be well, Aria.

You too, Aru. Take care of yourself.

Gabi

Gabi wiped her hands with the dish towel and removed the apron Okidu had loaned her. "Are you going to be okay on your own?"

"Oh, yes, mistress. It was most pleasant working side by side with you in the kitchen, but I have to confess that I prefer to work alone." He smiled apologetically.

She'd had to guilt the butler into letting her help, but most of the food was ready, the kitchen was clean, and all that was left to do was to watch over the few items that were still in the ovens.

Okidu could definitely handle that on his own.

Heck, he hadn't needed her help and hadn't wanted it, but Gabi wasn't the type of person who let others prepare a party for her while she idled.

Leaning closer to the squat man, she kissed his leathery cheek. "Thank you. It's very nice of you to do all of this for me. I appreciate your hard work and your dedication to culinary excellence."

The butler froze in place as if she'd unplugged him from the wall. Had she overstepped a boundary?

"Are you okay?" she said as she tried to look into his eyes. "I'm sorry if that offended you."

"I am not offended, mistress." He lifted a hand to his cheek. "No one has ever kissed me before. It is a strange sensation."

The poor guy had never been kissed? What kind of a mother had he had?

Perhaps he was an orphan?

"That's a travesty that needs to be corrected, and if you allow me, I will kiss your cheek every time I say hello and goodbye. Is that okay with you?"

A bright smile illuminated his face, and for a moment, he looked much younger than before. "I would like that very much. Can I kiss your cheek in return?"

"Of course." She turned her cheek toward him and tapped it with her finger. "Right here."

He hesitated for a split second before touching his oddly cold lips to her cheek and quickly retreating. "Thank you, mistress."

"You're welcome." She gave him a smile before walking out of the kitchen.

"Such an odd guy," she murmured on her way to the bedroom. "But sweet nonetheless. How could he have never been kissed?"

Shaking her head, Gabi opened the door to the bedroom and froze in her tracks.

The room was large, with a massive bed that sat on a raised platform and faced a fireplace with a big screen hanging over it. There was also a sitting area with a couch and two armchairs, and two bookcases filled with well-used books. But the most impressive thing in the room was the male spread out on top of the covers, wearing nothing but a pair of tight-fitting boxer shorts.

"No one ever deserved the name god more than you." She kicked off her shoes, shimmied out of her jeans, tossed them aside, and climbed on the bed in her tight T-shirt and underwear.

"Gabi." Aru wrapped his arms around her and pulled her under him. "You took longer than five minutes."

Staring up into his impossibly gorgeous face, Gabi forgot for a moment why she'd delayed. "I'll tell you about it later. Now, kiss me."

"Yes, mistress," he imitated the butler's voice.

"You're so bad." She laughed, but then his lips were on hers, and all she could do was feel.

Closing her eyes, she moaned into his mouth.

When he let go of her lips, she tried to chase his by lifting her head, but he was out of reach.

"Open your eyes and look at me," Aru said.

She did as he asked and gasped. "Your eyes are glowing."

It wasn't a subtle glow either. It was so strong that his eyes looked like they had flashlights inside of them, and instead of the dark chocolate ring and the black iris, all she could see was white light.

"My fangs are also elongated." He bared them. "Do they look scary to you?"

"A little." She lifted her hand and brought a finger to his mouth. "May I?"

"Yes, you may, but be careful. They are very sharp, and you could nick your finger."

Gabi smiled. "Now, that's a way to conduct the immortality test. Do you think we can forgo Julian's scalpel and use your fangs instead? It can be a new tradition, but I'm not sure whether it's any less barbaric. Probably more so, but it's also sexier."

Aru chuckled. "Just do it. But be careful."

"I don't want to be careful." She touched the sharp point with her finger, and a moment later, a drop of blood welled up on the tip.

Aru swiped it away with his tongue, and the tiny sting was gone.

"Now look what you have done. Your saliva has healing properties, so we won't know whether you healed me, or my body did that all on its own."

"No, we won't." He scraped those sharp fangs over her neck, somehow managing to do it with their blunt side and without drawing blood. "Let's save the testing for later. What I'm more interested in now is tasting rather than testing."

"Are you now." She lifted her pelvis and rubbed her mound over his delicious bulge. "Maybe I'm interested in some tasting myself."

"That can be arranged." He licked a spot on her neck. "As long as you don't exert yourself."

"Of course." Her eyes rolled back in her head. "We wouldn't want that."

Aru

Gabi's proposition was too good to turn down, but it would have to wait for another time. She'd already exerted herself in the kitchen, and Aru's plan had been to pleasure her until she screamed his name in ecstasy, but without her moving a muscle.

Thankfully, the penthouse had amazing soundproofing, so Gabi could be as loud as she pleased without his teammates or the Odu hearing her.

It was a great plan, but after seeing how Gabi had convinced the Odu to let her help him, he knew it would be a battle of wills.

Gabi was stubborn, and she overestimated what she could and should do right after her transition. The only way to ensure her compliance would be to tie her up.

The problem was that he had nothing to tie her with. His socks were not long enough, and twisting his T-shirts into ropes would produce uncomfortable restraints.

But wait a moment. Gabi had what he needed.

The Odu had put her carry-on in the bedroom, and if everything she'd had at the hotel was in there, he knew what he could use.

Dipping his head, Aru took Gabi's lips in a scorching kiss, his hands roaming all over her half-clad body. When he finally let go of her mouth, she was left flushed and panting.

"I'll take a rain check on your proposal." He kissed the tip of her nose. "This time is going to be all about you."

A mischievous smile curled her lips. "I know that you are new to Earth, but you must have heard the term sixty-nine."

He knew very well what she was referring to, and declining her offer was torturous.

"Not today, my love. The doctor said you shouldn't do anything physically strenuous, and I'm adamant about following his orders. In fact, I want to secure you to the bed to ensure compliance."

"Do you, now?" The scent of her arousal intensified. "I'm game for that, but no blindfold. I want to see you in all of your godly glory."

"Good. Do I have permission to open your luggage and take out a pair of stockings?"

She nodded and then giggled. "How many pairs are you going to use?"

He glanced at the ornate headboard and smiled. "One should do. I'm only going to secure your wrists to one of those iron swirls."

Lifting her head, she looked at the headboard above her. "How convenient."

"Indeed." He moved with his godly speed to get the stockings out of her carry-on and get back in bed.

Her eyes had stayed on him. "I'll never get tired of looking at you, and the thought that this magnificent body is never going to age is just mind-boggling. How lucky can a girl get?"

"I hope that was a rhetorical question." He tugged her shirt over her head and disposed of her bra almost at the same time.

Gabi laughed. "I've never been undressed so quickly."

He looped the stocking around the iron swirl and then slowed down to wrap the nylon around her wrists. "Comfortable?"

As she tugged on the restraints, her slender hands nearly slid through, but Gabi didn't want to get free. She liked the game they were playing as much as he did, and maybe more.

Straddling her upper thighs, he hooked his thumbs in the elastic of her panties, and as he pulled them down, the sweet scent of her arousal hit his nostrils, making him dizzy with desire.

"I forgot to lock the door," Gabi said. "Can you lock it with your mind?"

He chuckled. "I'm not a vampire, my love."

"You sure look like one from here."

She'd meant it as a joke, but Aru could detect a slight note of fear in her tone, and that wouldn't do. "I'm not going to bite you down there if that was what has gotten you thinking about vampires. At least not today."

Aru had no plans of biting Gabi anywhere before the ceremony. He didn't know whether immortal females blacked out from the bliss like human females did, and he couldn't risk having the star of the festivities passed out for the night.

Gabi's eyes widened. "Are you planning to do it some other day? Because if you are, I'm not on board with that at all." She tugged on the loose restraints, changing her mind about freeing herself when her hands were halfway through the loops.

Gripping them in her hands, she looked as if she was hanging from the headboard by nylons.

"Noted." He pressed a soft kiss to her inner thigh. "I will not do it unless you ask me."

Gabi frowned. "Not going to happen, and don't even think of thralling me to agree to that."

That was another thing that wouldn't do. "I will never thrall you, Gabi. The only reason I did that before was because I couldn't let you see my fangs and glowing eyes." It was a strange conversation to have while he was between his female's thighs, the enticing aroma of her arousal making him salivate, but these things had to be said. "I will never do anything to you without your explicit consent."

Gabi

Well, that wouldn't do.

Gabi had planned on asking Aru to use his thralling in a very specific way. She wanted him to bring to life the naughty dreams she'd had while at the clinic, and that required granting him access to her mind.

"I didn't say that you can never thrall me. I want you to thrall me when I ask you to." She smiled. "Remember those dreams I told you about?"

He arched a brow, which looked comical with his head peeking from between her spread legs. "You never told me what they were about." He kissed her other inner thigh, so close and yet so far from where she wanted him.

"In my dream, you created phantom limbs and tongues in addition to the real ones to touch me all over. It was incredible."

His eyes, which had been glowing already, looked like they were burning, or rather, emitting fire.

"It never occurred to me that I could do that." He grinned at her with those enormous fangs on display, and yet, he didn't scare her. "But that's an incredible idea. May I give it a try?"

Gabi sucked in a breath. "Yes, please."

If it was even half as good as in her dreams, she was in for one hell of an orgasm.

When two phantom tongues wrapped around her nipples at the same time, it was so much more intense than what she'd dreamt about that she nearly climaxed. But when he penetrated her with his fingers, real or phantom, and licked at her most sensitive spot, Gabi exploded like a firecracker.

"Incredible." Aru kissed her quivering flesh. "That took less than thirty seconds." He looked up at her with a satisfied expression on his handsome face.

He should have been terrifying to her with the fangs and glowing eyes, but he wasn't.

She was still panting, trying to catch her breath after the explosion. "Give me a moment to recuperate," she managed to say between one panting breath and the next. "I'm sorry that I didn't last longer."

"Nonsense." He smirked. "That was just the first of many more to come." His words were coming out slurred, probably because of the fangs that didn't allow his mouth to close. "Thank you for giving me the idea."

She glared at him. "Only with me. No one else."

"Oh, sweetheart. There will never be anyone else. You are it for me." His hands caressed her sides as he moved on top of her and propped his arms on the mattress on both sides of her.

Pulling her hands out of the restraints, she put her arms around his shoulders. "I promise to lie as still as I can."

He hesitated only for a moment before aligning himself with her entrance and surging all the way in.

Gabi gasped, the fullness of their joining so perfect that it brought tears to her eyes.

Aru dipped his head and kissed her eyelids one at a time while rocking gently into her.

It was just perfect, but one thought prevented her from surrendering to the bliss.

Was he going to bite her with those huge fangs?

She didn't remember the other bites because he'd thralled her to forget them, so she didn't know how painful they had been or, conversely, how pleasurable.

"What's the matter?" he murmured against her ear, still rocking gently inside her.

He was such an accommodating and thoughtful lover. Who would have ever thought a god could be so kind?

The thought amused her.

Who would have ever thought that she would be making love with a god?

"Everything is perfect." She rubbed her hands over the strong muscles of his back. "It's just surreal that you are here, making love to me, and about to bite me again, but I can't remember what it felt like the other times you bit me, so I don't know if I should be afraid or not. Kaia said —"

He stopped her tirade by claiming her mouth, and it was a claiming. His sinfully talented tongue thrust between her lips, mimicking the action below, and tasting herself on him only added to the erotic moment.

When he'd gotten his fill, or maybe when he ran out of air, Aru lifted his head and smiled down at her. "I'm not going to bite you this time, but I'm going to release your memories of the other times."

She was relieved but also disappointed. "Don't you need to bite me?"

"Oh, I do, but you have a ceremony coming up, and I don't want to have to explain to your family why you passed out and can't attend."

"Oh."

He laughed. "Yeah, oh. Now look into my eyes."

"Where else am I going to look?"

"Concentrate for just a moment."

She did, and as Aru's luminous gaze bored into her eyes, it felt as if a door was cracked open, letting the wind rush in. It carried with it memories of pleasure so indescribable that they were enough to trigger another orgasm and snap Aru's control.

As his thrusting turned urgent, she had to hold on to the ironwork of the headboard for purchase, and when he found his release, she climaxed again and called his name.

"Aru." She let go of the headboard and wrapped her arms around his trembling body. "I love you," she murmured into the crook of his neck.

He groaned. "I love you more than words can describe, but I need a cold shower."

Gabi frowned.

She could feel his essence dripping out of her, so she knew that he had found release. Why did he need a cold shower?

"Aru?" She stroked his hair. "Are you okay?"

He lifted his head, and as she saw his pained expression coupled with the enormity of his fangs, she got her answer. "You need to bite me."

He nodded. "I do, but I can't."

She cupped his cheeks. "Later tonight, after everyone leaves, we are doing this properly. The memories of your bites were awesome, but I want to experience the bliss in real time."

Aru

After Aru and Gabi had both showered, not together because he had been serious about taking a cold shower, he had convinced Gabi to lie down on the couch until her guests arrived.

"We can watch a show together." He sat next to her and clicked the giant screen on. "What are you in the mood for?"

"I'm not much of a television watcher. I prefer to read." She eyed the overfilled bookcases.

He remembered her telling him that during one of their dinners together, but he'd hoped to seduce her into watching something with him. "It doesn't have to be a show. We can watch a movie." He clicked on the menu. "A comedy, perhaps?"

She waved a feeble hand. "As long as it is not a war movie or horror, you can choose whatever you want, and I'll watch it with you. A comedy is fine."

He had a feeling that Gabi was going to fall asleep during the first few minutes, but that was fine. They had two and a half hours until their guests started arriving, and it would be great if she napped for most of it.

"It has been a long day. You can take a nap. Do you want to get in bed?"

She shook her head. "But it would be wonderful if you bring me one of those fluffy pillows." She glanced at the bed that she had put back in order before they had headed to the shower. "It's such a beautiful bed. Do you think Kian will let us live here?"

They hadn't discussed the future yet, and even though Aru had given it some thought, he wasn't sure how they would make it work.

"Kian said that we can stay here, but he didn't specify for how long. He usually rents the penthouse out, so he might be amenable to renting it to us if we decide to stay here. Do you mind rooming with Negal and Dagor?"

Gabi turned to look at him. "I don't mind. This primary bedroom is nearly the size of my entire condo in Cleveland. We can have privacy here, and when we want to hang out with our friends, we can be in the living room. My family will surely visit a lot too, and this place is gorgeous, but can you afford it? I can pitch in after I rent out my condo. I'll probably get at least three thousand a month for it, but this place is probably in the tens of thousands. Do you think Kian will give us a discount?"

As usual, Gabi talked a lot when she was nervous. It seemed like she'd made some life-altering decisions, so it was no wonder that she was anxious, but when had she had time to think and arrive at those decisions? Had she done it while working in the kitchen alongside the Odu?

"Don't worry about the cost. I can afford to pay whatever Kian charges for this place, and I don't need you to pitch in. But what about your clientele and your life in Cleveland?"

Gabi turned on her side and propped her head on her hand. "I'm immortal now, which means that I don't age, and sooner or later, my friends and clients will start to notice. I can probably stretch this out for a decade or so, excusing my appearance with extensive plastic surgery, but to what end? You are here, my family is here, and I can probably keep most of my clients even if I switch to virtual counseling. I'm already partnering with a laboratory that I send all my clients to. They do all the necessary blood work and urinalysis, and they email me the results. The only thing I won't be able to do are the in-person weigh-ins, and I can do without them." She closed her eyes for a moment and then opened them and leveled her blue gaze at him. "The big question is, what are your plans, and what part do I play in them?"

Aru took her hand and put it on his chest. "I want to spend every moment with you, but part of my mission is searching for the missing Kra-ell pods, and that involves travel. Sometimes, we have to hike for miles to get to a potential pod location, and we camp out, sleeping on the ground in sleeping bags and most times not even bothering with a tent. Would you be up for that?"

She smiled brilliantly. "I would love that. I love camping, and I love traveling to exotic locales." Her smile wilted a little. "I don't think I will be as terrified of flying as I was before my transition, so that shouldn't be an obstacle, but if it is, you can thrall me. But if I want to keep my practice while traveling, I will need a connection to the internet, so a satellite phone is a must."

"Of course." He lifted her hand to his lips and kissed her knuckles. "I love you, Gabriella Emerson. You are just as courageous as your name implies, and I'm so grateful that you are willing to accompany me on my travels. In fact, I'm overjoyed." He leaned down and took her lips in a gentle kiss. "The Fates have given me a perfect mate. I should offer them a prayer of thanks."

Gabi

"Oh, Aru." Gabi cupped his cheek. "I will add my thanks as well."

Gabi had had a few minutes to think about her future while helping Okidu in the kitchen.

Regrettably, the butler wasn't the talkative kind who shared juicy gossip about his employer, and she hadn't been able to coerce him into disclosing anything other than his recipes, which she had written down for when she and Aru lived together.

Okidu's steadfastness in the face of her questioning hadn't been a total waste of time, though, and since she'd had nothing better to do than think while washing dishes and chopping vegetables, Gabi had made some major decisions.

The most important one was that she was not going back to Cleveland. Her friends could help her wrap things up, and the truth was that not much was needed. Her condo was perfectly furnished and decorated and would be really easy to rent out. All she needed from there was her wardrobe, but since she'd grown half an inch in three days and was still growing, she would probably need new clothes anyway.

The biggest question had been Aru and his plans for the future. She knew that he had to return to the patrol ship in one hundred and fifteen years, but until then, they could spend all of their time together, provided that he wanted that.

She hadn't been sure about that until now, and she couldn't be happier about what Aru saw for their future. The next one hundred and fifteen years would be wonderful, full of love and adventure, and Fates willing, a solution would present itself that would allow Aru to stay.

"Here is your pillow, love." He gently lifted her head and placed the pillow under her cheek.

She loved it when he called her his love.

"I didn't even notice that you moved." She reached for his hand. Perhaps if she held on to it, he wouldn't be able to sneak out as stealthily as he did.

"You dozed off." Aru leaned down and kissed her cheek. "Sleep, my love. You need it."

She tightened her hold on his hand. "Don't leave me. You can watch television while I nap."

He looked conflicted. "I need to check up on Dagor and Negal and see if the butler needs anything."

"Then do it quickly and come back." Gabi brought Aru's hand to her cheek and rubbed his palm over her skin. "I promise that I'm not usually this needy and clingy. It's just that everything is in flux, and every time I wake up, I'm faced with a new reality. You are my anchor, Aru." She smiled. "You wanted to be my rock, and that comes with certain responsibilities and limitations."

"I love being your rock." He toed off his boots and lay next to her. "Dagor and Negal can wait. I'll hold you in my arms until you fall asleep."

"That's truly lovely." Gabi closed her eyes and let Aru's warmth envelop her.

They hadn't had moments like this before. It had been about pleasure and satisfaction, and they had cuddled only once and only after sex.

This was different.

This was about affection, not attraction, and about love, not lust.

Not that there was anything wrong with attraction and lust, but it was nice to have the softer side of togetherness as well.

Thinking back, she hadn't had many moments like this with Dylan. They'd had passion, they'd had all the outward expressions of love like words and gifts and grand gestures, but she couldn't remember them ever cuddling on the couch just for the sake of being together and not as a prelude to sex.

"You're not sleeping." Aru brushed his lips over her forehead. "What are you thinking about?"

She didn't want to bring Dylan into this precious moment between them.

"The different languages of love. I think mine is time. To show me love, you need to spend time with me."

He chuckled. "I have no problem with that. Isn't that a universal expression of love, though? Don't all lovers want to spend time with each other?"

"It depends how they want to spend that time. Some just want to have sex all the time, and when sex is not on the table, they lose interest and walk away. I'm glad you are not like that. It means a lot to me that you are content to just be with me without expecting anything other than closeness."

Aru

Aru waited until Gabi was fast asleep before reluctantly sliding off the couch.

He would have loved nothing more than to keep holding her in his arms until it was time for her to wake up, but he didn't like the idea of his teammates alone with the Odu.

Aru knew what the thing was capable of. He was fully aware that the propaganda painted a false picture, but he didn't know what the true picture was.

The Odu appeared as the dutiful servant he had been originally designed to be, but there was more to him, and that was what worried Aru.

The cyborg was so human-like that it appeared sentient, and sentient beings were even less trustworthy than machines. That being said, machines were made and programmed by unreliable sentient beings, so there was that.

Aru was about to push his feet into his boots when he felt Aria tug on their communication channel.

As he opened it on his end and let her in, her voice sounded in his head, *Can you talk?*

Yes. Leaving the boots by the couch, he walked over to the bed and lay down. *Do you have news?*

I do. I spoke with the Supreme, and I have instructions for you. You are to stay as close as you can to the immortals, learn as much as you can about them, and report back.

If only he could do that, it would solve many of his problems, but he served more than one master, and the commander expected Aru and his team to produce results.

My mission is to follow the Kra-ell and find the other pods. I cannot do both.

Yes, you can. Make your base of operation among the immortals or in their vicinity if they still do not welcome you into their secret village, and from time to time, go on excursions or send your teammates to search for the pods alone. The Supreme suggested that you involve the Kra-ell from Gor's compound in the search. They can accompany Negal and Dagor while you stay behind. Do the minimum required to fulfill your official duties or just a little more. You are to be our liaison to the immortals.

That wasn't going to be simple. How would he explain to his teammates why he was neglecting his duties? He couldn't tell them that he was following the Supreme's instructions. Besides, his clock was ticking, as the humans liked to say.

What about when I get picked up in one hundred and fifteen years? Who is going to be the liaison then?

Aru held his breath as he waited for Aria's response.

I do not have an answer for you at the ready, but I am sure the Supreme will find a way for you to stay on Earth and continue this most important task. Aria sighed. *I am going to miss you terribly, Aru, but I am happy for you. You will get to stay with your truelove mate. That is more important than a sister's loneliness.*

Aru's heart, which had soared to the stratosphere just a moment ago, sank down to the pit of his stomach.

One day, you will meet your truelove mate, Aria, and he will banish your loneliness. You will not miss me as much when you are in the arms of your mate.

Her laugh went through him like bubbles of champagne. *I do not need a truelove mate to enjoy the solace of strong arms around me. Do not worry about me, Aru. I keep myself entertained. One day, when our objectives are achieved, we will be reunited. Until then, we are blessed with this mental connection that allows us to talk with each other whenever we please. That is more than most gods get.*

He had said the same words to her many times, but it was the first time she had said them back to him.

It seemed that Aria viewed his connection to the immortals as the top priority, which must have reflected the way the Supreme viewed it. But why? What could these immortals do for the resistance?

The only thing he could think of was providing a secret base that could fly under the radar of the Eternal King, but the truth was that the resistance could do that without the immortals' help.

Can you find out what the Supreme has in mind in regard to these immortals?

Aria sighed again. *You know how the Supreme operates. Stealth and secrecy are the ways of the wise.*

Indeed. If you find out anything more concrete, let me know.

Of course. Be well, Aru.

You too, Aria.

As he closed the channel, Aru got up and walked over to the couch where he had left Gabi sleeping.

Crouching next to her on the floor, he looked at her beautiful face, and his heart swelled with love and hope. If the Supreme wanted him to be the resistance's liaison to the immortals and remain on Earth indefinitely, one way or another, it would be done. The Supreme always found a way. The question was how to tell Gabi about it without revealing his telepathic connection to his sister or lying about some other secret method of communication.

He would have to wait until the Supreme's machinations found their way down the chain of command and he received a notice from his commander that he would not be picked up in one hundred and fifteen years.

What about Negal and Dagor, though?

They wouldn't want to be stuck on Earth with him. They had loved ones they wanted to return to as much as he had wanted to return to his sister and their parents until he found his truelove, fated mate.

The Supreme wouldn't care about that, and if he stayed, his teammates would probably have to stay as well.

They wouldn't like it.

The good thing was that he wouldn't be the one to have to tell them that they were staying on Earth. The order would come from the patrol ship after their commander received it from Anumati.

Perhaps he should use the same excuse with Kian and tell him that the order included a coded message.

Except, that would only work if the Supreme moved fast and the commander contacted him soon, which wasn't likely. It also occurred to him that the Supreme hadn't commented on the Odus. Perhaps Aria hadn't had the chance to mention them yet or had forgotten what he had told her.

Gabi

"It's time to wake up, love." Aru kissed Gabi's cheek. "Your family will be here in fifteen minutes."

Gabi sat bolt upright. "Why did you let me sleep so long? You said that you would wake me up half an hour before the ceremony."

"I did." He smiled apologetically, but the apology wasn't genuine. "You murmured something about a few more minutes, so I let you sleep a little longer."

For some reason, Aru seemed to be in a much better mood than he'd been before she'd fallen asleep, and given that they had made love shortly before that, he should have been in the best mood then.

Was he excited about meeting the rest of her family?

That wasn't likely. Most people were intimidated by large families with small children, and as a god, Aru probably had zero experience with kids.

But wait, perhaps he hadn't been in such a great mood after their lovemaking because he hadn't bitten her? It was such an integral part of sex for his kind that it must have been very difficult for him to refrain.

But what had changed since then?

It wasn't as if he could have taken care of that himself. Biting his own arm probably wasn't fun.

Whatever the reason, she needed to hurry up and get ready. Aru was wearing jeans and a T-shirt and looking like the god he was, but she would have liked it if he put on a dress shirt and slacks for the ceremony.

Then again, the one person she wanted to approve of Aru had already met him, so perhaps he didn't need to change.

Gabi, on the other hand, needed to put on makeup and fix her hair so she wouldn't look like Cinderella before the fairy godmother sprinkled her magic dust over her. The dark circles under her eyes and the unexpected weight loss that had made her cheeks look hollow was not an attractive look.

Dashing to her carry-on, Gabi flipped it open and started taking things out.

"Do you want coffee while you are getting ready?" Aru asked.

She turned to look at him over her shoulder. "Did I tell you already how much I love you?"

His grin could have illuminated a football stadium. "I will never tire of hearing you say that." He crouched next to her and wrapped his arms around her. "I love you."

Given how his eyes were glowing, Gabi had a good idea where this was going, and if she wasn't pressed for time, she would have been a hundred percent on board, but the clock was ticking—not the biological one, though, thank goodness. That one was taken care of.

"Stop." She put her hand on his chest. "Save it for after the party."

"Right." He dropped his arms and pushed to his feet. "I'll get the coffee."

Gabi smiled. "You are an angel. Oh, wait, that's a downgrade for you. You are a god."

"You can call me anything you want, and I will love it." He opened the door, walked out, and closed it behind him.

"I must be the luckiest girl on Earth to score a guy like Aru." She lifted her face to the ceiling. "I don't know what I did to deserve such a gift. Thank you for giving Aru to me, and please, never take him away."

As usual, no one answered her plea, but perhaps this time it had been heard.

Looking back at her modest selection of clothing, Gabi chose a short-sleeved blue dress that wasn't too short so it wouldn't ride up if Julian demanded that she lie down while he administered his test.

The truth was that she wasn't scared of the cut, and she didn't care if it took her palm a minute to heal or five, as long as it healed faster than it would have while she'd been fully human.

"Here is your coffee, love." Aru handed her the cup.

"Thank you." Gabi took a sip and closed her eyes. "This is so good. What brand do they use?"

"I'll ask Okidu. He made it for you." He chuckled. "He was so happy when I told him that you wanted coffee. If I didn't know better, I would have thought that he was in love with you."

It must have been the kiss.

Poor guy. How could someone go through life without being kissed?

"I was nice to him. That's all."

Aru frowned, looking like he wanted to tell her something, but then shook his head. "I'll leave you to get ready and see if Okidu needs help." He straightened up and walked out of the room again.

Something must have gotten lost in translation, but Gabi wasn't sure what it was.

In the bathroom, she brushed her teeth and her hair and applied moisturizer. She was pale, but her skin looked smooth, and other than the dark circles under her eyes and the hollow cheeks, she looked great.

"The model look." She chuckled. "And I might even grow tall enough."

After applying concealer under her eyes, she dusted a little bronzer over her cheeks, did her eyes with eyeliner and mascara, and finished with the bright red lipstick that had Aru mesmerized every time she put it on.

Her hair was no longer as smooth and well-behaved as it had been when she'd stepped out of the salon, but it still looked good enough to leave loose around her shoulders instead of braiding it.

When she walked out of the bathroom, her eyes darted to the nylons that were still tied to the headboard, and she contemplated taking them down and putting them on.

She had other pairs in her carry-on, but wearing those particular ones would keep her smile turned on throughout the ceremony and drive Aru crazy.

By the time her guests went home, Aru would be wild with desire for her, and she would finally get to experience the bite in real time and not as a retrieved memory.

Aru

"I have everything under control, Master Aru." The Odu stood in the entrance to the kitchen. He smiled his fake smile. "Is there anything you require? Perhaps a little snack before the guests arrive?"

The Odu was appropriately accommodating and subservient, but Aru detected an undercurrent of hostility that the cyborg shouldn't be capable of, and even if he was, he had no reason to direct it at Aru.

Unless the Odu was jealous over Gabi, but that was even less likely than him being hostile. Then again, his face had lit up upon hearing her name.

He needed to speak with Kian and ask him whether the Odu had been modified in any way because it was giving him the creeps.

Come to think of it, he'd forgotten to ask Aria whether she'd mentioned the Odus to the Supreme. He was curious to hear whether the Supreme had a theory regarding their appearance on Earth.

"No, thank you." Aru returned the butler's fake smile. "The coffee will do for now." He reached for the cup he'd left on the counter.

The Odu bowed. "Very well, master."

Coffee cup in hand, Aru walked over to the living room couch and sat down next to Negal. "You know that Gabi's family will be here shortly, the doctor, of course, and Kian might show up either alone or with his wife and daughter. If you want to avoid meeting them, you should go to your rooms."

"I want to stay." Negal put down the magazine he'd been leafing through. "Are all the members of Gabi's family immortal?"

"The young ones are not, and neither is Gilbert's mate. Gabi told me that Gilbert's fangs and venom won't be operational for another five months, and until they are, he can't induce his mate."

"How do they induce men?" Dagor asked. "I hope it's not the same way that females are induced."

"I have no idea." Aru put his coffee cup on the table. "There is much more that we need to find out about these people. The question is whether you want to hang around all these immortals and try to get some answers."

Dagor lifted a brow. "Is that part of our mission?"

"It is now."

Dagor nodded. "Then it is our duty to mingle with the immortals and find out as much as we can."

"It would appear so."

Aru would have preferred this evening to be about Gabi and only Gabi, but his friends were right.

Her family of immortals and humans lived in the secret village, but they were civilians and, therefore, less guarded. They might reveal things that Kian and his advisor wouldn't.

"They are all arriving at the same time," Aru said. "Kian said he would arrange for a bus." He looked at his teammates. "They will ask a lot of questions as well, so be on your guard and don't say anything that you are not a hundred percent sure is okay. When you are not certain or just want to avoid answering, send them to me."

"Good deal." Negal lifted the magazine off the table and opened it to the page he'd earmarked.

"What are you reading?" Aru asked.

"Nothing important." Negal showed him the page. "It's an article on interior design and how to choose complementary colors."

"He's bored," Dagor said. "You need to find him something to do."

Aru raised a brow. "What about you?"

"I'm not bored." Dagor looked in the direction of the kitchen. "I'm studying the Odu," he whispered. "He's acting very strange for a cyborg. Have you noticed?"

Aru nodded. "He seems to have clear preferences for some people. He adores Gabi and is slightly hostile toward me."

Dagor cast another quick glance toward the kitchen before lowering his head and whispering, "He also hums as he works."

"Hums?" Aru asked. "Like in a machine noise? Maybe there is something wrong with him."

"He hums melodies of songs I recognize, and sometimes he sways to the music. That's not something cyborgs do."

"How do you know?" Negal asked. "The models we are familiar with don't sing, but maybe the old models were programmed to learn songs and repeat them? It's not like the technology is available to study. We don't know what they were capable of."

"True," Dagor admitted. "But I don't think the old Odus were programmed to enjoy and appreciate music. It would have been a waste."

As the bedroom door opened down the corridor and a moment later Gabi walked into the living room, Aru's heartbeat accelerated.

She looked beautiful in a blue dress and black heels, but what got his throat to go dry was the pair of pantyhose she'd put on. He recognized the pair he'd used to tie her to the headboard.

Pushing to his feet, Aru walked up to Gabi and wrapped one arm around her narrow waist. "That was a very naughty move, love," he whispered in her ear.

"Not at all." She lifted a pair of mockingly innocent eyes to him. "It's just a reminder of the unfinished business we need to attend to after the ceremony."

"Umm," Dagor cleared his throat. "I hope Aru told you that we have exceptionally good hearing. Same goes for eyesight and sense of smell."

He was going to throttle Dagor.

Unperturbed by the comment, Gabi leaned sideways to peer at Dagor and smiled. "I'm well aware of that, but I was told that gods and immortals are not shy about certain matters. Besides, we are going to be roommates for a couple of weeks, if not more, so we'd better get used to hearing things we shouldn't and pretending that we didn't."

Gabi

"**I**'m so glad that you brought the little ones." Gabi hugged Karen. "I just hope that they won't get scared when Julian makes the cut."

Karen squeezed her tight. "I'll keep the boys in their stroller so they won't see over the crowd, and Idina is not easily spooked." Karen let go of Gabi and patted her daughter's head. "I don't know whether she will grow up to be a surgeon or a general."

The girl gave her mother a wicked smile. "I don't want to be either. I want to be a witch."

"You already are." Kaia picked her sister up and planted a sloppy kiss on her cheek. "The question is whether you are a good witch or an evil one."

"Good one." Looking offended, Idina pulled out a pink wand from her pocket and waved it at Kaia. "Evil witches don't have pink wands. You can only do good magic with a pink wand. The silver wand is for dark magic."

"You are absolutely right." Kaia let the girl down and pulled Gabi into her arms. "Where is Aru?" she whispered in Gabi's ear. "I've seen the picture, and he's gorgeous, but I want to see him in person."

Gabi turned around and stretched up on her toes. "Gilbert and Eric cornered him. Come, I'll introduce you." She took Kaia's hand and led her to where Aru stood talking with her brothers.

The penthouse elevator could transport only so many people at a time, which was a good thing because not everyone had arrived at once. It gave Aru a few minutes to recuperate between the groups of people who wanted to meet him.

"Make room." She patted Eric's arm. "Kaia wants me to introduce her to Aru."

"Hi." Kaia extended her hand to him. "I'm Gabi's niece."

Smiling, Aru shook her hand. "The genius who gave up a position at Stanford to move in with an older guy."

"That's me." Kaia looked over her shoulder and waved William over. "And that's my mate, who is the greater genius in the family."

"I'm not." William offered Aru his hand. "Kaia is much smarter than me." He leaned closer to whisper loudly, "Young brain and all that."

"I'm sure," Aru laughed.

Cheryl shook her head. "Imagine living with those two around." She offered him her hand. "I'm Cheryl, Gabi's other niece, who is not a science genius but who has a good head for business."

"So I've heard." He shook her hand. "Gabi told me that you are conquering social media."

"That's a slight exaggeration, but not for long."

As the door opened again and Kian walked in with Syssi, Allegra, and his bodyguards, Gabi reached for Aru's hand. "Come. We need to say hello to Syssi and Kian."

He followed her gaze, and his smile widened. "Look at that baby girl. She's adorable."

"I know, right? And she's wicked smart."

"How do you know?"

"I told you. I met Syssi and her daughter in a restaurant when I met Karen and Darlene. Syssi and Kian's sister work in the same university as Karen, and they organized a little daycare for all the little ones."

Allegra's too-smart eyes were focused on Aru, and she lifted her hand and waved at him.

He waved back, and the baby's smile grew bigger.

"Hello." Syssi gave Gabi a warm smile. "I know that I'm not supposed to say congratulations until the test is done, but I'll say it anyway." She pulled Gabi into a one-armed embrace. "Congratulations." She let go of her and turned to Aru. "It's nice to finally meet you in person, Aru. I'm Syssi. Kian's wife."

"It's my honor to make your acquaintance." He dipped his head as he took her hand.

"The honor is all mine." Syssi held on to his hand. "By the way, I've seen you and your friends in a vision."

Aru

A cold shiver rushed down Aru's spine.

That was very bad news. Visions could reveal things that should remain hidden, and there was no way to shield himself or Aria from them.

"Are you an Oracle?" he asked hesitantly.

If she was, wouldn't the Supreme have known that she had a sister on Earth?

Syssi laughed. "Thank the Fates, I am not. I don't give divine counsel on things big or small, and Kian doesn't seek answers from me on strategy or the outcomes of battles. My visions are sporadic, unpredictable, and often too enigmatic to make any sense of. Once in a while, though, I get a glimpse of something useful. I believe that the Fates sent me a vision of you and your friends so I could tell Kian that your intentions were peaceful and that he shouldn't shoot first and ask questions later."

Aru dipped his head again. "Thank you for your intervention."

Thank the merciful Fates that Syssi was only a seer and not an Oracle. Nevertheless, he would inform Aria as soon as he got the chance. Perhaps the Supreme might be able to shield the telepathic connection between him and Aria from the seer.

"You are most welcome," Syssi said.

"Aro." The baby girl stretched her arm and reached for his cheek. "Ari."

This time, the shiver was so powerful that he was sure Syssi and Kian had noticed.

Was the child a more powerful seer than her mother?

Foresight ran in families.

Perhaps he was reading too much into the baby's babbling.

Swallowing hard, he plastered a smile on his face. "Hello, Allegra."

The child's regal, satisfied smile reminded him of someone, but thankfully it wasn't the Supreme. Was it similar to Kian's?

Perhaps when he was younger and less reserved, Kian had a smile like his daughter's, but right now, it was very different than that.

Behind Syssi and Kian, Julian lifted his hand high in the air. "Can I get everyone's attention, please?" When the chatter quieted, he continued, "I need you all to sit down wherever you can find a place. Gabi's had a long day, and she needs her rest."

"I'm okay," she assured her guests. "But I'm curious to see how fast I heal, so let's do it."

"Hop on the counter," Julian instructed. "So everyone can see."

Gabi looked at the counter and frowned. "Can someone bring me a chair? Actually, I'm immortal now, so maybe I can try hoisting myself to sit up there."

Before she could do that, Aru put his hands on her waist, lifted her, and deposited her on the counter next to the surgical tray that Julian had left there.

"Thanks." She smiled at him.

No one had followed Julian's request to sit down, and they were all standing next to the kitchen counter, crowding Gabi.

"Everyone, please take several steps back," Julian commanded.

When his command was obeyed, he picked up a stop-watch from the tray. "Who wants to time how fast Gabi is healing?"

"I do." Cheryl took the timer.

"Next, we need someone to film the test for posterity."

"I'll do that." Eric pulled out his phone.

"Aru." Julian looked at him. "You can hold Gabi's other hand."

Glad to be given a task, Aru clasped her hand in his while she extended the other one to the doctor.

Julian cleaned her palm with something that smelled bad and then lifted a tiny blade from his tray. "Eric, start filming. Cheryl, start the timer when I say now."

Gabi looked away but then changed her mind and looked at her palm. "I'm ready. Do it."

"Now!"

As Julian made the cut, Gabi didn't jerk or try to pull her hand away. Instead, she watched as blood welled over the incision.

It seemed like everyone in the penthouse was holding their collective breath as the stopwatch kept running, including the two little boys in the stroller and their toddler sister, whom Gilbert was holding so she could also watch.

As Julian took another square of white gauze and wiped the blood off, and Aru saw that the skin underneath was already knitting itself together, he let out a relieved breath. "Thank the merciful Fates. You are immortal."

"It's not healed yet," Gabi murmured. "The stopwatch is still running."

"One minute and forty-seven seconds," Cheryl said when the cut had disappeared completely.

"Congratulations," Julian said. "Welcome to immortality, Gabi."

Gabi

"Thank you." Gabi kissed Eric's cheek. "Can you send me the video of the test?"

"Sure. I'll also send you all the other pictures and videos I shot today. You can create a transition album." He lifted a finger and tapped it on his lips. "Here is an idea. You can ask Julian to send you the footage from the clinic. You can pick a few clips to add to the album so you'll have the whole experience." He turned to Darlene. "Come to think of it, we should do it for our own transition as well."

Darlene cleared her throat. "I'd rather forget all about it and pretend that I was born immortal." She offered Aru her hand. "It was nice meeting you. Welcome to the family."

Gabi tensed, expecting him to say that he didn't belong with her family, but he surprised her by taking Darlene's hand and saying thank you.

"I have a question." Aru looked at Eric's phone. "Isn't it dangerous to keep moments like that on the web where everyone can access them?"

Eric smiled indulgently. "This is a clan phone, and it's connected to a private satellite network. I don't understand much about encryption, so I can't tell you what kind of protocol William deployed, but we can communicate with each other without worrying about Big Brother watching."

"That explains a lot." Aru wrapped his arm around Gabi's waist. "I wondered why Kian and the rest of you were using a cheap knockoff of a popular brand."

"Not cheap at all." Kian stopped by their group and clapped Aru on his back. "We make them in-house, so they don't cost us a fortune, but they have the best components money can buy." He turned to Gabi. "Congratulations again, and welcome to the clan. Regrettably, I can't invite your mate to visit the village, but you are invited." He glanced at Aru. "Don't even think about attaching a bug to her. I'll have her searched with a magnifying glass, a millimeter at a time."

Aru put his hand over his chest. "I vow on my honor that I will never try to find out the village's location. Even if I find a way to stay on Earth and never return to Anumati, I don't want to know where it is. I don't want to risk it." He pulled Gabi closer against his side. "I was meaning to ask you if I can rent this penthouse. Gabi likes it here, and it's a convenient location for her family to visit, but I don't want to take advantage of your hospitality for more than the couple of weeks that you offered."

Hope surged in Gabi's chest. Aru had just implied that there might be a chance he wouldn't have to return to his home world.

Kian eyed him with a small smile. "The first month is on me. After that, we will figure out something." He cast a glance at Negal and Dagor, who were hanging back but listening to everything that was being said. "Are they going to live with you?"

Aru nodded. "Gabi doesn't mind."

When Syssi arched a brow, Gabi confirmed, "I really don't. The master bedroom alone is nearly the size of my condo in Cleveland, so I will have all the privacy I need." She leaned to whisper in Syssi's ear, "With how good the soundproofing here is, I really don't have to worry about a thing."

Given Negal's chuckle, he'd heard, but it didn't bother Gabi.

Aru's teammates were nearly as gorgeous as he was, and they seemed like decent guys, so she expected them to bring ladies over to spend the night quite often.

Turning around, she mock-glared at the duo. "As long as you behave and don't turn the place into a disgusting bachelor pad. No empty pizza boxes, beer bottles, and articles of clothing strewn around. Also, if you bring your lady friends to stay the night, I don't want to see anyone parading around the living room in their underwear or birthday suits. If any of these rules are broken, I'm kicking you out."

"Understood." Negal saluted her. "But you don't need to worry about any of that. We are soldiers, and we are trained to keep things tidy."

"What about the underwear rule?" Dagor asked. "Is that negotiable? What if I want to swim in that lap pool on the terrace?"

"You can buy a pair of swimming trunks." Kian took the sleeping baby from Syssi's arms. "Goodnight, and good luck." He wrapped his other arm around Syssi's waist and motioned with his head for his guards and the butler to follow.

"Goodbye, Mistress Gabi." Okidu bowed. "It was a pleasure serving you and your family tonight."

"Thank you, Okidu." Gabi pulled out of Aru's arm and embraced the butler. "You are a priceless asset to your employer." She kissed his cheek. "Goodnight."

This time, he didn't look as stunned as the first time she'd done it, but she could tell it made him happy.

Aru

As totally uncalled-for jealousy washed over Aru, he wondered whether he should tell Gabi that Okidu wasn't a real man. Perhaps she would be less inclined to kiss his cheeks when she realized that she'd kissed a robot.

The Odu had looked decidedly smug, too.

When the door closed behind the last of their guests, Gabi looked at him with a sheepish smile. "Congratulations. You survived your first encounter of the fifth kind with my family."

Aru frowned. "The fifth kind? It was the first time I met them."

Gabi put a hand on her hip and struck a pose. "You're an alien, so you should know the alien encounters terminology scale." She lifted one finger. "Encounters of the first kind are visual sightings of unidentified flying objects. I didn't see the ship you arrived on, so I can't claim that one." She lifted a second finger. "The second kind is some form of physical impact from those vessels, like crop circles or chemical traces, etc. Again, can't claim that." Gabi lifted a third finger. "The third kind is meeting an actual alien." She smiled. "That's me and you, and the fourth kind is an abduction by an alien, but I can't claim that one either. The fifth kind is when people are actually communicating with aliens. That's us, and that's you and my family, but the joke was that they were the aliens you encountered."

He smiled. "I can't do anything about the first and second kinds of encounters, but I can rectify the fourth." He picked her up by her waist and threw her over his shoulder. "Consider yourself abducted."

Laughing, she banged on his back. "Put me down, you oaf. Negal and Dagor will see you carry me off." She was kicking her legs up, and her shoes went flying.

"They are out on the terrace relaxing with a couple of beers, and the less commotion you make, the less chance there is of you attracting their attention."

"Oof." She tried to slap his butt but reached only the upper part.

It was the perfect excuse to respond in kind, and as his hand landed on her upturned bottom, she uttered a little squeak that sounded more like an invitation than a protest.

Walking into the primary bedroom, Aru closed the door with his foot and continued to the bed. He lowered Gabi gently on top of the comforter and sat next to her. He smoothed his hand over her nylon-covered legs. "I've been fantasizing about taking these off the entire evening."

"Then what are you waiting for?" She lifted her arms, folded them, and tucked her hands under her head. "You have my permission."

He bowed his head. "Thank you, oh kind mistress." He mimicked the Odu's fake British accent.

"It's not nice to make fun of Okidu. He worked very hard today."

"That's his job, love." Aru snaked his hands under the hem of her dress and pulled the pantyhose down her hips, dragging her tiny panties along with them.

Just the feel of her bare skin on his knuckles was enough to make him hard enough to hammer nails.

"He went above and beyond his job description," Gabi said. "I doubt Kian paid him overtime."

There was no gentle way to say it.

With a sigh, Aru dropped his head. "It might come as a shock to you, but Okidu is a cyborg. He doesn't get paid, and he doesn't get tired."

Gabi's eyes widened and, a moment later, narrowed. "You are toying with me."

"I'm not, and if you don't believe me, call your niece, the scientist. She knows what Kian's butler is. They were made on my home world, but the technology was banned."

Fear sparked in her eyes. "Why?"

That was not what Aru wanted Gabi to feel right now, and the cyborg was not what he wanted to talk about, but he had started it, so he needed to finish it.

"The Odus were created to be house servants, but there was a flaw in their design. They could be reprogrammed by unscrupulous individuals to become weapons. But I assume that Okidu is safe if Kian lets him around his daughter."

"Does he know?"

"He knows." Aru smoothed his hands over her outer thighs, going up. "No more talk about Odus. We have unfinished business to take care of, but only if you feel up to it. If you're tired, we can cuddle naked in bed instead."

It would be torture, but he'd rather suffer than cause her discomfort.

A mischievous gleam sparked in her eyes. "I am a little tired, but I have no problem repeating what we did this afternoon. You don't even have to tie me up. I'll just keep my hands right under my head and let you do all the work. I only have one condition."

Here it comes.

"What is it?"

"I want you to strip for me, slowly, so I can enjoy watching you getting naked."

He could do that.

Smiling, Aru rose to his feet. "Your wish is my command, Mistress Gabi."

Gabi

The room was dim, illuminated only by the moonlight streaming through the windows, which had been thankfully left uncovered, but it wasn't enough for Gabi to see Aru clearly.

Her eyesight had improved after her transition, but not sufficiently for her to see well in the dark. Julian had told her that it would come and that her healing time would improve as well, but that wasn't helping her at the moment.

Regrettably, Aru wasn't in the direct path of the moon's gentle glow, and Gabi had to make do with the ambient light.

A playful smirk lifted his lips as he reached for the button of his jeans, and as he leaned down to toe off his boots, his dark hair cascaded over his forehead.

"Shirt first," Gabi instructed.

He arched a brow. "Do you want to choreograph my striptease?"

Some men had a problem with following directions from a woman, but Aru was so confident that he probably wouldn't. Still, customs might be different where he'd grown up, and it was better not to assume but to ask.

"Would it bother you if I do?"

"Not at all. It turns me on."

She gifted him with a brilliant smile. "I thought it would, but I wasn't sure. It's better to ask, right?"

"Always." He reached for the hem of his T-shirt and tugged it up with the fluidity she now associated with gods and immortals. He paused with the fabric covering his beautiful face. "Am I going too fast?"

A little, but although Gabi could stare at the sculpted muscles of Aru's chest and his defined abs forever, she wanted to see his face, and she also wanted him to feel comfortable going at his own pace.

"You're doing great, my sexy god. Take the shirt off."

Aru tugged it over his head and tossed it all the way to the couch.

"Now, the bottom part," she breathed.

As Aru pushed his jeans down his muscular thighs, he tried to go slow, but he was either unable to slow down much or was impatient to get going.

When he turned around to push his boxer briefs down and gifted her with the sight of his ass, Gabi swallowed.

She'd seen his erection before, and it was impressive, but just like the rest of him, it was a sight to behold that she would never get tired of watching.

Never before had she considered that part of male anatomy as visually appealing. It was useful, and it served a function, but she would never say it was beautiful.

Until Aru.

Everything about him was perfect.

When he finally spun around, and she got a full frontal view, Gabi licked her lips. "Come here, my love." She beckoned with a finger.

"Tsk, tsk. You were supposed to keep your hands behind your head."

"Okay." She shifted to her knees and put her hands behind her neck. "I guess that you will have to feed me."

Aru's eyes, which had been luminous before, turned blazing, and his fangs punched over his lower lip, but he still hesitated.

The lack of panties underneath her dress only added to Gabi's arousal. She undulated her hips, trying to create some friction to relieve the ache, and her inner thighs got moistened with her juices.

Aru's nostrils flared.

"This dress is pretty, but it needs to go." He grabbed the hem and pulled it over her head.

Her bra was gone in the next split second.

When she mock-glared at him, he shrugged. "You didn't ask me to go slow while undressing you."

She hadn't, but with how fast he had done that, he could have torn her dress or damaged her bra. Besides being fast, he was also incredibly strong. She opened her mouth to tell him so, but he took the opportunity to fulfill her previous request and fed her his erection.

Only the tip at first, but then he wrapped his hand over hers at the back of her nape to hold her in place and started to shallowly pump in and out of her mouth.

Had he done it to shut her up?

The truth was that she didn't care why he had done it, only that he had. His body was so responsive, shuddering with pleasure as she took him deeper.

It was so arousing to be at his mercy like this, with her hands behind her head and him using her mouth as he pleased.

Aru

With her nipples peaked, her inner thighs glistening, and her mouth stretched over his girth, Gabi was a vision of lust.

Aru combed his fingers into her hair and fisted it, holding her head in place as he fed her his erection a fraction of an inch more with every forward thrust. When he got as deep as she could take him, he cupped her jaw and withdrew almost all the way before pushing back in, but not as deep as before. Gabi was struggling, but given the strong scent of arousal she was emitting, she enjoyed the game no less than he did.

Her hands were still behind her head, and seeing her like that was sexy as hell, but it couldn't be comfortable in this position.

"You don't have to keep your hands behind your head," he told her. "You can do with them as you please."

Anyway, there wasn't much she could do while on her knees, with him feeding her his shaft.

He relaxed his hold and let her hands fall, but they didn't stay down for long.

Groaning around his length, she lifted them to grip the back of his thighs for purchase.

He planned to give her a few more moments of this before flipping her on her back and devouring that nectar that was being wasted on coating her inner thighs instead of his tongue.

But Gabi had other plans, and as her hand closed around his balls from behind and kneaded, he growled a deep-throated groan and jerked deeper into her mouth.

She must have liked his response because her fingers tightened around his balls.

If this continued for another minute, he was going to climax, and that wouldn't do. His venom glands were full to bursting, and his fangs itched, but this position didn't lend itself to a proper bite that would bring them both pleasure.

Pulling out of the wet heat of her mouth required a herculean effort, especially since she didn't want him to go. Groaning in protest, she gripped his butt cheeks to keep him in place.

"Some other time, my love." He removed her hands from his ass and, in one swift move, repositioned her so she was on her back.

When he spread her thighs and dived between them, she moaned but didn't protest, and when he licked into her, she cried out and shuddered with pleasure.

"Nectar of the gods," he murmured against her slick folds before lapping it up.

Gabi stretched her arms above her head without him having to say a thing, and as he covered her entire cleft with his mouth, she arched up to get more.

"So greedy." He fluttered his tongue over her swollen nub and then rimmed it before applying gentle pressure again.

Adding his fingers to the action, he thralled her to feel two phantom mouths sucking on her nipples, and as her body started quaking, he added two more phantom mouths with fangs that gently scraped along the sides of her breasts.

The quaking became violent, and Gabi erupted with a scream. Through the tremors, he kept sucking and licking gently until the trembling subsided, and she pushed on his head.

"No more. I'm too sensitive."

Gabi

As Aru climbed on top of Gabi, her eyes were riveted to his beautiful face. His eyes were blazing white light, his fangs were fully elongated, and his skin was stretched over his high cheekbones and strong jaw. He was power and lust and love tied together with a ribbon and offered to her like a gift.

"I love you." She cupped his cheek.

"Gabi." He eased into her much more gently than she'd expected.

He was a big male, and she was slightly smaller than the average female, but after her climax, she had no trouble sheathing him comfortably. The fit was a little tight but not painfully so, and as he remained wedged deep inside of her without moving, her body adjusted to his size.

Reading her responses, he started moving the moment she was ready. His hands gripping her hips and pinning them to the mattress, he started a punishing tempo.

Thrusting hard and fast, it took only moments for her to climb all the way to the edge, and as he released her hip to palm the back of her head, the anticipation of what was coming next was enough to trigger an explosive climax that had her screaming his name.

As he grew impossibly big inside of her, she knew that he was close, and from the retrieved memories of the other times he'd bitten her, she knew the bite was coming.

The anticipation was both terrifying and carnal, and her body flooded with another wave of heat.

As Aru moved her head, tilting it sideways and elongating her neck, Gabi fought the urge to close her eyes. She was terrified but also curious, and she wanted to see those monstrous fangs sinking into her flesh.

When he pressed his fangs against her throat, she thought he would bite right away, but he kissed and licked the spot before uttering a snake-like hiss and striking.

The searing pain was enough to make her black out, and if not for the hand clamped on the back of her head, she would have jerked away and torn her neck on those instruments of torture. But then the initial heat was replaced with the cooling sensation of the venom entering her bloodstream, and the pain was gone as if it had never existed.

A tsunami of lust was next, triggering a chain of orgasms or maybe one long one, and when that ended a lifetime later, a wave of euphoria washed over her.

The sense of peace and buoyancy was incredible, and soon she was soaring on a fluffy cloud and passing over psychedelic landscapes rich with colors that didn't exist on Earth.

Perhaps she was seeing Aru's home planet?

Or maybe she'd been catapulted into another dimension?

The second one seemed more likely because the people waving at her from below didn't resemble humans, immortals, or gods. They were translucent and glowing and, at the same time, substantial.

Perhaps they were ghosts?

Willing the cloud to glide down did not work, so she couldn't ask them who they were, and all she could do was wave back.

It was so beautiful and peaceful that Gabi was in no hurry to return, but in the back of her mind, she remembered that Aru was down there on Earth, waiting for her to float down to him and that this trip was just one of many she would go on throughout her life with him.

She would be back soon and could explore this strange world at leisure, but right now, she needed to get back.

This time, when she willed the cloud to turn around and float back to where it had picked her up, the little puff obeyed, zipping through the psychedelic landscape much faster than it had on the way there.

With a gasp, Gabi opened her eyes and gazed into Aru's relaxed face. "Hello."

He smiled. "Welcome back. Did you have a nice trip?"

"The best. How long was I gone?"

"About an hour. Why did you come back so quickly? Weren't you having fun?"

"It was amazing, but I remembered that you were waiting for me, and I knew that I would have many other opportunities to travel through the alien fields and cities, so I willed the cloud to take me back."

He grinned happily. "You must really love me to shorten your euphoric trip to return to me."

"Duh." Gabi rolled her eyes. "Isn't that obvious? I love you more than anyone and anything."

The glow returned in full force to Aru's eyes. "I love you more than anything, too. You are my truelove mate."

"I know." She cupped his cheek. "And you are mine, and no force in the universe can keep us apart."

Syssi

"That's the last of it," Syssi murmured as she walked out of the closet in a simple, comfortable summer dress.

Then again, calling it simple might be an affront to the designer. The cut was perfect, the fabric so luxurious that she couldn't stop touching it, and the color was gorgeous. The only two things that were simple about it were the loose fit and that it was machine washable.

All the other outfits she'd gotten on her shopping excursion with Amanda were the kind that required dry cleaning, which was not practical for a mother of a nine-month-old baby. Still, there were many occasions that required a dressed-up look, like Perfect Match board meetings, celebrations of all kinds, and the occasional date night with Kian.

Lately, all they could manage was dinner at Callie's, which was fine with her. The food was excellent, and the company was even better.

Who needed to schlep to the city for an outing?

"I love it," Kian said quietly, not to wake up Allegra, who had fallen asleep in his arms. "It looks chic and comfortable."

Kian and Allegra had enthusiastically complimented all the new outfits she'd modeled for them, with Allegra showing her appreciation by clapping her hands and Kian by giving her sultry, glowing looks.

"Thank you." Syssi turned in a circle, trying to imitate Amanda's model moves but failing. "It's supposed to be an everyday dress, but given how much it costs, it will feel decadent wearing it around the house."

Kian glared at her. "I don't want to hear how much it cost. If you like it, wear it. In fact, I'll ask Amanda to order six more for you, one in every color."

Chuckling, she sat down next to him. "It only comes in three colors, and charcoal was the nicest."

"Then I'll order you six more of the same color. You'll have to wear them then because if you don't, it would be a waste."

He knew her too well. "Don't. I promise I'll wear this one until you are sick of seeing me in it. I might get the light gray, too, though."

"That's my girl." He wrapped his arm around her.

Leaning down, she kissed Allegra's tawny head. "Let's put her in her crib."

Kian sighed. "I love holding her, but she'll be more comfortable in her bed and sleep better."

When their daughter had a good afternoon nap, she was an angel for the rest of the day. If she didn't, she was grumpier than her father on his worst days.

As Kian pushed to his feet with Allegra in his arms, Syssi got up as well and joined him.

In the baby's room, she lifted the blanket and moved the mobile aside so he could gently lay their daughter down and then covered her. For a long moment, they just stood there, looking at their sleeping bundle of joy.

Kian moved first to activate the baby monitor, which gave Syssi an idea.

"Remember that I wanted to summon a vision today?"

Kian's shoulders immediately tensed, and he turned toward her. "I do. Where do you want to do it?"

She was glad he was standing by the deal he'd made with her and wasn't trying to dissuade her from attempting it.

"I can do it here, and you can watch over me through the baby monitor."

He arched a brow. "I thought that you couldn't concentrate and get into the special headspace when someone was with you in the room."

"That's true for everyone except for Allegra when she's asleep. The sounds of her breathing are so soothing to me that I can reach the meditative state effortlessly."

He hesitated for another split second before leaning down and kissing her cheek. "Good luck, and don't try too hard. If the vision doesn't come, don't try to force it."

"I won't."

Syssi waited until Kian left the room and closed the door behind him.

Her options for sitting were the rocking chair or the carpet on the floor, and given that she was wearing a dress, the rocking chair won.

For the first couple of minutes, she thought about Aru and his friends, then her previous vision of the brightly glowing goddess and her servant, and then took several long breaths.

As she'd told Kian, listening to Allegra's breathing made finding the receptive headspace effortless, and soon, a vision started playing in her head, clearer and more vivid than any she'd had before.

Kian

It was nerve-wracking watching Syssi looking comatose in the rocking chair. Kian had cranked the baby monitor volume up so he could hear them both breathing, which was reassuring up to a point.

The fact that Syssi was breathing didn't mean that she was conscious, and he never wanted to see her unconscious again.

He would lose his shit.

It would remind him of her fighting for her life during her transition. If not for his mother's timely intervention, Syssi might not have made it, and the thought of that possibility still haunted him years later.

Stop it. She is fine. Kian walked over to the wet bar in the master bedroom and poured himself a shot of whiskey even though it wasn't one in the afternoon yet. *Syssi is immortal now. A vision can't kill her.*

The glass of whiskey in hand, Kian paced their sizable master suite while darting glances at the monitor and hoping to see Syssi with her eyes open.

How long was she going to be in a trance state?

He hated not having anything to do.

Well, that wasn't true. He had a pile of files to go through over the weekend, but he hadn't been in a rush to retire to his home office and hadn't made a dent in that pile yet. Spending time with his wife and daughter took priority.

As a deep inhale followed by a loud exhale announced the end of Syssi's vision, he didn't wait for her to open her eyes and rushed to Allegra's room.

Opening the door as quietly as he could despite the urgency, he walked into the room and was greeted by his wife's smiling face.

"It was incredible, and I didn't suffer any ill effects." She turned her head and looked at their sleeping daughter. "Do you think being near her enhanced my vision? I've never had one that was so clear."

"It's possible." He crouched in front of the rocking chair and put his hands on her thighs. "We know she has your gift. Are you sure you are okay?"

"I'm great." She took his hands in hers and used them for leverage to get out of the chair. "Let's go to our room, and I'll tell you what I saw."

"Did you see the goddess?" Kian asked as they sat on the couch in their bedroom with another shot of whiskey for him and a glass of sparkling water for Syssi.

"I saw a goddess, but I don't think it was the same one as before. I couldn't see her face this time either because of the intense glow she was emitting. Her bearing was different, though, also regal but not as rigid." Syssi took a sip of water. "You know how my visions are. It's not just about the visuals. It's also about the impression they leave, the feelings they evoke, etc., although the visuals in this one were stunning. The cavernous room was illuminated by torches, so I assumed it was a glimpse into the past. Massive pillars held the domed ceiling, but their capitals weren't done in any style I could recognize." She smiled. "And I should know since I studied the different architectural styles of various epochs and civilizations."

"I didn't know that they taught history in architecture school."

"Of course, they do. Everything we know is built on top of previous knowledge. History is important."

"Naturally." Kian took another sip from his whiskey. "So, there was nothing modern at all in the room this time?"

In her previous vision, Syssi had seen a contemporary-looking gold vase.

She shook her head. "The goddess wore a toga-style outfit that was pure white with a gold clasp holding it gathered at her shoulder, so maybe the vision was from Greece or Rome, but given the capitals, maybe it was from somewhere else." She chuckled. "Like the lost world of Atlantis."

"Or Mount Olympus," Kian offered.

"Could be." Syssi laughed. "The glowing goddess sat on a throne-like chair on top of a dais that was less than a foot tall. A couple of petitioners knelt at the foot of the dais."

"How do you know they were petitioners? Your visions are mostly soundless. Did you hear them talking?"

"I did, but I couldn't understand their language. The tone, however, was easy to interpret. They were pleading for something. The goddess rose to her sandal-clad feet, walked over to them, and put her hands on their heads. For long moments, no one said anything, and then she spoke in a deep and resonant voice that almost sounded like she was singing. The female petitioner clasped the goddess's hand and kissed the ring on her finger, and her mate did the same with the goddess's other hand."

"How did the couple look?" Kian asked. "Maybe that will give us a clue as to the location."

Syssi frowned. "They were both beautiful, but they didn't glow, and they were so grateful to the goddess. The female started crying, they embraced each other, and then thanked the goddess with a deep obeisance."

"Wait." Kian lifted his hand. "You said that they didn't glow. Are you implying that they were gods, just not luminous?"

Her eyes widened. "Yes, they were gods. They must have been commoners. Once they thanked the goddess again, they rose to their feet, and that was when I noticed a scribe sitting next to one of the massive columns. She didn't have a glow either, but since she was in the shadows, I couldn't see her face." Syssi shook her head. "Strangely, she sat on a pillow on the floor, and she had a small table in front of her with a big book open on it, and she was writing in it with something that looked like a stylus. When the couple left the chamber, the goddess told her something, and she wrote that in the book as well."

"If not for the lack of technology, I would have thought that the vision was from Anumati. It couldn't have been from Earth in the era of the gods because all of those on Earth had a glow. Maybe the vision showed you one of the gods' colonies, and the supplicants were members of the resistance."

Syssi regarded him from under lowered lashes. "Are you seriously suggesting that, or are you joking?"

He'd been serious. But apparently, Syssi found his suggestion ludicrous. "Why are you dismissive of the possibility?"

"I'm not. But nothing in the vision indicated that it was taking place on Anumati or some other planet the gods had colonized."

"I'm just speculating. What else did you see? Maybe the clue is still to come."

Syssi shrugged. "After the couple, a lone male god entered, and he had a little bit of a glow. He also knelt in front of the goddess and lowered his forehead to the floor in obeisance. He spent a few minutes talking and pleading, but the goddess didn't rise from her throne-like chair and didn't put her hand on his head. The answer she gave him didn't bring him joy either. He thanked her and left the same way the couple did, and then the vision ended."

Kian leaned back, taking Syssi with him. "So, what is your vision trying to tell us? Who was that goddess, and why was she glowing so intensely that you couldn't see her face?"

"She must have been a royal like the other one, and it must have been Anumati despite the lack of technology. I don't think that beautiful reception hall was in one of the colonies."

Kian arched a brow. "A moment ago, you dismissed my suggestion that it had to do with Anumati or one of its colonies."

"I know, but there was a clue in my previous vision that I didn't pay attention to at the time. In today's vision, torches illuminated the goddess's reception hall, but there were none in the previous one. The room was well illuminated and not because of the glowing goddess. I remember seeing a light fixture directly over the golden abstract-shaped vase. You know, like the spotlights we use to illuminate art pieces."

"Now, I'm confused."

Syssi nodded. "Perhaps what I was shown was a temple, and for some reason, technology was not allowed inside."

"That could be. Perhaps it is time to tell my mother about your visions. She might be able to help us interpret them and solve the mystery of what they are trying to tell us."

COMING UP NEXT
The Children of the Gods Book 77
Dark Voyage Matters of the Heart

To read the first 3 chapters JOIN the VIP club
at ITLUCAS.COM —*To find out what's*
included in your free membership, click HERE or
flip to the last page.

As Annani and Syssi set out to unravel the mysteries of Syssi's visions about the gods' home world, the long-awaited wedding cruise sets sail with Aru, Gabi, and Aru's teammates on board.

While the gods find themselves surrounded by immortal clan ladies eager for their affections, they soon discover that destiny has a different plan for them.

Coming up next in the
PERFECT MATCH SERIES
THE CHANNELER'S COMPANION

A treat for fans of *The Wheel of Time.*

When Erika hires Rand to assist in her pediatric clinic, she does so despite his good looks and irresistible charm, not because of them.

He's empathic, adores children, and has the patience of a saint.

He's also all she can think about, but he's off limits.

What's a doctor to do to scratch that irresistible itch without risking workplace complications?

A shared adventure in the Perfect Match Virtual Studios seems like the solution, but instead of letting the algorithm choose a partner for her, Erika can try to influence it to select the one she wants. Awarding Rand a gift certificate to the service will get him into their database, but unless Erika can tip the odds in her favor, getting paired with him is a long shot.

Hopefully, a virtual adventure based on her and Rand's favorite series will do the trick.

———————

I hope Dark Encounters of the Fated Kind have added a little joy to your day. If you have a moment to add some to mine, you can help spread the word about the Children Of The Gods series by telling your friends and penning a review. Your recommendations are the most powerful way to inspire new readers to explore the series.

Thank you,

Isabell

Dark Encounters Of The Fated Kind is a work of fiction! Names, characters, places and incidents are products of the author's imagination or are used fictitiously and are not to be construed as real. Any similarity to actual persons, organizations and/or events is purely coincidental.

Copyright © 2023 by I. T. Lucas

Published by Evening Star Press

EveningStarPress.com

ISBN: 978-1-962067-04-1

Also by I. T. Lucas

<u>PERFECT MATCH</u>

The Children of the Gods Series Sets

Books 1-3: Dark Stranger trilogy— Includes a bonus short story: **The Fates take a Vacation**

Books 4-6: Dark Enemy Trilogy —Includes a bonus short story **The Fates' Post-Wedding Celebration**

Books 7-10: Dark Warrior Tetralogy

Books 11-13: Dark Guardian Trilogy

Books 14-16: Dark Angel Trilogy

Books 17-19: Dark Operative Trilogy

Books 20-22: Dark Survivor Trilogy

Books 23-25: Dark Widow Trilogy

Books 26-28: Dark Dream Trilogy

Books 29-31: Dark Prince Trilogy

Books 32-34: Dark Queen Trilogy

Books 35-37: Dark Spy Trilogy

Books 38-40: Dark Overlord Trilogy

Books 41-43: Dark Choices Trilogy

BOOKS 44-46: DARK SECRETS TRILOGY

BOOKS 47-49: DARK HAVEN TRILOGY

BOOKS 50-52: DARK POWER TRILOGY

BOOKS 53-55: DARK MEMORIES TRILOGY

BOOKS 56-58: DARK HUNTER TRILOGY

BOOKS 59-61: DARK GOD TRILOGY

BOOKS 62-64: DARK WHISPERS TRILOGY

BOOKS 65-67: DARK GAMBIT TRILOGY

BOOKS 68-70: DARK ALLIANCE TRILOGY

BOOKS 71-73: DARK HEALING TRILOGY

MEGA SETS
INCLUDE CHARACTER LISTS
THE CHILDREN OF THE GODS: BOOKS 1-6
THE CHILDREN OF THE GODS: BOOKS 6.5-10

PERFECT MATCH BUNDLE 1

CHECK OUT THE SPECIALS ON
ITLUCAS.COM
(https://itlucas.com/specials)

JOIN THE VIP CLUB

To find out what's included in your free membership, flip to the last page.

TRY THE CHILDREN OF THE GODS SERIES ON
AUDIBLE

2 FREE audiobooks with your new Audible subscription!

FOR EXCLUSIVE PEEKS AT UPCOMING RELEASES & A FREE COMPANION BOOK

JOIN MY *VIP CLUB* AND GAIN ACCESS TO THE VIP PORTAL AT ITLUCAS.COM
TO JOIN, GO TO:
http://eepurl.com/blMTpD

INCLUDED IN YOUR FREE MEMBERSHIP:

YOUR VIP PORTAL

- **READ PREVIEW CHAPTERS OF UPCOMING RELEASES.**
- **LISTEN TO GODDESS'S CHOICE NARRATION BY CHARLES LAWRENCE**
- **EXCLUSIVE CONTENT OFFERED ONLY TO MY VIPs.**

FREE I.T. LUCAS COMPANION INCLUDES:

- **GODDESS'S CHOICE PART 1**
- **PERFECT MATCH: VAMPIRE'S CONSORT** (A STANDALONE NOVELLA)
- **INTERVIEW Q & A**
- **CHARACTER CHARTS**

IF YOU'RE ALREADY A SUBSCRIBER, AND YOU ARE NOT GETTING MY EMAILS, YOUR PROVIDER IS

SENDING THEM TO YOUR JUNK FOLDER, AND YOU ARE MISSING OUT ON **IMPORTANT UPDATES**, **SIDE CHARACTERS' PORTRAITS, ADDITIONAL CONTENT, AND OTHER GOODIES.** TO FIX THAT, ADD isabell@itlucas.com TO YOUR EMAIL CONTACTS OR YOUR EMAIL VIP LIST.

**Check out the specials at
https://www.itlucas.com/specials**

Made in the USA
Las Vegas, NV
05 November 2023

Made in the USA
Las Vegas, NV
05 November 2023